What Matters Most

GWYNNE FORSTER
What Matters Most

ARABESQUE®

WHAT MATTERS MOST

An Arabesque novel

ISBN-13: 978-0-373-83106-7
ISBN-10:   0-373-83106-4

www.kimanipress.com

Printed in U.S.A.

Dear Reader,

You are about to enjoy some of our most extraordinary romantic fiction in a new series called Novels of Love & Hope, written by two of Arabesque's best-loved authors. In this series—which includes *For All We Know* by Sandra Kitt and *What Matters Most* by Gwynne Forster—great romance combines with heartwarming, compelling story lines that help raise awareness about health issues that affect our community. In partnering with St. Jude Children's Research Hospital for this series, we hope to enlighten as well as provide some insight into the research and medicine practiced at this preeminent research facility.

The first book in the series, *For All We Know,* tells the heartfelt story of two people whose love is tested as they care for an HIV-infected teen. The next novel, *What Matters Most,* is a story of romance that defies family pressure and reveals what it truly means to be committed to improving health care for the poor. Both books offer messages of love and hope in the face of tremendous struggles. Indeed, Arabesque is proud to be a part of this campaign launched by St. Jude, and we trust that it will spark interest and awareness among our readers.

All the best,

Evette Porter
Editor
Arabesque/Kimani Press

To the staff of St. Jude Children's Research Hospital, whose kindness, love, tenderness and caring for the children they serve I observed, and who impressed me with their professionalism and their pride in the hospital and its work.

Chapter 1

Melanie Sparks opened her bedroom window wide and breathed. The crisp April night air couldn't banish her problems, but she needed the psychological effect of clearing her head it seemed to give. If her father thought that challenging her every time she came home could break her, she'd show him. Nearly exhausted from typing students' term papers, studying during the day and attending evening classes at Towson University in Baltimore—a two-hour trip by bus between her home and the university—Melanie just wanted to go to bed and stay there. But challenges were merely invitations to hang tough.

Melanie had wanted to be a nurse since she was seven years old. Now, at age thirty-one, the coveted degree was finally within reach…provided she could pay her tuition. And with the prize so close, she was not going to allow anything to get between her and her bachelor's degree and certification as a registered nurse. She had been tired, but the thought was as calming as a warm bubble bath.

She arose early and prepared breakfast for her father and herself. Her father hated to eat alone, but he was not by anyone's measure pleasant company, so she finished as quickly as possible and went to her room to work on the student papers. It wasn't fun, but it was plentiful, and the money supported her, and allowed her to attend nursing school. And best of all, she didn't have a boss. Unfortunately, she didn't make enough to pay for her tuition.

She dashed out of the apartment en route to school that evening and ran down the stairs to avoid seeing her father, who stepped off the elevator just as she reached the staircase. She knew that, if he saw her, she would be late for school. He always found a way to delay her with questions that didn't require an answer, or he nagged her to get a full-time job and forget about school.

At the university, she ran into Greta, one of the few students with whom she maintained a friendly relationship, a young woman whose situation appeared to be as desperate as her own. She didn't make friends since she dared not bring them home. That evening, Greta's face bloomed with a rare smile.

"Guess what, Melanie? I got a job, a real one. And I

only work four hours a day. Now, I'll be able to pay my tuition. Girl, I feel like dancing."

"I'm happy for you. At least one of us is sure to graduate. I don't even want to think about how much I owe."

In her enthusiasm, Greta grabbed Melanie's arm a little too tightly. "I'm going to work at a clinic in a senior center. They didn't need a registered nurse, and since I'm a licensed practical nurse I got the job."

"We have to talk," Melanie said. "I'm an LPN, too. But if I don't get to class, old lady Harkness is going to have my head."

"Good luck," Greta called after her.

Melanie stopped. "Don't worry. Even if I have to work two jobs seven days a week, I'll be in that line when the dean starts passing out sheepskins."

"Wait a minute. Check the bulletin board. That's how I found my job."

Melanie thanked Greta and headed for her class.

After the lecture, she went to the student lounge, looked on the bulletin board and made a note of the ads that interested her. She was so busy, she missed the nine-thirty bus and got home an hour later than usual. As she'd expected, her father was on the warpath.

"You comin' in here later and later. I wanna know what's goin' on besides this school you claim you goin' to."

"I was checking out jobs, Daddy." She figured that would calm him, but rather than take a chance, she grabbed a banana from the kitchen counter and went to her room. Peace and quiet meant more to her right then than a full stomach. Two of the ads were good prospects, and she put the listings on her night table.

As soon as her father left for work the next morning, she telephoned a Dr. Ferguson, whose answering machine said to leave a message or to call him after two o'clock in the afternoon. She left a message asking him to call her before four o'clock. The other ad seemed less appealing. Although she didn't have a class that evening, she wanted to speak with the doctor before her father came home. She had never made so many mistakes typing papers as she did that day. Suppose he didn't call.

When she answered the phone at a quarter of three, she could barely catch her voice. "Hello."

"This is Jack Ferguson. Who am I speaking to?"

"Oh! Thank you for returning my call, Dr. Ferguson. I'm Melanie Sparks, and I'm answering your ad. I'm a licensed practical nurse, but I don't have much experience. I'm studying at Towson University three evenings a week, and I should have my degree by the end of the school year. But right now, I need a job."

"Thank you for responding to my ad, Ms. Sparks. I must say I like your honesty. What days are you in school?"

Here we go, she thought and worked hard at hiding her nervousness when she told him, "Monday, Wednesday and Friday evenings and Saturday mornings. In the day, I work at home typing term papers and theses, but it doesn't pay enough."

"I imagine it doesn't." The more he talked, the more

interested she became in knowing if the man was anything like the warm and comforting voice. "I have an office in the Bolton Hill area," he said, "but I'm opening one in Southwest Baltimore, and I need a nurse in that office."

"And you can't get a registered nurse to go there because it's not the greatest neighborhood." Her hopes began to rise. "If you're willing to take a chance on me," she told him, "I certainly don't mind working there. And after I graduate in June, you'll have a registered nurse."

"I like what I'm hearing, Ms. Sparks. But before we firm this up, I think we ought to meet. Can you come to my office at ten tomorrow morning?" He gave her the address.

"That's quite a distance from where I live, but I can make it by ten."

"Good. Take a taxi, and I'll reimburse you."

She thanked him, hung up and leaned back in the old chair. Such a kind and reassuring voice, and such a deep, velvet voice. She wondered how old he would be and what he looked like. The voice that she heard most often—her father's—was neither kind nor velvetlike, but cruel and harsh from guzzling beer.

"Ms. Sparks, Dr. Ferguson will see you now." A glance at her watch told Melanie that it was exactly ten o'clock. She had expected a long wait, and the doctor won points for punctuality.

"Dr. Ferguson, this is Ms. Sparks," the brusque receptionist said.

The man stood, and walked toward her with his right hand extended in her direction, smiling as he did so. And what a smile! She knew she was not easily flustered, and she did her best to summon her composure and return the smile. The touch of their hands produced what seemed like electricity, and both his eyebrows shot up. She had no idea what happened to hers, so she straightened her shoulders and raised her chin. She hadn't expected such a man, and the prospect of working so closely with him flashed through her mind.

Jack Ferguson thought he'd moved toward Melanie Sparks, because she was closer now, but he wasn't sure. He touched her hand to shake it and felt a shock run through his body. She reacted to him as he reacted to her. But hell, he needed a nurse, and they'd just have to work around it. She found her voice first, that same soft, sweet voice that he remembered from the afternoon before and had anticipated hearing again.

"I'm glad to meet you, Dr. Ferguson," she said, without an inkling of any physical reaction, and he relaxed. He had either misread her or she was a consummate actress. In any case, she lessened the tension, and that suited him. He told himself that he was capable of ignoring the tall, dreamy-eyed and perfectly stacked woman who would be working with him in his office, because he had to have a nurse.

He let a smile float over his face, or at least he hoped he had. "Please have a seat, Ms. Sparks. Thank you for coming. How much was your taxi fare?" He didn't want to forget that. She told him, and he opened his desk drawer, counted out twice as much and handed it to her.

Melanie looked first at the seventy-five dollars in her hand and then at Jack Ferguson. "That will take care of your fare back," he answered her silent question. "Mind telling me why you don't hesitate to work in that neighborhood? There's a lot of crime around there."

The neighborhoods around South Baltimore were worlds apart from upscale Bolton Hill. "Dr. Ferguson, I grew up in a poor neighborhood, not unlike South Baltimore, so I'm used to it and to the people who, like me, are working hard to make it. I've wanted to be a nurse most of my life."

He crossed his legs at the knee, leaned back and made a pyramid of his fingers. "My office is open from five to eight on Tuesday and Thursday evenings." He quoted a salary, and she felt her eyes widen.

"That's more than fair, Dr. Ferguson."

He relaxed visibly. "Then it's a deal. You'll get an advance for the cost and cleaning of your uniforms and your transportation to and from the office."

Working in an office where, often, it would be only the two of them could be a problem. She knew nothing about him, and his apparent gentleness and kindness could be an act. She wasn't cynical. But to be forewarned was to be forearmed.

She leaned back in the chair, crossed her legs, feeling comfortable with herself. She looked around at the opulent space. "Do you mind if I ask *you* a question, Dr. Ferguson?"

"Not at all. What's on your mind?"

"You have a posh office here in a rich neighborhood. Why would you open another office in one of the poorest sections of the city? You certainly won't make money down there." His smile and relaxed manner told her that he welcomed the question, though she sensed that he was not used to being challenged. Obviously, she'd earned his respect.

"No one was more surprised than me, Ms. Sparks, when I decided to open an office in South Baltimore. But I'm more proud of it than of all my accomplishments. It didn't happen by accident, and definitely not on a whim. A couple of months ago, well after midnight, as I was leaving the hospital, and old woman reached out to me, asking me to help her grandson. She'd been in the emergency room almost three hours trying to get help for him, but she had no money and no insurance. The admitting nurse didn't know what to do with her. I examined the child, found that he had double pneumonia, put him in the hospital and took care of him. After he was released, I treated him in this office until he was well. A couple of weeks after I discharged him from the hospital, the woman came here and brought me three of the most beautiful silk ties I'd ever seen. She made them from remnants that she was able to purchase. It was her way of thanking me. I can't tell you how that touched me. I knew she couldn't afford to buy quality silk, not even silk scraps.

"I'd never given serious thought to poverty or what it did to people. I'd always supported organizations that helped those less fortunate, but I had considered my success, talent and station in life as my due."

His eyes glistened with the excitement of a man who had just made a great discovery. She leaned forward, enraptured by his enthusiasm and his apparent eagerness to share his thoughts with her.

"What happened to change you? Something did."

He picked up a gold pen. "My father gave me this twenty-two-carat-gold pen when I graduated from medical school," he said under his breath, and began tapping it on his desk blotter. "Yeah. Something changed me, all right. Plenty. After the woman who gave me those ties left me that day, a cloud of guilt hung over me, and I couldn't shake it. It stayed with me through the night. I couldn't sleep. The woman was in her late sixties at the least, and she walked as if she carried the world on her shoulders. But she'd found a way to thank me. And I knew it was the widow's mite. The next day I got into my Porsche and drove through the neighborhood where she lived. I was born in Baltimore, but I'd never seen it.

"That was in March. I drove through the Morrell section of South Baltimore and saw areas where it seemed that most houses were boarded up. Broken glass was strewn around the streets. Children played near piles of garbage. The stench was mingled with the odor of frying fish and men drank openly from bottles on the corner. People sat on stoops and in chairs in front of their houses, as if they couldn't bear to be inside.

"I drove back to Franklin and on out Bolton Hill

Avenue to the park, pulled over and stopped, over-
whelmed by the tragedy. Nowhere in the neighborhood
did I see a doctor's office or even a pharmacy. I had been
vaguely aware of the conditions that existed right here
in Baltimore but had never seen them.

"It kept me awake in bed that night. Over and over
in my mind's eye, I remembered the lines from the last
letter my mother wrote me. 'You're blessed with an exceptional mind, son: skill, wealth, the best education,
advantages and opportunities that few people have. You
are my pride and joy. Don't ever forget your less fortunate brothers and sisters.' The next morning, I pulled out
the letter and read it in its entirety. I remembered her so
vividly then."

He shook his head slowly and, Melanie thought,
sadly. "I miss her sweet, gentle ways. She would want
me to do this."

He abruptly halted his reminiscence and looked at
her. "When can you start?" He had knocked the wind
out of her with his private revelation, and now he was
all business. Yet all that he had said only reassured her
that she would be lucky to work for him.

"Today's Tuesday," Melanie said, "so I'll be there at
five. Thank you for confiding in me. I won't let you down."

"I know. I'm a very good judge of people." He
walked with her to the door. "See you at five."

"Dr. Ferguson, your eleven o'clock is here."

"Thanks, Marnie. Show her to room A. I'll be there
in five or ten minutes."

John Hewitt "Jack" Ferguson closed his office door, went back to his desk and flopped down in the chair. Whew! The woman had thrown him for a loop. And it wasn't just the way she looked, it was everything. Lord, a man could drown himself in those eyes and love every second of that sweet death.

He shook his head. That Melanie Sparks appealed to him didn't surprise him. Besides her looks, she had a shapely body and a soft, sweet voice. Just the type of woman he liked. And she possessed a quiet strength that came across when she challenged him. He wasn't used to challenges from women, or men for that matter. Normally, he didn't like it. But she wasn't strident, and he hadn't minded at all.

What he couldn't understand was his confiding in her personal things about himself, things that he had wanted to tell his father, but hadn't because he didn't expect his father would approve. But as he'd talked, she leaned forward, her magnificent brown eyes sparking with excitement, and he wanted to open up to her. He'd found a kindred soul, a person like himself, and he hadn't sensed that kind of bond since his mother died.

He'd surprised her by asking when she could start work, because her dreamy eyes widened. Almost immediately her long lashes half hid them, sending a jolt through his body. He had to be careful with Melanie Sparks. She'd shaken him up. But he'd deal with it. He washed his hands and headed for examining room A.

If he'd had a choice, he probably wouldn't have hired her. Oh, hell! Why should he kid himself? She was a beautiful woman without the cosmetic enhancements of the women he treated and usually dated. She was the real thing, and he'd bet that svelte body was God-given, that she'd never been near a dermatologist, never had her body nipped and tucked or her breasts augmented. He told himself to snap out of it and to keep his mind off her. He reminded himself that a man shouldn't hit on women who worked for him. Still, five o'clock couldn't come fast enough.

By the time Melanie became fully aware of herself, she had walked from Jack Ferguson's Bolton Hill office almost to Liberty Heights. Four long blocks. Nothing she had experienced in her thirty-one years had prepared her for Jack Ferguson. He was more than six feet, four inches tall, muscular and the epitome of masculinity, and when she stepped into his office and looked at him, she was mesmerized. The man was the definition of sex itself, and sex wasn't something she spent a lot of time thinking about. But looking at him, there it was—in your face, blatant masculinity. And oh, those eyes. Large, long-lashed brown eyes that sent a bolt straight to her feminine core. Lord, the man had half smiled, and she caught herself moving toward him. She'd never seen quicksand, but after being near him, she knew what it was like.

She sat down on the steps of the nearest row houses and enjoyed a good laugh. Nobody in that neighborhood ever sat on the stoop. She opened the envelope Ferguson had given her and counted out seventy-five dollars. The taxi to his office had cost thirty-five dollars with tip, but she'd told him thirty, because it had seemed a bit high.

I wonder if it's a mistake to work for that man. I think he's nice, but he's so handsome. When I looked at him, I thought my heart was going to jump out of my chest. If I had any sense, I'd call him and tell him I don't want to take the job, but I need the money. I just pray that he doesn't get next to me.

She got home shortly before noon, changed her clothes and got to work at her computer. She had never studied juvenile crime, but she knew more about it than the graduate student who had written the paper she typed. She knew the seeds that gave rise to it, something to which this master's degree candidate had paid only passing attention. She'd almost finished when she realized she'd better start her father's dinner. If he didn't smell food when he walked into the house, she'd never get to Ferguson's office on time, and she didn't want to be late for her new job.

She smothered four pork chops in gravy, stewed turnip greens in the pressure cooker and prepared some candied sweet potatoes, baking the potatoes first in the microwave oven to save time. She took the leftover apple pie out of the refrigerator and placed it on the counter, set the table and dashed up to her bedroom to put on her uniform.

"Where do you think you're going in that?" her father asked when she came down stairs.

She was accustomed to his rudeness. "Hi, Daddy. I got a job in a doctor's office Tuesday and Thursday evenings, and it's not too far from here."

"Any doctor with a chicken-shit office anyplace near here ain't worth crap, so don't hand me that."

She knew better than to object if she wanted to leave anytime soon. The more he talked, the angrier he became and the more likely he was to start storming around and acting out. "Did you like the pork chops, Daddy? Mr. Muggings had some pretty nice ones for a change."

"They were all right. Next time, put a little more salt on them turnip greens."

"Yes, I will. See you when I get back." She left the house before her father could pick on something else that would delay her departure.

It had been nearly a decade since her mother had finally given up after battling years of fragile health and bouts of depression. She had promised her mother that she would stay with her father at least until she finished school. But she had exhausted her patience with his behavior, and especially his manners. It was too much to ask of her. When she got her RN, she intended to move.

She reached Jack's office shortly before five o'clock. "You going to work with the new doctor?" a boy of about seventeen asked her.

"Why, yes, I am. This will be my first evening on the job. Who are these people?" she asked about the fifteen or more sitting on nearby stoops.

"Looks like they're waiting for the doctor. My mama said she's been living here for thirty-nine years, and there's never been a doctor's office anyplace near here. These people gon' work you to death, lady."

She patted the boy's shoulder. "We're here because Dr. Ferguson saw a need and decided to do something about it." She decided to make friends with the teen. In this neighborhood, you couldn't have enough of them. "I'm Nurse Sparks. What's your name?"

"Terry Jordan. If I bring my kid sister here, you think the doc will look at her? She's been sick for weeks, but we can't afford to see no doctors."

She didn't know the answer, but she'd find out what Dr. Ferguson was made of. "Terry, I learned this early in life—if you don't try, you can't win. Go get your sister."

He hopped off the ledge. "Yes, ma'am."

When the Town Car drove up a few minutes later, a small boy ran to move the two orange traffic cones, and the people who sat on the nearby stoops stood and formed an orderly line. It relieved her to see that Terry and his sister, who looked to be about five, were third in line. Like ants following sugar, the line increased to about forty people within minutes.

Jack Ferguson jumped out of his car, waved to those who waited for him and, to her amazement, they all waved back. His smile, when he saw her standing there, would have weakened the strongest woman. He unlocked the door, stepped aside and ushered her to precede him inside.

"I'm not usually late," he said. "If I'm lax about my office hours, people will think I don't care. But I had to get a couple of extra keys made." Jack handed Melanie one. "Now, you won't have to wait outside."

"How're you going to handle this crowd in three hours?" she asked him.

"I'll stay till I've seen everyone. This is only my third evening, and there are a lot of people with health problems here." That devastating grin again. "You don't know how happy I am to see you. Last Thursday night, I almost went nuts."

"That may happen yet," she said under her breath.

"I heard that," he said. "Trouble is you're right."

"When should I let patients in?" she asked.

"Give me a minute to get ready." He finished washing his hands and looked off in the distance. "These people define the word *patient*. It makes a man humble."

She stared at him, but when he looked at her, she quickly turned away. She didn't know what her facial expression might reveal. "Should I ask them to come in now, sir?"

"Absolutely, and please don't call me sir. I'm only thirty-four."

She went to the door, opened it and let in the patients, who soon filled the waiting room.

"There's a young boy out there with his little sister, Dr. Ferguson. He said she's been sick for weeks, and they can't afford a doctor."

"That's no problem. If they have insurance, I take it. If they don't, I still do the best I can for them. I knew when I opened this place that most of the people wouldn't be able to pay. I don't mind."

He went out to the waiting room. "Thank all of you for being so patient. This is a lot for one doctor and a nurse to take care of in one evening. But I'll see every one of you before I leave here. I hope you don't mind if I take the children first. Ms. Sparks will ask you to fill out a form, because if I'm going to be your doctor, I need your medical history. Is that straight with everybody?" They all said yes in unison.

Is this man for real? thought Melanie. He had a posh office in Bolton Hill for wealthy patients, and could devote his afternoons to playing golf, tennis or just loafing around. But instead he chose to spend his free time helping people who had no health care. Melanie looked at the faces of the patients who sat in the waiting area looking as if Jack Ferguson was their savior. Not even the children seemed to mind waiting. She didn't know whether to attribute it to their need or to Jack's friendly manner.

Seven children lined up at her desk with their parents or guardians. She or the adult filled out the medical form. "Do you want me to fill in your sister's form, Terry?" she asked the boy.

"I don't know whether she's had all her shots. I can take it to my mama and be back in about fifteen minutes. Is the doctor still going to treat her?"

"He's going to see everybody in this room whether or not they have insurance or money. Now, run and take this to your mother."

"Yes, ma'am, Miss Sparks." He brought his sister over to sit beside Melanie and dashed out of the office. She filled out the forms after realizing that many of the patients didn't understand the questions and had to be asked in a different way or were unable to read. And she nearly cried when a four-year-old girl told her, "My mommy always kisses it and makes it better, but this didn't get better." She pointed to a spot under her armpit. "It hurts all the time."

As promised, Terry returned within fifteen minutes and gave her the form. No one had to tell Melanie that the boy's sister had been sick most of her life. She thanked him. "Do you have other sisters or brothers?" she asked Terry, wondering why his mother hadn't come with him.

"I have two little brothers. The baby one has a bad cold, and my mama didn't want to bring him out."

"We're open Thursday night, so you can stay with your brother and sister and let your mother bring your baby brother. Okay?"

"Yes, ma'am."

"Do you go to school?"

He stared at her. "Me? I'm graduating in June, and I'm class valedictorian. I got a couple of scholarships to college, but if I go away, I don't know what will happen to my mama."

The last patient left at twenty past ten. Melanie walked into the office and looked at the doctor, who looked tired. "That was your last patient, Dr. Ferguson. Let me tell you, tonight you definitely earned your wings."

He looked at her in a strange way. Lights seemed to dance in his eyes, and then his hypnotic eyes darkened from brown to umber. She could have sworn that she saw naked desire flash in those eyes. Only for a second, but it was there.

"You're the one," he said. "You were supposed to leave here at eight o'clock."

"How could I? If I'd left you here alone to take care of all those people, I'd have a hard time forgiving myself. Anyway, they needed us. I've already tidied up, so I'll see you Thursday at five."

"A few of the patients have serious problems. I'm beat, but I feel great," Jack said. "Have a seat while I call a taxi. You're not going home alone at this time of night."

She opened her mouth to tell him that she did so regularly, at least three times a week, but decided against it. The man winked at her, and in a self-mocking manner said, "I know I'm bossy, but don't take it personally. I mean well. If I become overbearing, tell me to back off."

"I can't imagine you being overbearing," she said, mostly because sitting there talking with him, just the two of them, made her nervous. In the stillness of the office, he seemed so powerful.

"Well, I can be." He rested his head on the high back of the tufted leather chair and laughed. "I certainly can."

Good Lord, the man is something to look at, Melanie thought. And when he laughed, stars seemed to dance in his eyes. When he abruptly stopped laughing and gazed at her, she knew that her facial expression reflected her thoughts of him. And he'd seen it. She got up to leave.

"Stay," he said. "The taxi will be here in a minute."

Still wearing his white coat, he locked the office, walked to the taxi with Melanie and paid the driver. "Thanks for your help. I don't think I could have gotten through this without you," he said.

"You're welcome. Good night." She was glad to leave. For the past five hours, she'd had a warm, tingly feeling every time she was near him—and she'd been close to him constantly all evening long. She released a long breath. Maybe in time, she'd get used to being around a man like Jack Ferguson. She certainly hoped so.

Jack carried the supper that Vernie, his housekeeper, left warming for him into the living room on a tray and sat down in front of the television to eat it. He'd barely begun to enjoy the meal of chicken, dumplings and string beans—one of his favorites—when the phone rang. He got up, looked at the cordless phone, saw the caller ID number and sat back down. He didn't feel like dealing with Elaine Jackson. He tuned the television to a talk show and enjoyed his supper while making a mental note to find out more about Melanie Sparks's personal life. Thirty-one years old and just getting her bachelor's degree. There had to be a reason.

"You're out of your mind," Jack's father, Dr. Montague Ferguson, insisted when they met for their usual Wednesday lunch. "It never occurred to me that you were serious. I and my father before me built the Ferguson name. And in the medical profession, that name stands for something. I want you to forget this madness and stick to your own private practice. Nobody over there in that neighborhood can afford to pay you. And since when did you think you had to solve the world's problems? You'll regret this. When your patients hear about this they'll desert you in droves."

Jack lifted his shoulder in a slight shrug. "Like rats from a sinking ship, eh? Not to worry, Dad. These rich women love to tell each other that I'm their doctor. It's like saying they drive a Lamborghini. They'll stick with me as long as that red Porsche sits in front of my office every morning from ten-thirty to twelve-thirty."

"Don't be too sure," Montague Ferguson added.

"If a doctor is six feet, four inches tall, single and knows how to smile, rich women—married or not—will always have some kind of ailment—real or imagined. And if they don't, there will still be people who really do need me."

Montague eyed his only child as though seeing him for the first time. "When did you get to be so cynical?"

Jack's smile emphasized his physical resemblance to his father. "I come by it naturally, Dad. Seems to me a physician is supposed to care for the sick, not just the wealthy who are sick." He chuckled to soften the remark. "I'm sticking with it, Dad."

After waiting half an hour for a bus, falling asleep past her stop and having to take a bus back, Melanie arrived home from class after midnight. She skipped up the stairs, ran a tub of hot water, added some bath salts and got in, feeling as if someone had just dropped heaven into her lap.

"Forty-two more days," she sang out, "and I'll be a registered nurse. I've been a waitress, babysitter, typist and Web-page designer, and I don't mind hard work. It's been worth it. Finally, I'm doing what I always wanted

to do. I'm a nurse, and I'll soon be a registered nurse."
She kicked up her heels, splashing the water on the
floor, and then created waves with her hand.

The warm water lapping over and around her body
gave her a tingling sensation, and she had a sudden
feeling of loneliness. In times past, she had longed for
someone to care for and who cared for her, a faceless
someone who would lift her out of her loneliness. But
now she imagined a face to sate this longing, a face that
belonged to Jack Ferguson. She'd had admirers, plenty
of them. But she let nothing stand between her and her
goal of becoming a registered nurse. Moreover, the men
who had pursued her hadn't made her pulse race and her
heartbeat accelerate like a runaway train as Jack
Ferguson had done the moment she saw him.

She got out of the tub, refreshed, dried her body, and
looked in her drawer for a teddy, her favorite sleepwear.
She thought better of it and slipped naked between the
cool sheets. She ran her hands over her breasts and
belly, wondering what Jack Ferguson would think of her
body. Suddenly, she sat up. She'd never done anything
like that before. *I'm losing my mind. The man is my
boss, and I had better remember it.*

At work the next Thursday, Jack helped her put
things in perspective when he surprised her with a
personal question.

Jack had never been shy about getting answers to
probing questions or going after anything else he wanted.
He didn't invade a woman's privacy. But Melanie Sparks

not only interested him, she was spending too much time in his head and he wasn't sure he liked it. She entered the examining room where he stood studying the results of a test. Her fragrance came close to making him weak in the knees. She smiled at him the same way she smiled at all the patients.

"Miss Sparks, what did you do before you entered Towson University? You're at least ten years older than most students."

Her eyes slightly narrowed, and she didn't try to hide the fact that his question irritated her. "I worked. Do you know how long it takes to save twenty thousand dollars when you're working at low-paying jobs? Well, Dr. Ferguson, that's what I was doing, working to save money to go to school and help pay my father's expenses."

His face creased into a deep frown. Testy, was she? "I see. You certainly were determined."

"Determination is a part of my character, Dr. Ferguson."

With her back to him, she opened a bottom cabinet drawer and removed a pair of surgical gloves. As she stood, her uniform outlined a pair of beautifully shaped hips. Going or coming, she got to him, but that didn't mean he had to do anything about it. Still, he had an unusual urge to delve into her background, to understand her, to know everything about her. He knew himself well enough to appreciate that he hadn't had such curiosity about any other woman.

"If you thought my question was out of place, Ms. Sparks, I apologize. I don't want to make you uncomfortable."

She turned and looked at him, but she immediately averted her gaze. "It's all right. I know you didn't intend to make me feel bad. It's just…" She shrugged, trailing off at the end of the sentence.

"It's just what?" He took a step toward her and, to his amazement, she stepped backward. He stopped himself just before he asked her if she was afraid of him. Women usually offered themselves to him almost as if it were their duty, but it only disgusted him. With her gentle, nurturing sweetness and—he was learning—her quiet strength, Melanie Sparks moved him as no woman had. Yet she kept him at a distance. And a good thing, too. She was his employee and therefore off-limits.

He repeated the question, but she smiled and said, "Nothing. I'd better get back to Mrs. Tate before she thinks I'm ignoring her."

He watched her swish out of the room, her head high and shoulders back, a queen unaware of her regal bearing. He laughed. If that was how he saw her, he was in trouble. The thought cooled him off and tamed his libido.

He made notes on the patient's chart and attached the lab report. Somehow, he had to instill in his South Baltimore patients the importance of coming to him at the first sign of illness. If they didn't have money, they didn't want charity, and they usually came to him only in desperation.

"Ms. Sparks, we have to approach this problem differently," he said when they had seen the last patient. "Since most of the patients come at the beginning of office hours, it would be good if you would give them a short talk about the importance of coming to the doctor as soon as they have symptoms and not waiting until they become really sick. What do you think?"

"I think it's a wonderful idea, and I'll spend five or ten minutes on it every Tuesday and Thursday till they get used to the idea."

He sat on the edge of his desk, thinking that he should be exhausted, but he wasn't. In fact, he felt good, as if he'd finally earned the money he'd made that morning in his Bolton Hill office.

She walked into the office and stored some drugs in the cabinet. "You must be exhausted."

"Actually, I'm not. There's something refreshing about knowing you've helped people in need."

She looked at him with an expression of admiration and appreciation for his efforts. "That doesn't begin to describe what you're doing here, Doctor. Already, these people love you, and well they should."

He thought of his mother and her wish for him. "I'm only doing what I should do, Ms. Sparks." He wanted to share his true feelings with her, but he couldn't. He dialed the cab company and ordered a taxi to take her home. "Come on, I'll see you to the taxi."

Melanie stood beside Jack at the door, waiting for the taxi. She didn't want to look at him, because she knew his gaze was on her. It was enough that he stood so close that the sleeve of his white coat brushed her arm.

"It's a beautiful night," he said of the moonlit and star-studded sky. "If it made any sense, I'd go for a walk." She looked up at him then. She couldn't help it, because she had detected a plaintiveness in his voice. He stared down at her, his eyes dark and stormy, and the heat in his gaze sent tremors plowing through her body. She grasped his arm for support, and he steadied her. The taxi arrived at that moment, and she heaved a deep sigh of relief. Heaven alone knew where they were headed.

Chapter 2

Jack drove his Town Car into this three-car garage and entered his house through the kitchen that adjoined it. Gray-blue marble-topped counters sparkled against chrome appliances and pale blue brick walls. Vernie, his housekeeper, would have been happy with much less. He thought about what it had cost him and how rarely he saw it and wondered if a man experienced a mental metamorphosis when he neared age thirty-five, because he'd been thinking a lot lately about what he had that his patients in South Baltimore couldn't even imagine having.

"I'm just tired," he told himself, checked the warmers he'd had built into the electric stove and smiled at the sight of beef stew, garlic mashed potatoes, turnip greens and sautéed green, yellow and red peppers. He filled his plate, poured a glass of red wine, sat down and concentrated on filling his long-empty belly.

After an enjoyable meal, he left the kitchen as neat as he found it and went upstairs to his bedroom. The red light blinked on his telephone, but when he phoned his answering service and found that he had no emergency calls, he checked his answering machine.

"Please call me the minute you get in. I rang your service and your personal cell phone a dozen times. Where are you? It's Elaine."

He wasn't about to call anyone other than his father at fifteen minutes past midnight, and he'd do that only if he knew his father needed him. He liked Elaine a lot, but she had a tendency to be controlling, and that accounted in part for the fact that he was still a bachelor. That and the fact that he imagined himself with a more feminine woman who was naturally sweet and sexy. Elaine's sexiness sometimes seemed to him contrived. Several times he'd started to tell her that if a woman wanted to control a man, she shouldn't be so obvious about it, especially if he was the man.

When his phone rang at six o'clock the next morning as he was heading for the shower, he kept going, thinking that Melanie would understand a doctor's need for rest and wouldn't call him so early knowing he'd had only a few hours of sleep. He went back to the phone and looked at the caller ID to verify his suspicion that Elaine was the caller. He thought back to the previous day and the wallop he'd got when he'd looked at Melanie Sparks for the first time. She hadn't displayed her sexuality like the Monday wash drying on the line. She didn't have to. It was an intrinsic part of her.

Melanie communicated softness, sweetness and comfort. And her eyes! He shook himself out of his reverie. Melanie Sparks worked for him, and he didn't dare dream of how giving she would be if he were ever wrapped in her arms.

Having forgotten about the phone call, Jack dressed, got into his Porsche and headed for the hospital. Still, Melanie Sparks preyed on his mind. She had handled his patients as if they were her own children, filling out the forms, answering questions, reassuring them and relieving him in other ways. And she knew a thing or two about medicine. They worked together as if they had done it for years. It was as if God liked what he'd started and sent him precisely the help he needed, for Melanie understood people and their needs far better than he did. She suited him as perfectly as did his hands and feet.

Jack drove to the doctors' parking area. "I'm getting the help I need," he said to himself, his thoughts still on Melanie, "but I'm also having a struggle that I *don't* need. She stayed with me to the end, two and a half hours overtime, and was cheerful every minute. That means she's loyal. If I'm not careful…" He didn't let himself finish the thought. He got a doughnut and coffee in the hospital's cafeteria and consumed it on the elevator en route to the operating floor.

Later that morning, he walked into his Bolton Hill office suite and stopped short. "Hello, Elaine. Is there a problem?" She knew he didn't socialize in his office or where he worked.

She rushed to him, but he stepped back from her, reminding her that she was in his office waiting room. "What's the purpose of this, Elaine? I'm late for my ten-thirty appointment."

"Oh, darling. Just tell me you don't intend to go through with this silly notion of opening an office in a run-down area of South Baltimore."

He stared at Elaine Jackson. She had never paid attention to anything about him other than his red Porsche and the size of his wallet. "Don't tell me you're interrupting my work to say that." Infuriated, he turned to his receptionist. "Give me two minutes and then send Mrs. Blount into my office. Ms. Jackson is leaving."

"Yes, sir." He did not imagine the triumphant expression on his receptionist's face, and he wondered what had passed between the two women.

After his office hours the next Wednesday, Jack met his father for lunch as he usually did on that day, and it depressed him that his father would not rejoice with him about his success the previous night, his joy in having treated all those people with their varied problems and ailments. He was dog-tired, but he felt better than he ever had about his work as a physician.

When his father arrived, Jack stood and embraced him. "How are you, Dad?"

"I'm fine, because I don't overtax myself. What about you?"

"I'm tired, but I've never felt better or been happier in my life."

Montague's left eye narrowed, and his fingers rubbed across his chin. "Is that a reason for you to brush off Elaine? She's a fine woman, and—"

Jack held up both hands to stop him. "She called you after she left my office? She knows I don't want her coming to see me where I work. She's never been in that office before. And how did she know about my South Baltimore clinic? *I* didn't tell her."

"Well, as I said, she's a fine woman—"

Jack leaned forward, put his forearms on the pristine white tablecloth and balled both fists. "Listen to me, Dad. I am neither married to nor engaged to Elaine Jackson, and I am beginning to realize that I never will be. No man wants a woman who runs to his father and tattles. I don't mind telling you, Dad, but I've lost my appetite for lunch."

Montague ground his teeth, a sure sign that he was seething with anger. "You're being pigheaded as usual, and you're going to regret it."

"I doubt it, but if I do, I'll put my tail between my legs and run and tell you," Jack said, his voice laced with sarcasm. The waiter cleared his throat.

"I'll have the special, thank you," Jack said and returned the menu to the waiter.

"But you don't like crayfish," Montague said.

"It doesn't matter, Dad."

He suffered through the meal and said goodbye to his father. Deciding that he had probably exhausted his supplies the previous night, he stored his Porsche at home, got on his Harley and headed for his other office. He hoped that none of the patients would see him, since he didn't plan to open on Wednesdays.

He arrived at the office around three o'clock, opened the door and stopped short. Melanie sat on a stool beside an open cupboard with pen and pad in hand, apparently taking inventory. He'd only seen her in nurse whites, and that had been enough to hook him. But in those tight, low-slung jeans, red T-shirt and sneakers, she was lethal.

Stunned, he stared up at her. "You're taking inventory?" he asked in a voice that sounded dry. "That's what I thought I'd do."

She looked down toward him, but not at him. "I hope you don't mind, Dr. Ferguson, but I got up thinking about that crowd in here last night and all the stuff we used up. I was just about to call you and tell you we're running low on supplies. What are we going to do?"

Not what will *you* do, but what are *we* going to do. Nothing could have told him with such certainty that she was with him all the way. He sat on the edge of her desk and tried to shift his attention from her to what she'd said. "How long have you been here?"

"Since around ten this morning. Why?"

He shook his head in wonder. She had worked five hours with no expectation of overtime pay, only because she wanted to help provide the best possible care for his patients. "So you didn't work on any term papers today, did you?"

She kept her mind on what she was doing, or so it

seemed, because she didn't look at him. "It's okay. I didn't want you to come here tomorrow and not find any swabs or cotton balls or…or whatever. You know." Her right hand shook nervously.

He thought about Elaine and her demand that he close the office and stifled the urge to lift Melanie from the stool and hug her. His father wouldn't approve, and he doubted that his friends or his well-heeled patients would understand. But this woman gladly gave her free time to help ensure his success.

He wished Melanie didn't look past him all the time, although he knew it was because she was afraid to make eye contact with him. Damned if he'd make it easier for her. The same bug that bit her had got him, and he was handling it, wasn't he?

"Ms. Sparks." She looked at him then, and he felt his heart take a tumble. "Can you figure out a way to work forty hours a week, including Tuesday and Thursday evenings? Then, you won't need to take any other work."

"I don't know."

"When do you study?"

"On the bus, the train, while I'm eating, whenever I can. But that's okay. It gets done."

"Do you want to work with me full-time?" Somehow, he couldn't bring himself to ask if she wanted to work *for* him, and that didn't make sense. "Melanie—" He hadn't addressed her by her first name before. "Look at me. I am not going to change into a pumpkin."

She looked at him, straight in the eye. "It might be a good thing if you did."

"What?"

"If I worked for you, Dr. Ferguson, my life would be easier. Much easier."

"Then so be it. You figure out the hours and let me know. And call me Jack."

She seemed to contemplate the idea for a moment, as if deciding whether to do it. Suddenly, her face relaxed into a dazzling smile. "All right. Is this an example of your overbearing behavior?"

He couldn't help grinning. "Believe me, I can do better. Much better."

"I can buy some of the supplies we need at a supermarket," she said, ignoring his reply, "but most of it has to be sterile."

"I can't let you do that, Melanie. You don't have a car. I'll call my supplier and read the order to him. If you can come around noon tomorrow to receive it, we should be in good shape, thanks to you."

"All right, but if there's a problem, call me."

Together, they finished taking inventory in about an hour. It occurred to him that she might be late for school. "What time is your class, Melanie?"

She glanced at her watch. "Six-fifteen. Oh, my goodness. I'd better go. Can you close up?"

"Sure." He phoned the taxi company. He was glad that he'd opened an account with the car service. "Are you going home first?" She nodded. He walked her out to the taxi. "Take her home, and then wait and take her to Towson University."

"Yes, sir," the driver said.

Jack looked at Melanie to thank her, but the expression on her face nearly weakened his knees. She may have been grateful, but her facial expression said something more intimate. "Thank you.... I...uh...thanks."

He started back inside to close up the office but turned when he felt a tug at his hand. He looked down and saw a little girl of about five years old.

"Hi, Doctor. My mama sent you this." The child handed him a plastic bag. He took it and hunkered beside her. "Tell your mama thanks. What's your name?"

"Keshani Jordan. That's my mama leaning out the window." She pointed across the street.

"Oh, yes, Keshani. I remember you. You're feeling better?"

She nodded. "Yes, sir."

He looked up, saw the child's mother, smiled and waved. The woman waved back, and he waited until the little girl crossed the street and went into the house. The bag didn't weigh much, and he couldn't imagine what was inside. He placed it on his desk, opened it and saw six exquisitely embroidered linen place mats with matching napkins. He looked through the names and addresses of his patients until he located Norma Jordan. He saw the address and made a note to write her a letter of thanks. He looked at the inventory list, phoned in the necessary items to his supplier, got on his Harley and headed home.

What a day it had been. He looked forward to Vernie's smile and a warm greeting and a good meal. What was missing was a woman's sweet warmth. He needed love as he'd never needed it before.

* * *

Melanie jumped out of the taxi, went inside the house and raced up the stairs. She dressed quickly and grabbed her purse and schoolbag. Downstairs, she took a frozen pizza from the freezer, turned on the oven to preheat, set the table for her father, locked the front door and ran to the waiting taxi.

"That was quick," the driver said, "but you didn't have to break your neck. The doc put it on his tab."

She hardly heard him. If her father had been at home to make his demands, she might have missed school in spite of Jack Ferguson's kindness. Jack. Such a strong, masculine name, and oh, how it suited him, she thought. Don't go there, her common sense preached, but she already knew that ignoring Jack Ferguson would take more willpower than she had just yet. If he weren't so kind and so gentle, despite his bossiness, not thinking of him would still be difficult. Lord, that man was something to look at.

When she'd walked into his office and gotten her first look at him, she had nearly swallowed her tongue. Her body had even warned her, *Girl, just give him whatever he wants. Don't even bother to try holding back. It's useless.* Thinking of that moment brought a smile to her face.

She enjoyed getting to school in comfort, for once, and sailed into the classroom fresh both physically and mentally. When she got home around ten-thirty that night, her father sat in front of the television with a glass of beer in one hand and a cigarette in the other.

"Hi, Daddy," she said, sounding as cheerful as possible considering her weariness after the long trip home.

"The pizza wasn't as good as usual. There's a new pizza shop about six or eight blocks down Fairmont. Get 'em there."

"Yes, sir." She went to the kitchen hoping that he'd left her a slice, but he'd dumped in the garbage what he hadn't eaten. She warmed three rolls, got a piece of cheese and a glass of tomato juice and went to her room. If he didn't see her, he'd be less likely to go on a rampage.

The next morning, after preparing her father his breakfast, making the beds and cleaning the kitchen, she packed her uniform, white shoes and stockings in a small bag. She dressed in a dusty-rose linen shirtdress and went to work. She was required to work that day until eight o'clock in the evening, but she knew she'd be there longer. She stopped at a supermarket and purchased a coffeemaker, coffee, tea, sugar and milk and a bag of fresh blueberry scones. On impulse, she bought a bunch of flowers—snapdragons, lilies and roses— and made it to work by ten-thirty. She had planned to be there by ten.

The telephone rang so frequently that she feared she wouldn't have time to create a folder for each of the patients that the doctor had treated. She needed to finish before five o'clock when the office opened. However, when Jack arrived at one-thirty, she'd only done half of them.

"Hi," he said, his face all smiles. "Say, these flowers are beautiful," he remarked of the arrangement, "and they give the office a welcoming touch. I didn't think of it. Did you have lunch?"

"Not yet. I'm trying to get these files in order before we open this afternoon. We've had a lot of calls this morning." She wished he wasn't so close. *I'm not a nervous woman, but this man makes me feel as if I'm in the middle of a tornado.*

"Come on," he said. "Let's get something to eat. I'm useless when I'm hungry."

"But I—"

"No buts." He looked at a couple of the files. "This is wonderful, but would you mind staggering the tabs a little bit? And while you do that, I'll start entering the essentials in the computer—after we have lunch, that is."

"Oh, no. You shouldn't use your time doing that."

"I probably wouldn't in my Bolton Hill office, but this is different, Melanie. It's not about money, but about doing what I can to help people in need." He covered her hand with his, which made her nervous. Her gaze flew to his and locked. She got the feeling that he wished he hadn't touched her, still his demeanor shifted from impersonal to intimate, though against his will. It appeared as if he was backtracking when he shook his head as if denying something. She tore her gaze from his, unwilling to let him see what she felt.

"Can we go to lunch?" he asked her, his voice soft and solicitous.

She laughed, as much to ease the moment as for any other reason. "I see the bossy Jack just took a walk."

* * *

Jack didn't know of a decent restaurant in the neighborhood, so he walked to his car, opened the front passenger door, looked at Melanie and waited for her to get in. Then, he did what he'd do for any woman riding in the front seat with him. He leaned across her and fastened her seat belt. He didn't have to do that, and when he heard her sharp intake of air, he realized that he probably shouldn't have. He closed the door, walked around and got in.

"What do you like to eat, Melanie?"

"Anything. Well, almost anything." Her wrinkled forehead suggested that she might have an idea. He was about to ask when she said, "It's been ages since I had a pastrami sandwich. Do you like them? Blake's on Franklin Avenue serves the best. It's not far." He couldn't imagine Elaine asking to be taken to a place that served pastrami sandwiches. She'd want lobster or filet mignon. "I love pastrami," he said, "and if they serve it with a good old-fashioned sour pickle, I'll be a happy man."

"Expect to be elated." She rested her head against the back of the leather seat and closed her eyes. "Five blocks north and four blocks to the east, and we'll be there."

He eased the car away from the curb and headed for Blake's. He didn't feel the need to talk and, apparently, neither did she. He liked that. The sun slipped behind the clouds just as he drove up to the restaurant.

"I think we're in for some rain, and that means it'll be busy at the clinic tonight," he said. "I intend to get a service to clean the office, but I haven't found one I like that's willing to work out here."

"One of the problems with workers, cleaners or anyone else is how to secure the drugs," Melanie said. "Would you consider putting a safe in your private office?"

"I hadn't thought of that. You're suggesting that someone might break in to look for drugs?" he asked her.

"In that neighborhood, it's something to consider."

In the restaurant, they found a table near the window. He hadn't expected luxury, but the neat, attractive setting pleased him. Glass covered the white tablecloth, and a bud vase held a pretty flower. They ordered the pastrami sandwiches, which arrived quickly, and she seemed to hold her breath while he bit into his.

"Well?"

"Fantastic," he said. "The best I've ever tasted. The coffee's great, too. By the way, give me a bill for all that stuff you bought."

She handed him a receipt for thirty-seven dollars. "The coffeemaker cost twenty-four dollars and tax," she said. "I didn't have time to check around for something cheaper."

He had to remember that they thought differently about money and value. However, since she seemed anxious that she'd spent too much, he said, "Twenty-four dollars? At that price, we'll be lucky if it works."

"It worked fine today," she said.

He didn't believe he'd ever seen anybody enjoy food the way she enjoyed that pastrami sandwich. She finished the sandwich, drank the remainder of her lemonade and smiled the smile of a satisfied woman.

"We'd better get back," she said. "We have a lot to do before five o'clock. We don't want the patients to think that because they're poor, they're not entitled to our best."

The thought that came to mind brought perspiration to his forehead. The thought lingered, and when he set the coffee cup into the saucer, his hand shook. *She's the perfect complement to me.*

"We're not going to let them think that, but right now I'm enjoying this sandwich, and I don't want to rush."

"Would you think it nosy of me if I asked what you did with your afternoons before you opened the office down here?"

"Nosy? It's a good question. I can't remember, at least not accurately. I guess I wasted a lot of time. Occasionally, I played golf, went to the club, went horseback-riding and found other ways to pass the time. Unless there was an emergency with a patient, my work day was over at one o'clock in the afternoon. If I was at home, I'd read, usually medical information. Why'd you happen to ask that?"

She shrugged her shoulders. "You're so low-key. I never have enough time."

"I can't afford stress, Melanie. A surgeon needs a clear head and steady hands, so I try not to carry a bigger load than I can handle." His cell phone rang. "Excuse me." She moved as if to leave the table, but he stopped her by putting his hand on hers. "Ferguson."

"Darling, where on earth are you this time of day?

Can you meet me for a drink? Dad's sponsoring a
cabaret theater, and we want you to join us. Your name
will guarantee its success."

He listened for a minute. "Sorry, I can't go into that
now. I'm in a restaurant, and I am not alone." He pushed
his chair back from the table and listened for a minute.
"I told you that I am not alone. We'll finish this some
other time." Jack hung up the phone.

"I'm sorry," Melanie said. "I could have left."

"No way. I said as much as I wanted to say. I realize
that that person is a source of stress." Elaine had begun to
annoy him, and she had overestimated her importance in
his life. Growing up, his parents had controlled him with
their love and by appealing to his logic, not by telling him
what to do and keeping tabs on him. He took the check,
walked around to Melanie's chair and helped her up. She
seemed surprised, but she'd get used to it.

At four o'clock, they had completed the files and
computerized them. Melanie looked down at Jack's feet,
clad as they were in only socks, and asked him, "What
happened to your shoes?"

He grinned in that devastating way of his, and she told
herself not to let him get to her. "Melanie, the first thing
I do when I get inside my house is kick off my shoes. I
like to be comfortable, and shoes and clothes make me
feel like a harnessed horse. A necktie is an abomination."

She certainly hadn't expected that. "Gosh, you must
be uncomfortable most of the time. It's a wonder you
aren't a radical. Oh, dear. I broke this tube. I'm sorry."

"No problem. You'll get the hang of it. What makes you think I'm not a radical-type? My father and certain of my friends probably think so."

"Why would they think that? Most radicals don't drive a Town Car."

"They don't approve of my opening an office here. My father is pretty close to being outraged."

"I'm sorry. I think he should be proud of you. What does he do?"

"My dad's an internist, physician to the rich."

"Come now," she said. "I'll bet I wouldn't find poor people lounging in the waiting room of your Bolton Hill office."

"That's true, but I have treated patients there from whom I didn't expect payment, and I'd do it again."

She couldn't help looking at him then. His voice had a plaintive tone that said he could hurt. Without thinking, she placed her hand on his bare arm. "I think you're wonderful, and I know your mother is proud of you."

"You're right. She was."

"Oh, Jack, I'm...so sorry. I know what it means to be without a mother. Sometimes it's..." She shook her head, wishing the subject hadn't come up.

He finished it for her. "Sometimes it's pure hell. My dad's been good to, but he doesn't easily show affection. And every kid needs that. He also thinks he knows best. And since I'm thirty-four years old, I'm damn sure *I* know best."

"That's part of being an adult." She looked around. "I wish we had a shower here," she said.

"All right. I'll call the architect and have him draw some plans for a shower. It's easy enough to enlarge that bathroom. If you want anything else, just tell me." His voice dropped a few decibels, but she knew he was not trying to seduce her. "I'll drive you home if you want to shower," he said

"I don't think there's time, but thank you. My uniform is in the closet. I'll manage to get clean." She changed into her uniform. Refreshed, she found him sitting on her desk, drinking coffee.

"I made enough for you. It's good. I can't believe that pot only cost twenty-four dollars."

"I'm sorry to tell you that it is definitely the quality of the coffee and not always of the pot that makes the difference, Doctor."

"A minute ago, you called me by my name for the first time. Do your best to remember it."

"Yes, sir. Back to bossy, eh?"

Jack tried to remind himself to keep his thoughts straight. He'd been thinking of Melanie nude in the shower less than twenty feet from his office, and he imagined steam jutting from his ears. But when she came back to the waiting room dressed in her white uniform, switching his mind back to an employer-employee relationship wasn't much of a stretch.

Her smile was a warm and loving thing, natural and spontaneous, and he enjoyed seeing it. She sipped the coffee and smiled. "Thanks for this. It really hits the spot."

"You are welcome. Tell me, Melanie, why do you

have so much trouble calling me Jack? You did it once, and I suspect that was because you saw that my defenses were down."

She looked at her watch, glad to focus anywhere but on him, and said, "You have twelve minutes to change and put your shoes on."

"Twelve is all I need. And don't think we won't get back to that question."

"Don't forget your shoes," she called after him, because she enjoyed needling him and he didn't seem to mind.

Twelve minutes later, he presented himself for her inspection. "How'd I do? I brushed my teeth, too."

Her eyes sparkled with amusement, and she walked up to him with a wide grin on her face. "You did? Let's see."

He hadn't previously seen that side of her, and excitement raced through him. Without thinking, he grabbed the hand that seemed headed toward his lips. "Be careful, Melanie. It wouldn't take much for me to step over the line. And if I ever do that, there will be no turning back for either of us."

"I… Jack…" Her gaze fastened on his mouth, and then, with what he witnessed as a display of awesome willpower, she forced herself to look away from him. He released a deep breath in relief.

"Sorry," she said. "I tease too much."

Jack made himself grin, although he was far from amused. "Let's get these folks in here."

Melanie walked into the waiting room, smiled and a chorus of voices sang, "Hi, Ms. Sparks."

She called the first patient, got the chart from the file

and took the patient in to see Jack. "How are you at drawing blood?" he asked Melanie in an aside.

"I'm not an expert, but I've done it. Want me to?"

He nodded and handed her a needle. "Easy now. That's it." He told the girl to make a fist and gave her a dancing monkey to distract her. "Slant it a little bit more," he said to Melanie. "Good. Perfect. Fill the vial."

"You're a great teacher," she told him later. "I've never been around anyone who shows as much patience as you do. It's really refreshing."

He stared at her. Would she say such things if she didn't mean them? The women he knew used flattery as social currency, and he'd long since found it distasteful. But he didn't believe Melanie was that type. "You're generous with compliments," he said, "and my ego loves it."

He had worked with nurses ever since he'd finished medical school. He'd liked some, disliked others and been indifferent about a lot of them. But this woman was different. Her professionalism at no time overshadowed her compassion and femininity. She separated the nurse from the woman, yet the nurse had her personality and value system. She would never believe how much he admired her.

He went back to the girl and patted her shoulder. "I'm going to give you some medicine that requires an injection."

Her eyes had a glazed look. "Will it hurt?"

He rested a hand lightly on her shoulder, hoping to communicate to her that he cared. "It will sting a little, but afterward, you can have some ice cream."

He named three flavors, and after she chose cherry, he gave her a shot of penicillin and told her mother to bring the girl back the following Tuesday.

"I can't be certain until we get the results of the blood tests," he told Melanie later, "but from what her mother tells me, it wouldn't surprise me if she has sickle-cell anemia. She has the symptoms. If that's the case, at first she'll need better care than I can give her. I'm not up on some of these diseases. I wish I had an internist here."

"You want to give the best health care, but until you came here, they would spend hours waiting in an emergency room. Many would become dispirited and leave without treatment. You're a godsend to these people, and someday they'll let you know it."

His heart seemed to expand. "*You're* a godsend, Melanie. With you here, I can't possibly become discouraged. You won't let me." He smiled to lessen the impact of his words.

"What'll we do if your hunch is right?" she asked him.

"Good question. I'll do some research to see what our alternatives are."

It was probably going to be a bad night. He knew that when he got tonight's tests results, he would find that at least four of his patients were seriously ill. "I'd better call your taxi," he said to Melanie at nine-fifteen. "You've had a very long day."

"So have you," she said.

Every muscle in her body screamed for rest; she had been exhausted before the first patient arrived. However, she didn't feel like going home. Intuition told her that her father would be on the warpath, and she didn't have the energy to face him.

"What do you think of Mrs. Lacey?" she asked Jack, postponing the time until they closed the office. She'd been concerned about the patient's breathing.

"Doesn't look good. She has an accelerated heartbeat, and her lungs aren't clear. She may need an ablation, but that may complicate her condition. I phoned one of my colleagues and asked him to give her an MRI and a CT scan tomorrow and let me know what he finds. She could get them at the hospital, but I don't want to wait that long. I think she's headed out of here."

"But she's got those three little kids, and she's a single mom."

"I know. Life's hard sometimes. We'll do all we can for her. Hey, don't… We'll take care of her. Melanie, for goodness' sake."

She turned her back to him and wiped the tears that rolled down her face. "Those children are in for it. The worst thing that can happen to a child is not to have a mother. It's—" The day Melanie came home from school at nine years old and discovered that her mother had died flashed through her mind, and her shoulders shook uncontrollably.

"Don't. Please don't cry. It will be all right."

Jack's hands locked on her in a steely grip. "Swee… Melanie, please…I…" He turned her to face him, and he folded her in his embrace. Her arms eased around his shoulders and locked. The sensation of his long surgeon's fingers stroking her back and her hair sent tremors throughout her body. "It's all right. I know how you feel, because I feel the same. Being without your mother is hell." She relaxed into the comfort of his arms, soaking up the warmth and tenderness that she needed so badly. His grip on her tightened, bringing her back to reality. The worst thing she could do would be to fall for this man. And, oh, how hard she would fall! She willed herself to pat his shoulder and step back.

He released her immediately, but when she didn't look at him, he gripped her shoulder. "Look at me, Melanie," he said, his voice stern and unrecognizable. "Don't pretend you didn't enjoy being in my arms. Tell me you think it was a mistake or that you wish it hadn't happened. But don't dismiss your feelings."

She looked him in the eye then, bristling at his words. "How can you suggest such a thing? You warned me of the consequences if you ever crossed the line with me. I'm not sure what you think would take place, but I know you are not ready for it. As for dismissing you, who was ever stupid enough to try it?" She softened her words with a smile.

"I'm going to call a taxi for you before I get into deeper trouble," he said, and she noticed that his gaze lingered on her mouth. *One of these days, he's going to say the hell with it, and I know I will remember it for as long as I live.*

Chapter 3

Melanie opened the door as quietly as she could in order not to disturb her father who, she knew, would be sitting in the living room watching television and guzzling beer or asleep, having drunk too much of it.

"You coming home mighty late," he said when he heard her footsteps.

"I just left work, Daddy. The doctor had so many patients tonight, and I couldn't leave before the last one."

"Yeah? Well, if you making so much overtime, where's the money? I wanna see some money. We gotta pay these bills."

"I get paid every two weeks, Daddy. Nurses don't get paid by the day."

"Don't you smart-mouth me, young lady."

In his present mood, she knew better than to try to defend herself. "I'm sorry, Daddy," she said, going into the kitchen to find something to eat. She couldn't go to bed without food, starved as she was, though she'd done it many times in order to avoid him. She made a cheese sandwich, got an orange and headed up to her room.

"You can't answer me?" he yelled up after her. "This college business is going to your head."

She went into her room, closed the door, hooked a chair under the doorknob and took a deep breath. She listened carefully, didn't hear his footsteps on the stairs and gave silent thanks. On many occasions, her father had stood at her bedroom door yelling at her. In less than a month, she would have her degree and her certification as a registered nurse, and now with her salary she would finally be able to afford her own apartment. She studied for one of her final exams, got ready for bed, crawled in and tried to sleep.

Memories of those few minutes when Jack Ferguson held her in his arms crowded out every other thought from her mind. Exhaustion fell away, and sleep deserted her as fantasies of herself with Jack invaded her mind and desire for him throbbed inside her. What would have happened if she hadn't moved, if she had given in to her feelings and eased her arms around his neck? Nobody had to tell her that. If they continued to work together, they would eventually consummate the passion that swirled around them.

She didn't believe that a man with Jack Ferguson's background, reputation and obvious wealth would settle for a woman born and raised in South Baltimore. She turned over and clawed at her pillow. *Why can't I make love with him just once and have that sweetness, that hot passion that I see when he looks at me? Why can't I know just once his driving power?* She chewed on the end of the pillow case and then pounded the pillow with her fist. *I want to feel him explode inside me just once.* She began to count sheep, but they all had Jack Ferguson's face, and they all bleated so sadly. She sat up wondering if Jack was as lonely as her.

"You wanna watch your behavior," her father said as they ate breakfast the next morning. "And you show me some money, or you get a job that pays. You're not letting some two-bit doctor work you to death for nothing."

"Yes, sir," she said, gulping down her coffee. "I'll ask for an advance."

"Where you going now? You don't type the term papers no more? At least they paid you the few pennies you earned."

She took a deep breath. "I work for the doctor full-time now, Daddy. That's why I get paid twice a month."

He glared at her. "We have to pay the light bill. Tell him you want to get paid every Friday or he should get somebody else. You bring some money home."

"Yes, sir. Bye, Daddy. I have to go." She didn't relax until she was out of the house. When she returned at four-thirty, she heated lasagna, sautéed a package of fresh spinach and broiled two halved tomatoes, set the table for her father and prepared to go to class.

Her father walked into the house as she reached the

bottom stair. When he threw his hard hat on the sofa, she knew he'd fought with his boss and that he'd be in a rage. "I see you're home at a decent hour," he said. "Where's the money?"

"I don't work tonight, Daddy. I'm on my way to class."

He towered over her like an angry bear. "So you didn't bring any money, and that's your excuse. School is all you think about. Get out of my sight."

He strode past her, and as she bounded out of his way, her shoulder hit the banister with a loud thud sending pain from her neck to the tips of her fingers. She picked up her schoolbag, stumbled out the door and closed it. If only she could survive until she got the degree! A promise was a promise, but her mother had asked too much. Now his anger and abuse gave her—in effect— permission to break her promise to her mother.

When she returned home from school, his snores greeted her, and she slipped past him to the kitchen, got a sandwich and a glass of tomato juice. A hot shower soothed her aching shoulder, and she slept soundly. The next morning, she dragged herself out of bed and dressed by sheer force of will. She'd had all she was prepared to take, and her anger mounted until it became a fierce, almost dangerous, thing with energy of its own. As she descended the stairs, she tallied her grievances against her father and left home without greeting him or cooking his breakfast. He'd gone too far.

On the way to work, Melanie bought some dough-nuts and decided to ask Jack if they could have a micro-wave oven. When she walked into the office, she realized she had come to regard it as home, for it was there that she was happiest. She made coffee and drank it in the waiting room, a place nearly as elegant as the waiting room in Jack's Bolton Hill office. Light brown leather sofas and chairs were grouped attractively with mahogany tables on which were silk-shaded brass lamps; beige-brown Bokara carpets, machine-made but beautiful, covered the floor. She looked around at the reproductions of Doris Price, Romare Bearden, Jacob Lawrence and Elizabeth Catlett, great African-American artists, and let herself dream.

"One of these days, I'll have beautiful things, too,' she said aloud. After finishing her coffee and two doughnuts, she placed orders for supplies by telephone, sent bills out for patients who had insurance, wrote checks for Jack's signature and sent thank-you notes to patients who volunteered to pay in kind.

"He's the doctor. It's his office and his business, but it's our job together," she told herself, "and I'm going to do everything I can to make Jack's dad sorry for not supporting him in this."

Jack arrived at the office shortly after three and greeted her with his famous smile. She vowed not to get too familiar with him, because she figured she would be the loser, but she smiled in return, because she couldn't resist his infectious grin.

"Hi. Looks like you've been busy as usual," he said, looking at the papers she'd placed on his desk. "I hadn't thought I'd need a secretary here. We could do this at my other office where I have a secretary and a receptionist."

She didn't want that. What else would she do for the three full and two half days a week when they weren't having office hours? "If I don't get it right, okay," she said, "but if you're satisfied, I'd like to do it here."

"I couldn't be more pleased," he said, and his grin assured her that he meant it.

"Thank you, sir."

He sat down, leaned back in his desk chair, picked up a pen and tapped it rapidly on the desk, reminding her that he could be impatient. "Melanie. I have asked you not to call me sir, and I don't want to hear that word come out of your mouth again when you're addressing me."

She looked straight at him, took in his thunderous gaze and said, "Sorry, sir. I'll try not to do it again, sir."

"Wh-what?" She glanced at him from the corner of her eye, saw the deep crevice in his forehead and the pensive expression on his face. He sat forward, ran his hands over his tight curls and only then did he look at her. "I can't decide whether to throttle you or kiss you."

"Want some coffee?" she asked him.

He slumped in the chair and roared with laughter. "You're priceless, and in more ways than one."

As usual, the waiting room filled up almost as soon as Melanie unlocked the door. "What's wrong with your shoulder?" Jack asked her, when she couldn't lift a two-year-old girl.

"It's…it's bruised, I guess. Nothing, really."

He looked at her strangely, as if he knew she hadn't

leveled with him. But he didn't say more about it. After they tended to the last patient around a quarter of nine, he walked up behind her and placed his hand heavily on her shoulder.

"Oh!" she exclaimed, wincing visibly.

With both hands, he turned her around to face him. "Now, what happened to your shoulder after you left here Tuesday night? Something did. What was it?"

"You don't want to know."

"Oh, but I do, and you're going to tell me. Unbutton this and let me look at it."

"But—"

"You don't want me to do that for you. Do you?" He didn't smile. Indeed, she'd rarely seen him so serious. She tried to unbutton the dress with her right hand, but pain shot through her right shoulder, and she had to use her left hand.

"I'll do it," he said. "Did you fall?" When she shook her head, a frown clouded his face. "Don't tell me somebody hit you."

Tears pooled in her eyes, and she tried to turn her back to him, because she didn't want him to see her fall apart, but he wouldn't allow it. "Talk to me, Melanie. I care about you." He slipped the uniform off her shoulder.

"My God! Who did this to you?" He examined the bruises on her shoulder and upper arm, careful not to cause her pain. "I don't know whether there's a fracture. If it hurts tomorrow, I want you to get a CT scan. All right?"

She could no longer restrain the tears, and sobs wracked her body. His hands reached out to her, but then he stepped back. "Who was it, Melanie? This is criminal."

"My…my father bumped into me, and I fell."

"Your *father?* Good Lord!" His arms enveloped her, and she couldn't stop the tears. He picked her up, carried her to one of the leather chairs and sat with her in his lap.

"Tell me about it." She did, beginning with the day her mother died. He soothed her as best he could, but they both knew she wasn't sitting on Jack Ferguson's lap because of what her father did.

"Why do you stay with him?"

"Because my mother begged me not to leave him until I finished school, and because he gave me a home, such as it was, even though he expects me to pay for it."

"I want you to get your own apartment. If you continue to stay with him, one day he may endanger your life, even kill you. You don't owe him a damn thing. Do you want me to go home with you tonight?"

"Oh, no! That would really set him off. He'll be furious when I get there, but he'll see a different Melanie. I've always been respectful, but not tonight. I'll give him as good as he gives me."

"If you're sure, but I'm here if you need me. He's a bully, but he won't take me on. Please don't provoke him."

She stood, looked down at him and wondered why she wasn't in his arms. Without thinking of the implications of what she did, she reached down and stroked his cheek. "You're such a good man, a wonderful human being. A prince."

His eyes darkened as his gaze locked on her, and she knew at once that she'd done and said the wrong thing. He bounded out of the chair. "You think I'm a prince, do you?" His stare challenged her to lie.

She'd never stammered before, so why couldn't her words come out. "You kn-know…wh-what I mean."

"No, I don't." He brought her to him so quickly that she didn't know how it happened.

"Jack…I—"

He tightened his hold on her. "You knew it had to happen. You knew it the minute we met," he whispered, and his lips, sweet and hot, burned her mouth, and wave on wave of heat seared her. "Open up to me, Melanie." Tremors laced his voice.

Shivers raced through her in anticipation of the feel of him inside her at last. She parted her lips, and he went into her, testing, tasting and sampling every crevice, ever centimeter of her mouth. She sucked his tongue deeper into her mouth, and as his long fingers stroked her back, she feasted on it. Her nipples tightened against his chest, and she rubbed on him in frustration. Her groans mingled with his, and suddenly she pushed him away from her. But, as quickly, he brought her back into the cradle of his arms as if to soften the brunt of their separation. Her eyes and her cheeks bloomed beneath the sweetness of his lips.

"I don't know what we're going to do about this, Melanie, but I do know that I wanted you the minute I saw you. I thought I could control it or that it would wear off, but I've been learning how unlikely that is. Are you all right?"

She stared at him, feeling not one bit angelic. "Apart from frustration, you mean?"

The sound of laughter began deep in him and slowly rumbled out of his throat. "Your choice. I know how you feel. Will you call me when you get home? I'll stay right here until I hear from you. Tomorrow, you take the day off and look for an apartment."

"Hmm. I see the bossy Jack is back with us. I already know where I want to stay. It's a development that opened several weeks ago. I'll call them in the morning."

He took both of her hands and looked into her eyes. "I'm counting on that, Melanie. I don't want to think of you living there any longer. You've paid your dues, and he owes you a better life than he's given you. I don't mean financially, because I don't know his circumstances, but he owed you a father's love and protection from abuse and harm of any kind. I find it hard to forgive him for causing you to fall and hurt yourself. If you need money for the rent, phone me, and you can have a salary advance."

He called for a taxi and, to her astonishment, he kissed her lips before walking with her to the taxi. She didn't look at him, but merely stumbled into the cab and listened dumbfounded while Jack gave the driver her address. She supposed he remembered it from the information she'd given him the day he'd hired her.

"Thanks," she remembered to say as the taxi pulled away.

* * *

"You're late again. Where's the money?" her father called when she entered the house.

She didn't run up the stairs like a scared rabbit as she usually did when he began one of his tirades, but walked into the living room and faced him. "I have always respected you as my father. Last night, you almost broke my shoulder. If you ever touch me again, you will regret it for as long as you live."

He stared at her, his eyes wide in an expression of disbelief. "You got a mouth on you. I'll close it for you."

She didn't move. "Don't try it, Daddy. I'm not taking any more of your abuse. Good night."

His demeanor seemed rigid, almost as if he were suspended in disbelief, as he seemed to decide whether to challenge her. For once, she didn't fear him. It occurred to her that a man who would push a woman around was probably a coward. She walked into the kitchen and telephoned Jack.

"It's all right," she told him. "He began his usual harassment, but I called him on it, and he backed down. I won't be at work tomorrow morning, because I'll be renting that apartment." After they talked for a few minutes, she hung up, made a sandwich and got a glass of milk, sat down and ate it. Then she went to her room, closed the door and began packing her things.

By noon the next day, she had the keys to a two-bedroom apartment. She phoned a company that promised to deliver a mattress within two hours, included some bed linen with her personal belongings, got a folding chair from the kitchen and telephoned for a taxi. She didn't leave a message. "If he doesn't know why, telling him won't help," she told herself. That night, she slept in her own apartment.

Melanie awakened the next morning, dressed and went shopping. With so little money, she could only buy kitchen essentials and food for the weekend. She found a pay phone and called Jack.

"Where are you?" he asked, and she hoped that his urgent tone reflected his concern for her, not as his nurse, but as a woman.

"I'm in the supermarket. I don't have a phone yet, so—"

"What do you mean you don't have a phone?"

"Sorry. I got ahead of myself. Late yesterday, I moved into my own apartment. It's—"

"You what? With what? How?"

"With a taxi. I only have a mattress and a folding chair, Jack, but it's mine. It's quiet and peaceful, and I'm so happy I could cry."

"Do you have money for furniture and other things you need?"

"Some. Monday, I'll know how much of a salary advance I need."

"Good. What's your new address?" She told him. "Terrific," he said. "Now go to this place and get a cell phone right now. I'll call there and tell them you're coming. Just give your name."

"But I can't let you—"

"I need to be in touch with my nurse."

"I don't think so, Jack." She was already obligated to him, and she didn't intend to get further in debt to him.

"Consider it partial pay for your overtime."

She thought about it for a minute, and decided that it made sense. "All right. I can do that, and thanks so much for your help."

"I haven't done anything to earn your gratitude," he countered. "Call me as soon as you figure out what you'll need in order to get your apartment livable."

"Okay. See you Tuesday."

"Woman, let me tell you something. You and I can work together as professionals, and we'll make a great team. But we will never again be who we were at ten minutes to nine Tuesday night, a minute before you pulled my tongue into your mouth," he said in the voice of a person thoroughly exasperated. "And don't you forget it. We'll never be the same."

At least *she* wouldn't, and where did that leave her? Too annoyed with him to cover her tracks, she spoke from her heart. "What do you think I am, Jack, a piece of wood?" She didn't heed his gasp. "I do not need to be reminded of the way I felt in your arms. Goodbye."

Jack listened to the dial tone and slowly shook his head. He had no choice but to learn how to follow Melanie's lead. And maybe that wouldn't be such a bad thing. The chemistry between them threatened to cause an explosion, and after that sample of her fire and passion for him, he knew they would eventually make love. She wanted him as badly as he wanted her, and because she was without guile and wasn't coy, she either couldn't hide what she felt or didn't consider it.

He had spent too much time with women who pretended what they didn't feel, said what they didn't mean and behaved as if a man was their whole world when, in fact, an intelligent child could see right through their chicanery.

When his cell phone rang immediately after Melanie hung up, he answered without checking the caller ID.

Thinking he would hear Melanie's voice, he said, "Did you call to apologize for hanging up on me?"

"What? Who do you think you're talking to?" He recognized Elaine's voice, closed his eyes and looked toward the ceiling. "What can I do for you, Elaine? I hope you didn't call to chew me out about my second office, because—"

She interrupted him. "That and you've been avoiding me these past days. Can't you find some other way to waste your time? Honest, Jack. This is too much."

From honey to gall in one minute. He took a deep breath, hooked his foot under a chair to drag it closer to the table and took a seat. "Yes, Elaine, I agree that it's too much. I'd rather not have this conversation with you over the phone, but since you brought it up, so be it. I am not wasting my time when I care for the sick. I took an oath to do that. I've been avoiding you while I figured out an easy, gracious way to tell you that I don't want to see you anymore." He ignored the sputters on the other end of the line. "It isn't working for me. In fact, it never has. I wish you the best."

"You can't do this to me," she screamed, "I won't let you."

"You made the mistake of behaving as if you own me. I don't need to be possessed. I need to be loved, and you're incapable of loving anyone but Elaine. We're neither married not engaged, and I have never professed to love you. We were pretty good friends until you decided that my work is…I believe you said, 'ridiculous.' My work is who I am, and I do not need friends who tell me to my face that I'm ridiculous."

"How can you say that? What will all our friends think?"

"You'll eventually find another guy with a Porsche. Nothing you can say will change how I feel, Elaine. I'm sorry."

He hung up, his relief almost palpable. Elaine Jackson represented a lesson that he did not expect to learn again. He hadn't chosen her; she'd chosen him, and it had been convenient to associate with a woman who belonged to his social set, a legacy from his socially conscious father. More like his mother than his father, he had never judged people wholly on the basis of their material trappings. He had always known that his mother would have disliked Elaine, just as he knew she would have loved Melanie. The passing of seventeen years had not lessened his need for his mother's counsel, understanding, warmth and affection.

The following week, after having performed a long and tedious operation on a man he had known for years, Jack met his father for their usual Wednesday lunch. He wanted to discuss the young girl in his South Baltimore office whose tests showed that she had sickle-cell anemia. His father would know the best course of treatment, but he didn't feel like a lecture about his office in that neighborhood. So, their conversation centered on the banal. However, Jack knew his father would have a point to make, because he always spoke his mind when something wasn't going his way.

"I got a call from Elaine last weekend," Montague said. "She was completely distraught."

Jack didn't stop eating the raspberry sorbet that he loved. "Yeah. I can imagine. Discussing my personal affairs with my father is one of the reasons why she had reason to be distraught. The other reason is that I have never loved her. How could I? She's too calculating and too possessive. Please don't mention her to me again."

Montague sipped his espresso, something he insisted on having after every meal except breakfast. "All right," he said. "But you're making a mistake. She's a fine woman."

Jack struggled to control his facial expression. He honored his father and didn't want to appear rude. "You would want your son to spend his life with a woman he didn't love? I don't believe it."

Montague threw up his hands. "Enough said. But it's time you got married and started a family. I want some grandchildren."

"Now, that I can agree with." He looked at the bill and pushed it toward his father. "I paid last time." They embraced at the front of the restaurant, and Jack leaned against the post that supported the restaurant's canopy and watched his father get into his Cadillac De Ville and drive off. He'd swear that there wasn't a speck of lint or dirt anywhere on that car, not even on the white walls of its tires. Montague Ferguson would sit on a Harley about as quickly as he'd jump into a seething volcano. Jack shook his head in wonder. *If I wasn't the spitting image of him, I'd wonder about our blood ties.*

He had an urge to get to his other office. It was unusual, he knew, because he'd never been consumed with a desire to get to his Bolton Hill office. But what the heck!

Having that second office added a new and exciting dimension to his life. *Go ahead and fool yourself,* his conscience needled. *You love the work, but it's the woman who's pulling you there right now.*

He drove the Town Car to his office and, to his surprise, he found the space in front of his office blocked off at three-thirty in the afternoon. Two boys dashed over from nowhere and removed the orange cones.

"Hi, Doc," they said in unison. "We don't let nobody into your space."

He thanked them, unlocked his office and went inside. She stood on a ladder changing a lightbulb. "Melanie, for goodness' sake, what are you doing up there?" he asked her. "Couldn't you wait till I got here?"

Her smile warmed him all over, and he admitted to himself again that she was the reason why he was there and not at the club, swimming.

"Hi. You're early. If I don't have light, I can't see how to work, so I'm putting in some new lightbulbs."

"That's fine, but hop down. I'll change the others." He opened his arms. "Come on. I'll catch you. Don't you trust me?"

From the sudden tension in her shoulders, he guessed that she was about to be stubborn, and she proved him right. "I trust you implicitly, but I want to get some work done, and playing house with you won't cut it. Besides, that's not why we're here."

He knew he was getting to her, that she felt the heat of his body, that she was sensitive to him, and he meant to see how far he could go before she got her back up. She had some compunction about letting herself go with him, and that was probably wise, but he didn't give her high odds for succeeding.

He grinned at her. "We wouldn't be playing house. This isn't the kind of house I play. Come on. You could work while I do that. My arms are wide open and I'm a strong guy, so don't be afraid. I won't hold you too close."

As if she'd planned it—and he knew she hadn't—her foot slipped, and he caught her. Whether she was embarrassed or merely disgusted, he wasn't certain, but hard as he tried, he couldn't control the laughter. He set her on her feet, stepped on the ladder and inserted the track lights.

"How's your apartment coming?" he asked her.

"Wonderful. It's livable, it's mine and I'm the only one who lives there."

He signed the checks she'd written to pay several bills and decided that he'd be wise to leave. "I'll see you tomorrow," he told her.

"Uh, Doctor. Midge's mother has called here twice about her condition, and—"

He looked at her. "You didn't want to bother me? Melanie, I'm that child's doctor. Always let me know when a patient calls about something serious. Midge's condition is very serious. What's her address? Phone her mother and ask her if she wants me to go there and have a look at the child."

He looked at the address that Melanie had written on the back of one of his cards. "How far away is this?"

"A little over two blocks. Midge's mother wants you to come." She gave him directions.

"I'll walk. See you later." He got two half-pint containers of ice cream from the freezer, left the office and covered the two short blocks in about five minutes. As he waited for Midge's mother to answer the door, he wondered what he'd find. He had never entered the home of a really poor person, and when he walked into the small apartment—one of two on the first floor of what had once been a single-family home—he realized that its neat appearance surprised him.

He shook hands with Alice Hawkins and followed her to a sparse but tidy bedroom, where Midge lay in bed. He sat beside the bed, took the girl's hand and smiled when she opened her eyes.

"How are you, Midge? Remember me? I'm Dr. Ferguson."

"Hi, Doctor. Did you bring me any ice cream? In the office, you have ice cream."

"Yes, I did. I remembered that you like raspberry. It's

my favorite, too. Where do you hurt?" She pointed to her chest, and he took out his stethoscope and examined her. "Does it hurt especially when you cough?"

"Yes, sir."

He knew she had a fever, but he took her temperature nonetheless. "Well, Midge, I have to give you some medicine, and it comes in a needle. It didn't hurt much the last time, did it?"

"No, sir, but can I have the ice cream first?"

"Absolutely." He gave it to her and prepped her arm while her eyes gleamed in anticipation of enjoying her favorite treat. After giving Midge the antibiotic and taking her temperature, he gave the thermometer to her mother and showed her how to use it. "She's at a hundred and one degrees. It should drop now. If it doesn't, or if it climbs the slightest bit, call me." He handed her his card. "We'll have to work out a plan for her. In the meantime, give her two of these tablets every four hours and one of these vitamin compounds each morning at breakfast. If she's feeling well enough, bring her to my office tomorrow during office hours."

He gave Midge the other cup of ice cream, patted her hand, turned to leave and stopped. Alice Hawkins trembled and tears cascaded down her face. "Now, now, Mrs. Hawkins. Don't worry. She'll be fine."

The woman shook her head. "You're the only doctor who's ever been in this apartment. Doctors don't visit the sick, Dr. Ferguson. When I called, I just wanted to ask you what I could do for Midge, and when Miss Sparks said you'd come if I needed you and asked me if I wanted you to come here, I almost said no. I won't even try to thank you. You know I don't have any money and no insurance. I don't want public assistance, so we live off what I can make with bake sales, but with Midge so sick these past few days, I haven't been able to bake a thing."

Her eyes nearly doubled in size when he gave her two twenty-dollar bills. But he quickly explained. "Ms. Sparks orders four cranberry scones and four doughnuts—two plain and two chocolate—every Tuesday and every Thursday, and we'd as soon have you as our supplier."

"I'll do that gladly, Doctor, but I can't let you pay me, not after the way you've been taking care of Midge for nothing."

"Put it in Midge's piggy bank, then. I refuse to take it back. See you tomorrow night."

The following day, Thursday, he arrived at the South Baltimore office a few minutes before five o'clock, having decided to keep his emotions in check where Melanie was concerned. That morning, he had performed a difficult operation that had exhausted him so much he canceled his Bolton Hill office hours and went home to rest.

As he opened the door of an examining room, having told the patient to dress and come to the office, he noticed a young boy whose age he estimated to be around nine come into the waiting room carrying a baseball bat as if it were buried treasure.

"Ms. Sparks, can I see Dr. Ferguson?" he heard the boy say.

"All right," she told him, "but he has a patient. He can see you in half an hour or so. How are you feeling?"

"Oh, I'm not sick anymore, but I want to see Dr. Ferguson."

Jack went into the waiting room. "What may I do for you?" he asked the boy, looking down at the sketch pad in the boy's hands. He recognized the beginnings of real talent. "Nice drawings."

"Thanks. I guess you don't remember me, sir. My grandmother—actually, she's my great-grandmother— told me you saved my life. She said everybody at the hospital ignored her but you. I brought you this." The boy handed him the baseball bat. "My name is Tommy."

Jack scrutinized first the boy and then the bat. "Oh yes, I remember you, Tommy, but I can't accept this. It's very valuable."

"I know that, sir. Derek Jeter signed it for me one day when it was raining, and you have to take it. Please. I want you to have it." The boy's eyes beseeched him.

Jack hunkered beside the boy whose illness had changed Jack's life, awakening him to a world that he knew existed, but hadn't understood or cared to investigate. The child gazed at him as if he were regarding a saint. He draped his arm around Tommy's shoulder. "Thank you, Tommy. I'll cherish this. I see you like to draw."

"Yes, sir, and I can draw you. Can you sit there for a minute?"

He didn't have time, but how could he say no? "Yes, but only for a couple of minutes."

A few minutes later, the boy tore off the sheet from

the pad and handed it to Jack, whose jaw dropped when he looked at it.

"This is unbelievable. It's definitely me. Would you sign it, please? I'll give it to my father."

Tommy signed the drawing. "Friends?" he asked.

Jack felt his face crease into a wide, happy grin. "Good friends. How's your grandma?"

"Fine, except she's always tired. I have to bring her something from the store. See you next time."

"Thank you for the bat, Tommy." He made a mental note to see that Tommy didn't slip through the cracks. His guardian was a woman in her late eighties or early nineties, and the boy would need support.

At home that night, anxious for some quick answers, Jack ate his dinner sitting at his computer. He wanted to learn as much as he could about St. Jude Children's Research Hospital in Memphis, because an idea had begun to form in his mind, and he believed it had merit. Children under age twelve constituted half of his patient load, and he was even less of a pediatrician than he was an internist. Melanie was a quick study, and she could learn a lot during a six-week internship at the country's leading children's hospital. On the Internet, he found a telephone number and an e-mail address and, most importantly, encouragement to dialogue with St. Jude doctors about the health care of his patients. He made notes, signed off, went downstairs to the refrigerator and treated himself to a bottle of beer. He didn't know when he'd felt so good. His dad wasn't with him, but he could talk with doctors at St. Jude Children's Research Hospital who would sympathize with what he was trying to do.

The next morning as soon as he arrived at his Bolton Hill office, he telephoned Alice Hawkins and took a complete history of Midge's ailments and treatments. Since the girl hadn't been born in a hospital, but at home with the help of an old woman who served as midwife, she hadn't been screened for sickle-cell anemia. He made a note to revise the questionnaire he used for the children he treated in the South Baltimore office to include whether they had been screened for that ailment.

When he reached his office at three-thirty that day, Melanie greeted him with raspberry scones and coffee. "These are the best scones I have ever tasted," she said. "You only ordered them for Tuesday and Thursday, when *you're* here. How could you? What about the other days? What'll I eat then?"

He bit into the scone, savored it and let a smile drift over his face. "This is heavenly. I like you just the way you are, and eating two of these things five days a week would ruin your perfect figure."

"Will not."

"Will so. And nothing's worse than a good figure gone bad."

"You can't be serious," she said. "If I thought you were, I'd—"

"You'd what?"

She didn't answer, just sat there eating the scone, sipping coffee and licking her lips. When she put the last piece into her mouth, she slumped down in the chair and moaned lightly. "Boy was that good!" She crossed her knees and closed her eyes.

He stared at her, so soft and so sensuous. He didn't doubt that if they had been anywhere private other than his office, he'd have been inside her within five minutes.

"Why are you looking at me that way?" she asked him, her face the picture of confusion.

"You can't possibly know how sensual you are. Right now, I want you badly enough to steal you." She sat up, clearly stunned. "Don't worry, Melanie. I've been properly brought up."

"What good will that do?" she asked him as she removed the cups. "You were, but I was shortchanged."

His lower jaw hung. "What're you saying?"

"That it takes two to tango. Wish me luck."

Chapter 4

Jack pushed thoughts of Melanie from his mind. He looked down his little patient's throat, didn't see any evidence of a problem, confirmed that she should see a dentist and was about to tell the twelve-year-old as much when, to his amazement, she smiled and winked at him. He could see that she'd reached puberty, but he wouldn't have thought that she was already flirting with older men.

"What was that about?" he asked her.

"I just wanted to see if you'd notice."

"Really? What do you think your mother would say if I told her how fresh you are?"

"Please don't do that. She might tell my dad, and he'd kill me."

He adopted his most serious expression. "In that

case, I'll mention it directly to your father. I dislike young women who tease men, and I may decide not to treat you again."

"Oh, please, Dr. Ferguson. Please don't do that. You don't know my father."

"Well, since you know him, behave yourself and act your age. That's all for tonight."

It hadn't occurred to him that girls that young knew how to entice men. Just one more reason why children should be cared for by pediatricians. One day, he'd find one willing to share his office. For the time being, however, he'd do his best, and he refused to let anyone or anything—including a fresh, pubescent girl—disrupt his contentment and his sense of satisfaction with his work.

Toward the end of his evening office hours, Melanie rushed into his examining room. "Doctor, I'm sorry to disturb you, but I have an emergency. The patient is in the next examining room."

"Who is it?"

"Alma, and it's more than her asthma. It doesn't look good."

While they hurried to the other examining room, he pulled on a new pair of rubber gloves, nodded to the child's father and examined her chest. "How long has she been sick?"

"Since Sunday, Doctor, but I thought she'd get better. We gave her aspirin and tea with honey and vinegar, but she didn't get any better."

Jacked turned to Melanie. "Get an ambulance. She's got pneumonia." He called the child. "Alma, this is Dr.

Ferguson, your favorite doctor. How do you feel?" He tried several times, but she didn't respond.

A boy knocked on the door of the examining room. "The ambulance is here, Dr. Ferguson."

Jack went into the waiting room where two people waited to see him. "I have to take this patient to the hospital. Do you feel that you can't wait to see me until Thursday? If you can wait till then, you'll be first."

"I just need some more medicine, Doctor," one man said. "I don't have any more pills." He handed the empty bottle to Jack.

"The nurse will give them to you." He looked at the woman who sat across the room reading the newspaper. "I'm fine, Doctor. I just came tonight to read the paper. At least I get to read one twice a week."

He patted her shoulder, and handed the empty pill bottle to Melanie. "Get four samples and give them to Mr. Bond, please. I'd better hurry. Call the taxi when you're ready to leave and lock up, will you?" He beckoned to Alma's father. "We're going to General."

Jack knew that with chronic asthma, pneumonia in both lungs and a temperature at one hundred and four degrees, the child was in grave danger. He also suspected that she'd lapsed into a coma. He put on his professional face, the impassive expression he donned when a patient wasn't doing well. The worst part of being a doctor was pretending that you didn't want to scream and shake your fist at the heavens when Providence removed a patient's well-being from your hands, and all of your skill and expertise amounted to nothing.

He and the child's father rode in the ambulance. It wasn't something he'd ordinarily do, but he knew the man didn't have insurance, and he remembered the predicament in which he found Tommy's great-grandmother well after midnight alone in a waiting room ignored by all who passed her. Of course, help was available for the indigent; the problem was that they didn't know their rights. He had the child admitted and joined the father in the waiting room.

"Thanks for coming with me, Doc," the man said. "You don't know what it means to me. No way would they take my child in ten minutes if I came here by myself."

A little more than half an hour later, Melanie joined them. "Any news yet?"

Jack shook his head. "I'm sure they're doing everything possible for her." To the father, he said, "Would you like me to run down to the cafeteria and get some coffee and a sandwich? You probably didn't have dinner."

"Thanks. I won't forget your kindness, but I couldn't eat a thing. My wife is probably going out of her mind."

Melanie opened her cell phone and handed it to the man. "Do you want to call her?"

Jack moved to Melanie's side while the man went outside to talk with his wife. He had a feeling that the longer they waited, the worse the news would be. With his elbows resting on his thighs, he lowered his head to his hands. In eight years of practice, he hadn't lost a patient. Several had died, but not from an ailment that he treated. He hated the feeling of helplessness. Melanie's hand eased into his palm, and her fingers locked with his. Her other hand stroked his cheek. He looked at her, saw the compassion in her eyes, knew it was for him and leaned back in the seat, trying to come to terms with the inevitable.

The news they finally got did not surprise Jack. The child had come to him too late. Jack watched as Melanie sat beside the child's father, put her arms around him and tried to comfort him. After accepting her ministrations for a few minutes, he stood and shook hands with Jack. "You did everything you could, and I won't forget it."

"Come with us," Jack said. He called for a taxi, took the man home and he and Melanie went back to the office where he'd left his car.

"Maybe we should get something to eat," he said to Melanie. "It's almost midnight, and we haven't had dinner." He opened the front passenger door of the Town Car, fastened her seat belt after she got in and then seated himself. He sat facing the steering wheel, and finally circled it with his arms and rested his head there.

"I've never felt so lousy in my life," he said. "If he'd brought her to me night before last, she'd still be alive, but he hated asking for favors, and he didn't come until he was desperate. I have to find another way."

"Maybe if…" Her hand stroked his back. "Oh, Jack. It hurts me, too, but I know you feel it more. Maybe if you tell them to pay whatever they can afford, from a dollar on?"

"Some don't have a penny for medicine, Melanie. You know that. If they had to pay the cost of transportation to get to my office, half of them wouldn't come."

"Do you want me to drive?" she asked him. "I've never driven a Town Car, but I don't think I'd wreck it."

"Thanks, but I can drive."

He parked in front of an all-night White Castle. They ordered the famous hamburgers and coffee and sat beside each other in a booth near the window. "I wonder how that poor man faced his wife," Jack said.

"It couldn't have been easy," she replied and handed him a tiny envelope that contained a hand-sanitizing wipe, explaining that she always carried a few of them in her pocketbook.

"That's a good idea. Thanks."

Their hamburgers arrived, and Jack picked one up, bit into it and managed to chew, but he could barely swallow it. "I don't have an appetite," Melanie said, pushing the food away. "I love these burgers, but I just can't eat right now."

He slipped an arm around her waist and pulled her a little closer to him. "I know. I don't want any food, either. I almost choked on that." He sipped the coffee. "Is it all right with you if we go?"

"Sure." They didn't speak at all during the drive to the apartment building in which she lived. He parked near the front door of her building and turned to her.

Melanie knew that in Jack's present frame of mind, he didn't want to be alone. He felt the child's death as if it were his personal responsibility, and though the first loss of one of her patients cut her to the quick, her training in putting a distance between herself and the patients' condition helped her to put the incident in perspective.

Jack walked with her to the door of her apartment, and no one had to tell her that he didn't want to leave her. He closed his eyes, pulled her to him and tightened his arms around her. "I don't want to leave you," he whispered.

She didn't want him to leave, either, but she always thought ahead to the consequences of her acts. "Is it because you're depressed?" she asked him.

"I don't doubt that my defenses are lower, but I wouldn't want to leave you, even if nothing had happened tonight."

Her right hand went to his left cheek almost of its own volition, and, as he gazed down at her with all the pain, misery, passion and affection that churned in him reflected in his eyes, she couldn't have resisted him if her life had depended on it. "Come in for a little while, Jack. I don't know why, but I'm scared to death about bringing you into my apartment after midnight."

His famous grin did not materialize when he said, "Why? What can happen after midnight in your apartment that couldn't happen at twelve noon? If I know my facts, passion can go wild anytime, day or night."

"Excuse me. I'll be right back," she told him once they were in her apartment. "Have a seat somewhere." She went to the kitchen, heated two slices of pizza in the microwave oven, boiled water for drip coffee and was back in the living room in less than ten minutes.

"I want you to eat this, Jack. You'll wake up at three

in the morning starved. It's not much, so have some. Sorry I don't have any beer."

He never took kindly to being ordered to do anything. He hadn't, even as a child. But he realized that she wanted to take care of him right then, and he needed that care. He also needed her honest expression of it. He took the tray from her, put it on the coffee table and looked at her. "I'll eat it, and I appreciate your concern for me, but what I need from you most of all is some sign that you care."

Both of her eyebrows shot up, and she imagined that her face bore an expression of disbelief. "Jack, do you think I make coffee and heat food for just any man at almost one-fifteen in the morning? And do I kiss Tom, Dick and Harry as I've kissed you?"

"I tell myself I'm special to you, and I try to believe it, but you have a way of punching a hole in this balloon when I least expect it."

"Your pizza is getting cold."

"Yeah. By the way, I love pepperoni pizza."

She patted his hand, because she had to touch him, and any part of him would suffice. "So do I. I keep some in the freezer for the times I don't feel like cooking."

"Invite me to dinner sometime. I imagine you're as good a cook as you are a nurse."

"Thanks for the compliment. I'll graduate soon, and I'd like you to come to my graduation. I'm not going to invite my father, because he might cause a scene and spoil the occasion for me. But I want someone to be there for me. Would you come?"

"Of course I'll come. When is it?" She told him and

watched him make a note in his date book. "It will be my pleasure." He finished the pizza and drained the coffee cup. "I'll take this to the kitchen."

She rushed to take the tray from him. "Oh, no. You're my guest." He continued to the kitchen as if he hadn't heard her. But she knew him by now, and little that he did surprised her. She hastened to turn on the kitchen's ceiling light and bumped into him as he placed the tray on a counter.

"You're exactly what I needed, and I'd rather not leave. But I know that if I don't get out of here, I could ruin something that's very special. I... Oh, Melanie. I..."

He needed her. She knew it, and her arms opened to him. She tried to control the trembling of her lips when he brought her to him and locked her to his body. Tremors raced through her, and she knew he could feel her body shake. Her unsteady hands reached for his nape, and then his mouth was on her, fierce and hungry. She parted her lips to receive him and groans escaped her when his tongue began its lover's dance. He imprisoned her between himself and the wall, and his hand roamed over her arms and her back. Heat roared through her veins as her blood raced hot and fast to her loins. Her breasts grew heavy, and her nipples ached until, in need of relief, she rubbed them against him mercilessly.

He placed his hand on her left breast, and when she pressed his hand, he asked her, "What do you want? Tell me."

When she undulated against him, he lifted her and kissed her aching flesh. Out of her mind with desire, she ripped off the first three buttons of her dress, and seconds later screams tore out of her when his warm, moist mouth covered her nipple. She closed her eyes and let him have her.

"If you're going to send me home," he said, his voice low and guttural, "do it now."

Her senses returned at once, and she pressed against his shoulder. He set her on her feet and wrapped her in his arms. "I didn't mean to let it get that far," she said, "but you...you got to me. These feelings... I've never had them before. I hope you'll forgive me," she whispered.

With both arms still tightly around her, he said, "Forgive you for what? For being one hundred percent woman? I didn't push it, because I know you wouldn't be comfortable having me for a lover. Not yet, at least. But, honey, the chemistry between us is like lightning. When we make love, we'll be like a forest fire after a long, long drought."

A man shouldn't be that sure of a woman. She gathered herself, laid back her shoulders and looked him in the eye. "Did you say *when?* I'm not that sure."

"I am. This level of attraction is rare. It's also precious, and I'm wise enough not to let it slip by. You should be, too. We need more time to know each other, but if desire takes over..." He grinned. "You know the rest."

"I certainly do." She reached up and kissed his lips. "Go home."

He stared at her. "If you want me to go, that is definitely not the way to get me to do it. Walk me to the door."

With his hand on the doorknob, he looked down at

her. "I'll call you tomorrow morning around ten. All right?" She nodded. He caressed her cheek with the back of his hand, opened the door and left. She locked the door and went to the kitchen thinking for the first time that a relationship with Jack Ferguson might be possible. *She had begun to need him, but so much stood between them, even if he acted as if it didn't. Wasn't this what she'd feared from the outset?*

Jack drove home slowly, entered his house through the kitchen, emptied the still-warm food Vernie had left him into the garbage disposal, and went upstairs to his room. He had to get up at six, so he had four hours to rest following one of the most difficult experiences in his profession, but when he checked his calendar, he saw that he didn't have to operate that morning and set his alarm clock for eight o'clock. That would give him plenty of time to keep a consultation appointment at nine-thirty.

He showered, dried off and slipped into his king-size sleigh bed. The cool sheets, which Vernie changed every day, and the hard mattress soothed him only a little. Fire still raged in his loins from the fueling he'd received while he caressed, fondled and suckled Melanie. He didn't ask himself where he was headed with her, because he had already decided that she pleased him as no other woman had—morally, intellectually and physically. Moreover, she believed in him and supported his efforts. So, if what he felt for her developed to the point where he didn't want to be without her, he would embrace it and her. He wouldn't push it forward, but he wouldn't fight it, either.

He wished he could talk with his father and ask him how he dealt with the loss of a patient. After his one-hour consultation with interns later that morning, he went to the doctors' lounge in the hospital and telephoned his father.

"How are you, son? Ben and I are thinking of going on a fishing trip this weekend. I'd be glad if you'd come along with us."

"I'd like that, too, Dad, but I'm leaving Sunday evening for a medical convention in Atlanta. I'm doing a workshop, and I need Saturday to prepare for it."

"A workshop, eh? That's the way to get the respect of your peers. Have you closed that place in South Baltimore? That's what's taking up your time. If you hadn't been down *there,* you'd have finished polishing your lecture."

Montague Ferguson hadn't asked why his son had called him at ten-thirty in the morning, rather than in the evening when he usually called. Oh, what was the use! He hung up and phoned the doctor at St. Jude Children's Research Hospital with whom he had developed a dialogue.

"It's Ferguson," he said when the doctor answered the phone. They spoke for a few minutes before Jack asked the man, "How do you handle the death of a child who trusted you? I had my first experience with that last night, and it's eating me like acid. The father brought the child to my office when she was already in a coma."

"What was her problem?"

"She had chronic asthma and developed double pneumonia."

"I see. And she was in a coma, right? You couldn't have done one thing other than console the parents. I had to learn early in my practice that when I did everything I could, the loss of a child was not my fault, and that I cannot alter God's agenda. It hurts. You and I are human. We go the limit for our patients, but we do have limits, and we have to accept that."

He thought for a minute. "Thanks. I appreciate your words and your time. I'll be in touch."

"Any time, Doctor Ferguson. If I was of any help, *I* thank *you.*"

He phoned Melanie and waited impatiently for the sound of her voice. When she said hello, waves of relief and contentment washed over him. "How are you this morning? You didn't get much sleep."

"I'm in good shape. I've been waiting to find out how you made it. I prayed that you wouldn't have to perform heart surgery this morning."

"Thanks. I didn't have to operate this morning, and trust me, I was happy about that. This call isn't about work. I wanted to know how you are. But I remember that as I was leaving the office last evening I asked you to give Mr. Bond most of the samples of metoprolol that I had in the office. Would you please phone the company and get some more samples?"

"All right. We're getting calls already. I'll be out of the office for half an hour or so around noon, because I want to run over to the bereaved parents' home and take them some food. On occasions like this, lots of people come and sit with the family, and you have to have a lot of food for them."

"That's true. What are you taking?"

"I made biscuits and a big pan of candied sweet potatoes. I didn't have time to do more."

"What's the address?" She told him. "Thanks. I'll have something delivered." He surprised himself when he said, "We're off tonight. Why don't we make ourselves a picnic, get a blanket and enjoy it by the lake in Druid Hill Park? I haven't done that in years."

"It's a wonderful idea, but I hear that park has deteriorated. Maybe we shouldn't go there at night."

"Point taken. What'll we do? I want to spend the evening with you, and something tells me a public place is our best bet."

"Let's go down to the Inner Harbor, sit by the water and watch the boats and the people." He tried unsuccessfully to imagine Elaine telling him that she would enjoy such a simple evening, not to speak of suggesting it.

"If you know where we can be in a quiet place there, great," he said. "Otherwise, we can go for a drive to a great picnic place beside a lovely pond out near Owings Mills. If we're lucky, there'll be a jazz band or a string quartet there."

"Where you lead I follow," she said. "Who's packing the picnic basket?"

"It's my party. You bring the cookies. I'll be at your place at five."

It would be the first time he had been with her on a

purely social occasion, and he could hardly wait to see how they behaved with each other. He believed that their employee-employer relationship was a strike against him, at least to her mind, but he needed to know her a lot better than he did, and it seemed as if he also had a great deal to learn about himself.

At four o'clock, Melanie closed and locked the office, dashed home, changed into a white pantsuit, yellow tank top and white espadrilles. Dressed that way, she could go anyplace, even to the opera. She combed out her hair and let it hang to her shoulders, put a pair of gold hoops in her ears, put on some lipstick and looked at her watch. She hadn't been able to afford expensive clothes, but she shopped carefully and always appeared well dressed.

She opened the door when he rang the doorbell at five o'clock and looked at the breathtaking specimen of a man in white pants and a yellow polo T-shirt. Surprised, and not a little amused, she looked down and saw white sneakers on his feet. Laughter bubbled up in her.

"Hi," he said. "What's funny?"

"If I pull off this jacket, we'll be dressed alike."

He leaned forward, kissed her nose and said, "My white jacket's in the car. You're so beautiful. I've never seen your hair down. Gosh, I'm not sure I want to share you with a lot of people."

She certainly didn't want to share him, but he'd never hear her say it. She got the rum cookies that she'd made before leaving home that morning, hooked the strap of her white shoulder bag over her shoulder and looked up at him. "I'm ready."

"You mean we're going in this?" she said when he led her to the Porsche. "Gosh, I've never been within a mile of one of these."

He put their picnic supplies in the trunk of the car, fastened her seat belt and went around to the driver's door. "I'm in the mood for three scoops of ice cream in a cone," he said, as he got into the car. "I feel as if someone peeled years off me."

She heard what he said, and she understood its meaning, but she doubted that he did. Nonetheless, the confession gave her comfort. He felt young, and after that, his singing as he headed toward Reisterstown Road didn't surprise her.

"We're in luck," he said. "A string quartet is performing this evening. I hope you like Mozart."

"I love chamber music. In fact, I love music."

"You haven't asked where we're going. Your confidence in me is enough to rattle a man's nerves. We're going to Owings Mills. It's one of my favorite small towns. I once considered building a house there, but it's a long trip to my office, so I thought better of it."

He found a place near a tree facing a small lake and neither too close to nor too far from the music stand. "There may be mosquitoes, Melanie, so it's a good idea to apply this insect repellent lotion on any exposed parts." Her laughter wrapped around him like warm sunshine. "You laugh at the damnedest things. What's amusing?"

"What exposed parts did you have in mind?"

His expression was nothing less than withering. "That top you're wearing isn't exactly hugging your neck. Mosquitoes will kiss your neck as quickly as I will, and they love those veins around your ankles."

"Yes, sir." She accepted the lotion and rubbed it on her feet, ankles, arms, neck, hands and chest. "A mosquito bite aggravates me for at least a week, sometimes longer."

He spread the blanket, put the food down, went to the car and returned with two stools and two pillows.

"You went to a lot of trouble."

"It wasn't any trouble. I want you to be comfortable."

"Thank you, Jack. You're…"

"I'm what?"

"I don't know exactly, but whatever you are is very nice, indeed."

He placed the two stools side by side and motioned for her to sit down. He remained standing, looked down at her and said, "You can't possibly understand how important those words are to me." She patted the stool beside her, and he sat on it, but facing her. "All day, I've been feeling kind of like a chicken whose feathers have been plucked. I don't understand it, because it's a new feeling for me. I also don't like it. And then you say something like that, and I feel ten feet tall and bulletproof."

She patted his hand. "You just needed a hug." She was getting used to that expression in his eyes, but familiarity didn't lessen the heat that it sent roaring through her veins.

"You're right, and I still need one."

She couldn't help grinning at his sudden small-boy demeanor, and she didn't try to stifle the words that tumbled from her lips. "Will I do?" she asked and opened her arms to him.

"You're the only one who *will* do, as you put it."

She hadn't expected that, and she could barely contain the joy she felt. She put her arms around him and rested his head against her breasts. "Anybody as sweet as you are deserves a hug."

He raised himself up straight, evidently to see her face. "Are you telling me you think I'm sweet?"

She was suddenly unsure that she wouldn't regret what she'd started. However, she'd promised herself always to be honest, so she nodded her head. "Uh-huh."

"Look here, Melanie. I don't want any head nods. Do you or don't you?"

"I do, and quit pushing me."

"I'm not... Oh, baby. I'm sorry. I hope I'm not usually so self-centered."

She changed the subject as soon as she could find a good topic. "By the way, when I went to see the Waters family at noon today to take the biscuits and candied sweet potatoes, Mr. Waters told me you sent them a baked ham."

"I can't take credit for doing anything special, Melanie. It cost me a phone call and a few measly dollars. You went to them. That meant something."

The string quartet assembled onstage and began tuning their instruments. Jack looked at his watch. "It's almost seven o'clock. I have a little battery-powered light for us to eat by. If you're hungry, I'll set out the food."

"Want me to help?" she asked, not because she wanted to, but it seemed appropriate.

"No. I want to pamper you, and that means you sit over there and decorate that stool."

She put one of the pillows against the tree trunk, rested her back against it and stretched her feet out in front of her. "I am in no mood to reprimand you for being bossy," she said. "Besides, I'm not used to pampering, and I find that I like it."

When she tried to remove her jacket, he said, "If you take that off, I'd better put some of this lotion on you, otherwise you'll be full of mosquito bites." He eased the jacket off her, saw the tiny straps of the tank top that covered her shoulders and said, "I'd better take care of this right now. Sit up straight." She did, and he spread the lotion on her neck, back and arms. Looking her in the eye and pointing to her cleavage, he said, "You want to put it there yourself, or are you going to let me do it?"

She didn't look at him. She couldn't, for her whole body reacted to the memory of his warm mouth pulling at her nipple. "I think you had a reason for suggesting that our outing be in a public place, didn't you?" she said. When he didn't answer, she took the lotion that he held in his hand and began applying it.

"Why didn't you want me to do it?" he asked her.

"I like your hands, Jack, but if I didn't have a sense of propriety, you wouldn't be here with me."

"You're right. I wouldn't be." He positioned the pillow behind her back, dragged the other stool closer to her and put the picnic basket on top of it. He set out their plates, glasses and utensils on the blanket and opened an odd-looking heavy plastic bag.

"What's in that?" she asked him.

"Madam, I can offer you warm spinach-bacon quiche, crab cakes, hot cheese biscuits, a green salad, cherry tomatoes and pinot grigio wine. The hot food is in this bag, and the cold things are in that one."

"Oh, Jack, you're so thoughtful. I'll have some of everything."

He served them as the musicians began the sweet strains of Mozart's "Divertimento in B-flat." She hadn't realized that darkness had fallen, and when she glanced up, she saw the moon and the stars. Some of the most beautiful music ever written replaced the night sounds and the whispers of human voices, washing over her like waves of heavenly contentment. Lost in the moment, she chewed the delicious crab cake and sipped the wine that Jack held to her lips.

"What is it? What's the matter?" he asked her, his tone so urgent that it shocked her.

"What do you mean?"

"You're crying. What's wrong?" His fingers brushed away the tears that cascaded down her cheeks.

"I didn't realize it," she said, dabbing at her face with the handkerchief he gave her. "I don't think… I know I've never been as happy in my entire life as I am right now. As much as I dreamed of a beautiful life when I was a child and later as a teenager, I never imagined an evening like this."

He leaned over and kissed her cheek. "Nothing you've said to me has touched me like this."

She smiled, and then she laughed, because she didn't want to change the mood. "I haven't tried the quiche yet. If it's as good as the crab cake, I may sob. You're going to get me the recipe for these cheese biscuits, aren't you?"

"I promise to do my best. You know how cooks are with their secrets."

"If the cook is stingy, we can work it out. Cooking is like chemistry. You put together the ingredients that work and avoid those that don't. How are you at chemistry?"

His laughter surprised her, because she hadn't thought that he was back into a light mood. "As you can see, I don't control it. Oh, you're not talking about us, are you?"

She tweaked his nose. "Definitely not, and you know it."

He poured more wine into their glasses. "You're right about these biscuits. I could eat a dozen of them." Patting his flat abdomen, he asked her, "How do you feel about love handles?" and glanced at her from the corner of his eye.

"Never been attracted to them. It's the washboards that send my imagination into orbit." She reached over and zipped up the bag that contained the warm biscuits. "The salad and tomatoes are delicious, too," she said.

"Well, I certainly get that message. We can eat the dessert during intermission, unless you want it now."

"I'm stuffed. Let's wait," she said. He closed the picnic basket, put the food away, pulled her off her stool to sit on the blanket and lay down and rested his head in her lap. She looked down into his face, at his barely parted lips and searing gaze, and thought, *If he isn't for real, I'm lost!*

She closed her eyes and stroked his hair. His arm went around her waist, and she had to resist bending over and kissing him. Her fingers brushed his cheek and his hair with light, feathery touches as she hummed softly to the tune of Mozart's "Eine Kleine Nachtmusik," while the musicians gave the music life.

At intermission, she asked Jack, "What's for dessert?"

His arms tightened around her. "If you think I'm moving from here, you're nuts. You've been making love to me for the last twenty minutes, and I don't want you to stop."

"I have not. I was only—"

"You have so."

"If I'd been making love to you, there'd be no question in my mind."

He sat up. "You're damned right there wouldn't be."

He cut two slices of cheesecake, handed her a slice and opened a bottle of champagne. "We'll eat your cookies after intermission. How do you like the music?"

"I love music. When I was growing up, I wanted to learn to play the piano, but Daddy said there wasn't money for lessons. I would listen to the radio and long to play like some of the pianists I heard."

"You can still learn. All you need, it seems to me, is a piano and a teacher. It's amazing that, in spite of the apparent differences in our backgrounds, there's been such similarity in our lives," Jack said as he finished his cheesecake and lay down with his head in her lap again.

"This morning, I wanted to ask my father how he deals with patient loss. It was the first time I've needed him as a father since I've been grown. I needed his guidance, sympathy and understanding as a father and as a physician, because whatever he told me, I would believe.

"I telephoned him, and he didn't wait to find out why I called him. He told me of his plans for a fishing trip, urged me to join him and launched into criticism of my work in South Baltimore. I didn't bother to tell him how miserable I was, that I needed his guidance, his experience from forty years of practicing medicine."

He turned and buried his face in her lap. "Oh, what the hell! I wish I hadn't brought it up."

She understood then why he had called her and invited her to spend the evening with him. He needed what she gave him, her faith in him and her sympathetic understanding of his compassion for his patients. "Please don't hold it against him, Jack. One day, he will realize that he failed to share what may become the most important part of your life, and he will regret it. No matter how he acts, he's proud of you. Any parent anywhere would be proud to have a man like you for a son. I mean that."

She felt dampness on the tail of her tank top, leaned down and kissed his eyes. "At least you're precious to me," she whispered, mainly to herself.

Chapter 5

Jack nuzzled Melanie's lap, soaking up her sweetness, affection and, yes, loving, for there was nothing else to call it. He hadn't known such caring since his mother had died weeks after his eighteenth birthday. As Melanie's gentle stroking made his pain over the little girl's death the day before more bearable, it reminded him of his mother's tender and soothing care, and of the fact that almost seventeen years had passed since he'd received such unconditional love. He knew it was his fault, because of the company he kept, but he had only recently begun to notice the self-centeredness of the people with whom he associated. He hoped he hadn't been like them, people for whom any show of compassion was almost always perfunctory and definitely short-lived.

Melanie's faith in him seemed unbounded. Yes, his patients believed he could work miracles, but they needed to believe it; she didn't. His mother had believed in him. She had always told him that he could do anything he set himself to do, and he believed her. She'd said he was gifted with a fine mind, sturdy hands, inner strength and a will to succeed. But when he'd needed her encouragement most, during those awful days and nights of his first months at college, when he'd tried to be a good student while his classmates fought for popularity, she'd slipped away from him. Suddenly. Like the explosion of a cannon.

In those days, his father had wallowed in his own grief, seemingly forgetting that his son—an only child—had lost his mother. Yes, today he walked tall and sometimes performed what his colleagues at the hospital referred to as miracles. He wasn't a fool, and not much frightened him. He knew himself, and he knew he excelled at what he did. But that didn't mean he wasn't vulnerable, that he didn't need love, affection and a woman's tenderness.

Melanie's hands stroked and caressed his back, and, whether she intended them for his ears or not, her whispered words came to him clearly: *At least you're precious to me.* He didn't comment; when she wanted him to know it, she'd say it loud and clear. He slipped his arms around her waist, hugged her, kissed her belly and sat up.

"Do you think you can manage the office next week? I have to attend a convention. I'm conducting a workshop on the diagnosis of certain circulatory ailments, and I haven't found a doctor who's willing to fill in for me at my South Baltimore office. They'd happily take my Bolton Hill patients, but…well, you know the story."

"What will I do if someone really needs a doctor?"

"Send them to General, but phone first. I'll give you a message that should make their admittance easier, and you have my cell-phone number."

"You know I'll do the best I can."

He didn't like leaving Melanie alone to handle his office emergencies, but what choice did he have? He couldn't leave his patients with no care at all. Since he'd opened that office, he'd learned more about poverty and the plight of the poor than in his previous thirty-four and a half years, and the knowledge had changed him irrevocably.

"You can certainly phone me. But if it's an emergency like we had the other night, you may call a doctor whose name I'll leave with you. He owes me, and he should help."

"All right, but I hope I don't have one that I can't handle."

At the concert's end, he packed up, walked with Melanie to his car and stored the picnic basket and remains of their supper in the trunk. "I don't know about you," he said as he eased the Porsche from the curb, "but for me, this has been a delightful and revealing evening."

"I wouldn't have missed it for anything, Jack. It's been wonderful."

He stopped for a red light and looked at her, feminine

and sexy with her hair swinging around her shoulders. "And in the office tomorrow evening, you'll have your hair up and some little white pearl balls sticking in your ears." He allowed himself a slight shrug. "But I don't mind. Both women get to me." When he reached the building in which she lived, he accompanied her to her apartment and waited while she unlocked the door.

"You gave me something very special tonight, Melanie. I'll have to think about it for a long time before I'll be able to articulate it, but I've locked it right here." He pointed to his heart, leaned down and kissed her quickly on her lips. "Good night." It had been an evening that he would never forget.

The following morning, Friday, at his Bolton Hills office, when he saw his South Baltimore office number on his cell phone caller ID, his heartbeat accelerated, pounding like horses' hooves. Melanie never called him at this location.

"Hello, Melanie. Is everything all right? How are you?"

"Hi. I'm fine. I just got a call from Mrs. Hawkins. She said Midge got out of bed this morning and passed out as soon as she stood up."

"Hmm. What's her phone number?" Melanie gave it to him. "She's a very sick girl. I'll call her mother. Stay sweet."

"You do the same."

No matter what he prescribed for the child, she didn't improve. That she had sickle-cell anemia was a fact. But she also had a serious respiratory problem that she exacerbated by smoking pot. His father would know in a second what to do about the respiratory complication, but he didn't have the option of consulting him about a patient in his South Baltimore office. But he was learning, and he'd soon be as good an internist as he was a cardiologist.

He left his Bolton Hill office at the usual time, twelve-thirty, and went to visit Midge. "You'll feel better if you do as I tell you," he told the teenager, "and if you obey your mother. Smoking, including pot smoking, will kill you. Anybody who smokes knowing she has a respiratory problem is a fool. I'll be back to see you tomorrow afternoon." He gave the girl's mother two packages of pills and directions as to how Midge should take them. "Throw away every cigarette or joint you can find in this house. She can't tolerate smoking," he said to Alice Hawkins, left them and drove three blocks to his office.

Seeing him unexpectedly seemed to frustrate Melanie. She dropped the file she held, retrieved it and knocked over the clock that sat on her desk. "You should warn a person," she said.

He walked toward her, eager to hold her, but she warded off his advance. "I'll make us some coffee." With those words, she ducked out of the waiting room.

He started to follow her, and stopped. He didn't crowd women, not even one he wanted as badly as he wanted her. *Besides,* he thought, *I have to learn how to be with her and keep a lid on my feelings.* A few minutes later, she returned with two mugs of coffee and two of Alice Hawkins's cranberry scones.

"You haven't had time to eat lunch," she said, "and if you eat this, you may not want any."

"I've had nothing today but two cups of lousy coffee and one dry doughnut. Hungry as I am, I'll eat anything you put in front of me."

"In that case, I'd better be very careful. How's Midge?"

"She's very sick. I don't think her problem is life-threatening, at least not yet, but if she continues smoking cigarettes and pot, it will be. No matter what I give her for that upper respiratory ailment, it doesn't help, and I know I'm prescribing the proper medicine."

"Maybe you need to give it more time."

"That isn't it. Maybe sickle-cell complicates it. I'm not sure." He rested the mug on her desk, dropped himself into the chair beside it, leaned back and closed his eyes. "My dad would have the answer in no time. It's his specialty. I'm a good cardiologist and surgeon, and I know it, but here, with all these problems…I can't possibly have the most current information on all of them. It's a terrible feeling knowing that I can't give all of my patients the best care they could get."

He didn't know when she moved, but she was there behind him, massaging his shoulders, stroking his cheek and whispering, "You're as fine a doctor as these patients will get anywhere and at any time. You care, and they know it, and they recover, don't they?" She kissed the side of his mouth, went back to her desk and sat down. He opened his eyes and gazed at her until she looked at him and smiled. It hit him forcibly then that he needed her.

* * *

What could she do with a room full of patients and no doctor? She straightened her back and smiled when the first patient entered the office that Tuesday afternoon. "The doctor is away this week," she said to the twelve-year-old boy. After taking the child's temperature and questioning him as to how he felt, she decided that he needed to see a doctor and called the doctor whose name and number Jack left with her.

"He's pretty sick, Doctor," she said after explaining the child's ailments.

"Seems that way. Can you get him over here by six o'clock?"

She went into the waiting room and looked at the people who had arrived within the last few minutes. "I can't leave these people and go across town to Bolton Hill," she told him, "and he's too sick to go alone in a taxi."

"In that case, get an ambulance and send him to a hospital."

She had no faith in that solution, for she knew the child had no insurance and that, if she sent him alone, he could wait hours for help, get discouraged and leave. "This settles it," she said to herself. "I'm calling him, and if he refuses to come, he can answer to Jack and to God."

She dialed Montague Ferguson's home phone number, which she found after rummaging through Jack's desk. "Dr. Ferguson, this is Nurse Melanie Sparks. I'm at Dr. Jack Ferguson's office in South Baltimore. Dr. Ferguson is attending a meeting in Atlanta, and I have a patient here who needs to see a doctor. The doctor on call won't come down here. Can you please help me, sir?"

"Well…uh…I'm making other plans for this evening. Can't you take the patient to a hospital?"

"Dr. Ferguson, I have fourteen other people here, and I shouldn't walk out on them. Besides, this child could sit in the hospital waiting room for hours without getting medical attention. I need your help."

"I don't think I can make it."

"His temperature is a hundred and four. What shall I tell your son if this child dies after you refused to help?"

"I see you know how to play hardball, miss."

"Hardball? I figured that you're as proud a man as your son is. Will you come?"

"Call it whatever you like, miss, but I'm accustomed to some deference from nurses."

"I am sure, sir, that not only nurses, but your peers, as well, defer to you. You're a distinguished physician, and that's why I want you to help my patient."

"You're good at spreading butter, too. I'll be down there in twenty minutes. Let the patient lie down, and put a cold towel on his face and the back of his neck. I'd suggest an aspirin, but that might be contraindicated. Goodbye."

After hanging up, she said to the boy, "The doctor will be here in twenty minutes."

The boy looked at her with fevered eyes as she led him to an examining room. "Dr. Ferguson?"

"No. He's away on business, but his father is a doctor, and he's coming."

She understood the boy's disappointment, but if

Montague Ferguson treated the boy successfully, maybe it would all have been for the better. Maybe the man would see for himself what his son faced twice a week. She put cold towels on the boy's forehead and at the back of his neck and checked his breathing. At least it had not deteriorated.

Montague Ferguson walked into the office of Jack Ferguson, and looked around at what he estimated to be between fifteen and twenty people, all of whose eyes were trained on him. Not one of them seemed impatient or even anxious, yet he knew they were not sitting in that office for want of anything else to do.

"Good evening everybody, I'm Dr. Ferguson, your regular doctor's father. Where is Ms. Sparks?"

"I'll get her for you, Doctor," a little girl, who he estimated to be about ten, told him and ran out of the waiting room.

"Ms. Sparks, I'm Doctor Montague Ferguson. Where's that patient?" He didn't extend his hand, and she reprimanded him by extending hers.

"Thank you for coming, Doctor. Please follow me."

"Are you a registered nurse?"

She stopped walking and faced him. "Doctor Ferguson, I am an LPN, and I will not be an RN until June the fourth. Right this way."

He made a mental note to scold Jack about leaving his patients with an LPN, but within ten minutes, he changed his mind. Melanie Sparks had medical smarts superior to those of many registered nurses with whom he'd worked. She drew blood, took an electrocardio-gram and performed tasks that he usually assigned to his medical technician.

He gave the boy an antibiotic injection. "Are either of his parents here?"

"No, sir," she said. "His parents are separated, and his mother works at night as a cleaning woman in the bank."

"I see. I want you to take an aspirin every four hours," he told the boy, then took a thermometer from his bag and showed him how to take his temperature. "Take it every two hours. If it goes above a hundred and two, phone Ms. Sparks, and she'll get in touch with me."

Melanie Sparks looked at him expectantly, or was it accusingly? He couldn't tell. Damn! How could he walk out of here and leave the rest of those people unat-tended? He walked back into the waiting room, an ele-gantly furnished room suitable for welcoming the most discriminating individual, one that sent the message "I will do my very best for you in every way that I can."

"All right," he said. "Who's next?"

A boy limped up and showed the doctor a cut on the side of his foot. "I can clean and bandage that, Doctor," she said, "while you take care of someone else…unless you think he needs a tetanus shot." He questioned the boy, then told Melanie, "I'll give him the shot, and you clean and bandage his foot while I do something else. Do you have a crowd like this often?"

"Every Tuesday and Thursday afternoon and eve-ning. Sometimes we leave here after ten." She put an arm around the boy's shoulder. "Come with me."

"I see." But he didn't see at all. What had these people done before Jack opened that office? And it was ultramodern with the very best, up-to-date equipment and furnishings. The area needed a clinic, one that was staffed with doctors in all the major specialties. No one doctor, not even an internist, should try meeting the needs of so many people with such a variety of ailments. When he'd finally treated the last patient, he washed his hands and sat down, too drained to leave.

"I can make you some very good coffee, Doctor Ferguson, and I have some fresh strawberries and a couple of delicious cranberry scones. I know you haven't had any dinner."

"You know, I didn't even remember that I hadn't eaten. I feel like I did a good day's work, for a change, and it's a really good feeling. No wonder Jack enjoys this."

"He does enjoy it, sir, and these people would do anything for him."

"I can imagine they would. I'll take that coffee and whatever else you've got in there. Now that you've mentioned it, I'm starving."

When he got home, he warmed the leek soup that his cook had intended for the first course of his dinner, enjoyed it and got ready for bed. But sleep eluded him. He had been unfair to Jack about that office. He'd never seen people with that attitude of helplessness. Not one approached or beseeched him. They waited their turn and, considering the pain that a couple of them must have been experiencing, he didn't see how they could sit quietly and passively. Waiting with Job-like patience,

as if they had no right to make demands. And their gratitude was of such measure that it almost gave him a
feeling of guilt.

Throughout the night, he fought with his conscience
and, by morning, he had decided to do whatever was
necessary to improve health care in the area.

Melanie didn't expect Jack to call her while he was
in Atlanta, but he had telephoned almost daily, and she
always told him that she didn't have any problems. She
didn't want him to worry or to change his plans and
return earlier, as she knew he would have done if she
needed him. He telephoned her at home around four
o'clock Sunday afternoon.

"Hi. Can I come over? I just got in."

The bottom seemed to drop out of her. She sat on the
edge of the nearest chair and tried to compose herself.
"Jack. How are you? I... Sure, you can come over."

She recognized a slight pause before he asked, "Are
you... I mean, did you hesitate in answering?"

"Yes, I did. I'm practically in shock hearing your
voice, and then you ask if you can come over. Well, have
you ever seen a puppy spinning around? What time will
you get here?"

"I don't know how to take that. Will I be welcome?"

"Will thunder follow lightning?"

"I'll be there in half an hour."

She brushed her teeth, replaced her white T-shirt with
a red one and her house slippers with white sneakers,
combed her hair down—because he liked it that way—

and put a pair of silver hoops in her ears. True to his word, he rang her doorbell thirty minutes later.

"Hi," she said, and hated the seductive tone of her voice. He looked at her for a second, picked her up and walked into her apartment with her in his arms.

"I need a kiss," he said, wrapped her close and brushed her lips with his own. She opened her mouth for his tongue and got the impression that she'd done something wrong, because he dipped into her, and then moved away so quickly that she hardly felt the contact.

Miffed and not bothering to hide it, she said, "What's with you?"

"I was about to start something that we probably wouldn't finish before tomorrow morning, if ever. I quit while I could. Who was it who said, 'Know thyself'?"

She could see that he was thinking hard, something she'd never seen him do. "Socrates, Christ and a lot of other people. It's easier to know others than to know yourself."

"This is true. I think I could handle a kiss now. But don't lay it on too thick."

She raised her arms to him, and he gripped her shoulders, stared down at her and suddenly crushed her lips with his own, as a hoarse groan poured out of him. She opened to him, sucked his tongue into her mouth and loved him. He released her, walked to her living room window and gazed out of it.

"What is it, Jack?"

"I left you with a terrible burden. Oh, it was important that I be at that meeting, but I worried about you. Are you going to tell me that you didn't have a single problem?"

"No, I'm not going to tell you that, but you trusted me to run the office smoothly, and I did. I had a problem Tuesday night, and when Dr. Robb wouldn't come, I couldn't leave the other patients and take the boy to him. So he said take him to the hospital. I didn't want to do that, because I couldn't leave the office, and the boy was really sick, so…I called your father."

"You did *what?*"

"I did. And after I challenged him, he told me he'd be there in twenty minutes, and he was." Jack's mouth was agape, but she ignored it. "What's more, he stayed until after ten o'clock and treated every one of the twenty-one patients in that waiting room. He was there from five-thirty to ten-fifteen. He even forgot that he hadn't eaten dinner, and I can attest that he had coffee, strawberries and two cranberry scones for supper."

"Well, I'll be damned."

She went to him and put a hand on his arm. "Will you please call him and thank him? I don't know what I would have done without his help."

"Of course I will. I'll call him as soon as I get home. You mean he didn't resent it at all?"

"He was as gracious as a man could be. He was about to leave after taking care of the boy—I think his name is Joshua—but when he saw all those people waiting to see a doctor he dropped his bag on the floor and said, 'Who's next?' Jack, I called him because I knew he'd come, because no matter what he thinks or says, he has to be proud of you."

He walked from one end of her living room to the other and back to the window. "You know what I'd like? Suppose we get a bag of hot dogs, a couple of bottles of lemonade and some potato chips and go over to the Patapsco River. I want to be with you, but I think it's best we... I feel like enjoying the outdoors. What do you say?"

"Do you know a place that sells good hot dogs?" she asked him, not that she was a connoisseur of good hot dogs. "I'm happy right here, but if you'd like us to spend some time in a park or at a lake or a river, I'm all for it." She wanted him to know, without having to tell him, that if she wanted to keep them out of bed, she could do it.

"I definitely know a place. Let's go." She grabbed her straw hat and pocketbook, handed him her door key and told herself that she was foolish not to have put him to the test.

"Sure you don't mind?" he asked, sensitive to her change in demeanor.

"I love the outdoors, and especially near the water. I also like hot dogs." He locked her door, put an arm around her and headed for his Porsche.

At a quarter of eight that evening, after having rowed a canoe on the Patapsco River for two hours and punished every muscle from his waist to his wrists, Jack barely had the strength to kiss Melanie good-night. "I used muscles I forgot I had," he told her when they reached her apartment, "and if they weren't aching, I'd give you a proper kiss. Unfortunately, you'll have to settle for kids' stuff."

"Not to worry. I'll kiss you. I enjoyed every minute of our time together, Jack." She kissed him quickly on the mouth. "Don't forget to call your father."

"I won't. That's the reason I'm leaving you so early. He doesn't think the phone should ring after eight-thirty in the evening." He let his hand caress her face. If she had any sense, she could see in his eyes that he cared.

He parked in his garage and entered the house through the kitchen. If he ever redecorated, he'd get rid of everything that bore any shade of blue. It wasn't a happy color, and he was in a mood to be happy. He took a long hot shower, dried off, wrapped a towel around his waist, went to the mini refrigerator in his office and got a bottle of beer.

After opening it, he phoned his father. "Dad. I can't thank you enough for helping Ms. Sparks and taking care of my patients while I was in Atlanta. When she told me what you did, I was dumbfounded. You can't imagine how happy hearing that made me."

"Well, she's got a fast tongue, that one, and she's sassy, too, but she's as good a nurse as I've ever worked with. Those people look to her as if she's a saint."

"In some respects, she is. I know she can sass, but how do you know it?"

"She challenged me, and I don't remember the last time anybody took a shot at my pride as a doctor. But I was glad I went. I got a chance to see what's going on there. You're telling me you operate at seven, hold offices hours from ten-thirty to twelve-thirty and work down there from five to ten?

"It's only twice a week, and I don't operate every morning."

"Well, I never dreamed conditions down there were so bad. Twenty-something patients scheduled for a two-hour period, and such a variety of ailments and diseases. Why do so many kids down there have pneumonia and asthma? You need an internist. That's too much for a cardiologist to handle."

"I know that, Dad, and I've arranged with a pediatrician at St. Jude Children's Research Hospital to consult with me when I'm not certain about some of the problems the children have, especially sickle-cell anemia and HIV. I constantly bemoan the fact that I need an internist in that office, but right now, I'm all they have.

"Looks as if I'm learning internal medicine on the job, so to speak. Your patients and my Bolton Hill patients come to us at the very first sign that something's amiss. They don't wait half a day, and they are very well-informed about their health and their bodies. But in that neighborhood and other poor areas, people see a doctor as a last resort. Many of them don't have insurance and can't afford to pay for medical care, not even for medicine. So I get as many samples from pharmaceutical companies as I can.

"One woman made some elegant neckties for me. A boy gave me his bat signed by Derek Jeter. A woman does my laundry and mending. Others have polished my silver, cleaned my carpets, mowed my lawn, washed my car, trimmed my hedges, and I don't know what else. They don't want charity, so they do what they can for me. If I left my Porsche in front of my office unlocked, nobody would touch it. The neighborhood boys even protect my parking space. You didn't have to look for a space, did you?"

"No. When I drove up, two boys came to the driver's window and asked if I was substituting for Dr. Ferguson. When I said yes, they moved the orange cones."

"They're so protective of me, Dad, that I sometimes get a guilty feeling, especially when it's sizzling hot, and I see kids sitting in open windows trying to get cool. Wherever I am—in my car, home or office—I have air-conditioning."

"If you didn't have air-conditioning, it wouldn't make the people in that neighborhood any more comfortable," Montague said.

"I know that, Dad."

"Look, son. You built a fine office there with the latest and most modern furnishings and equipment, and you're doing a fine thing. After experiencing once what you go through twice weekly, and I suspect at other times, too, I admire you more than ever, and I'm proud of you. But, Jack, what that area needs is a full-time clinic. I've been thinking about it, and I can get the resources to build one. You could still run it as you see fit, because you started something that's needed."

Jack had to digest that, to make sure he'd heard his father correctly. Never had Montague Ferguson told his son that he admired him or that he took pride in him. Yet the words had flowed out of him as easily as if he said them every day.

As if he'd heard nothing out of the ordinary, Jack calmly replied, "A clinic would be an enormous financial investment."

"I can put together a group of silent partners to form a foundation, and you'd have enough money in no time, because they'd all take it off their income tax. You can work with an architect to build exactly what you want. Soon as the word gets around, you can get a couple dozen of the best doctors to spend three hours a week there, and you won't have to pay 'em a cent."

He had a tinge of anxiety. Would the people whom he'd come to regard as his patients and friends still get the personal attention that he tried to give them? Would the doctors consider going to Midge Hawkins's non-air-conditioned house? He shook himself. If he'd been after glory, he'd have practiced his guitar more diligently and become a rock star. If he wanted those people to get the best care available, he'd do all he could to support his father's idea of a clinic.

"Where would we put it?"

"In that vacant lot diagonally across the street from your office. That way, you could keep that office."

Lights seemed to go on in his head. "You bet. I'd reorganize it and fit it for a diagnostic laboratory. What do you say?"

"I say we're onto something. That would take care of the high cost of laboratory tests. I'll get on it first thing tomorrow morning. Get a lawyer to draw up papers for a silent partnership, a nonprofit foundation. I should have the group I want within a couple of days."

"I don't know how to thank you for this, Dad. I don't mind telling you that not having your support has been a source of painful grief to me. I…I feel as if my life has…that a light is shining on me now. I don't want to be maudlin, but I…I love you a lot, Dad."

He waited, holding his breath, and then he heard the words, "I love you, too, son."

Thirty-four years. How many people waited thirty-four years, a third of a century, to hear their father say that he loved them? At least he'd said the words. He wiped the tears that dripped from the corners of his eyes, took a swallow of the beer on his night table and dialed Melanie's number.

"I'm so happy for you," Melanie told him after he related to her the gist of his conversation with his father. "I couldn't imagine that a man of your father's accomplishments wouldn't be proud of you, Jack. If the two of you succeed in getting a clinic for that area, it will be a miracle and a blessing, and all because you tried to help."

"You can count that clinic as built, Melanie. My father has the connections and the clout, and he does what he says he will do. Besides, I got the feeling that he's taking it as his mission."

"What will you do with your current office there?"

"We'll refit it into a diagnostic laboratory. Gosh, I have my dad on my side at last. All I need right now is to have you here with me. If it hadn't been for your gutsiness in getting Dad to help you, none of this would have happened. Once he saw what I've been trying to do, his attitude changed. I need you to be with me right now, but we'll make up for it. Do you know what I'm saying?"

"I think I do." They talked for an hour about everything but themselves, but each knew that the feeling they shared was a time bomb that would explode one way or another. And soon.

When she and Jack left the office that Thursday night after having treated the last of twenty-two patients, she didn't want to remind him of her graduation. He had the invitation. So she said, "Do you remember that I won't be in tomorrow?"

"Of course I remember it, Melanie. At eleven o'clock, you are graduating from Towson University, and I'll be there to see you. I kept my calendar clear of appointments at my Bolton Hill office, so I'll be free all day. I expect there'll be a crowd. Where should I wait for you?"

"At the end of the ceremony, come up to the front. I'll find you."

The next morning at about ten minutes to twelve, the dean called her name. "Melanie Sparks, Registered Nurse." With her eyes blinded by tears of joy, Melanie could hardly make her way to the podium, but her voice rang out when she said to the Dean, "Thank you, ma'am." She turned to go to her seat, saw that a lone man stood, applauding, and thought her heart would bounce out of her chest. His smile eclipsed his face, and when she waved at him, he waved back.

At last, the ceremony ended, and she went to the foot of the podium to wait for Jack. To her astonishment, he didn't shake her hand or kiss her cheek, but picked her up, swung her around and around, laughing and hugging her, before he set her on her feet, took her hand and said, "Let's go. I have your whole day planned."

After a light lunch at the reception for the graduates and their families, he drove them in his Town Car to Harborplace at the corner of Light Pavilion Street. "We're taking a duck's-eye-view, historic, land-water tour of Baltimore, seeing it all in the same vehicle. It's great fun," he told her. After getting their tickets, he bought them triple-scoop ice-cream cones of their favorite flavors.

"Does the boat have wheels?" If it didn't, she couldn't see how it could travel on water and land.

"It does indeed. Wait. You'll see how much fun it is." He handed her a Wacky-Quacky that came with the tickets. As they sailed or rode past different monuments, their fellow travelers squeezed the Wacky-Quackys to sound like ducks, and she and Jack joined them, laughing and enjoying the outing, unencumbered by life-and-death problems.

She would not have thought that, as serious as he was about most things, Jack would consider using time in that way. *I know the public Jack and only a little of the private man, but whatever eases out of him is likeable.* When the vehicle returned to Harborplace, they walked hand-in-hand to his car.

"Can we have dinner together?" he asked her. "I have a place in mind that's really nice."

"I'd love that. How do I dress? Long, short or micro-mini?"

"Wh-what?" he stammered. "You in a *micro-mini?* You're probably pulling my leg, but I'm tempted to say that a mini would be great, because I'd like to see you in one. Long would be nice."

She couldn't help grinning. "Surprised you, didn't I? I'll have pity on you. Long it will be." She would have preferred to wear a short dinner dress, but she couldn't wait to see him in a tuxedo.

"I'll bet you don't own a micro-mini."

"I don't, but only because my father would have confined me to my room if he saw me wear one. In those days, having peace at home was my priority."

"Fortunately, that's behind you. Have you seen him since you moved?"

"No, but I will as soon as he finds my address. He wouldn't miss blasting me for leaving home."

"It may be easier if you get in touch with him."

"I know, and I'm thinking about it."

When they reached her apartment, he said, "I'll be here for you at seven," kissed her cheek and left.

She had a figure-revealing, melon-red, strapless chiffon evening gown, a sheath that she had bought at greatly reduced price for the graduates' ball before deciding not to attend it. She hadn't had a date and refused to use a service as some of the students did. But now she had a date for this evening, a forty-carat knockout of a man.

Chapter 6

I hope he doesn't come here expecting to see me decked out in wide-skirted baby-blue. I may not get another opportunity, so I'm going to use this one. I wish I had some designer perfume, but I don't, and I'm not going to ruin things with the flowery-smelling soap I usually use. She showered and pampered her body, gave herself a manicure and a pedicure, set her clock alarm for six o'clock and got in bed. Maybe she'd sleep, but with her heart racing and her head filled with images of what could be, she doubted it. Suddenly, fear gripped her, and after thrashing and turning for half an hour, she sat up. Suppose she'd been misreading his signals. Just because he wanted to help the poor wasn't an engraving in stone that he didn't mislead women.

She got out of bed, poured a glass of ginger ale and sipped it as she watched the six o'clock news without seeing or hearing anything. What was wrong with her? He wouldn't be the first man she'd dated, for Pete's sake. *Get your act together, girl, or you may fall flat on your face.* Tall order! She had to admit that she was enamored of him. With a shrug, she put her hair up in a French twist, brushed her teeth, put on the little pearl earrings—Jack called them little white balls—because they were the only appropriate ones she had, and shimmied into the sheath that transformed her into a siren.

When the bell rang at seven, she stood as if glued to the floor. Unable to move. When the bell rang a second time, more forcefully—not surprising in view of Jack's impatient nature—she told herself to move and to calm down. With her hand on the doorknob, she looked down. *Oh, Lord, I hope I'm not showing too much cleavage.*

She opened the door with a shaking hand and stared up at Jack Ferguson, eyebrows raised and wearing a white tuxedo, pleated white shirt and red-and-blue paisley tie and cummerbund. If she gaped at him, she didn't care. "Lord, you look g-gor-gorgeous," she stammered.

His grin didn't help things, nor did his whistle. "Good evening. Is Ms. Sparks at home?"

"Is…" A few seconds passed before the comment sank in. She tried to limit her reaction to a smile, but within seconds, laughter poured out of her. "She's here somewhere. Come in."

"You are so beautiful, Melanie. I wasn't sure that I should wear this tux, but I decided that if you said *long* you meant that. I'd love to hug you, but it's too tempting—you look like a sumptuous feast. An elegant one. I'm ready when you are."

She got the little silver purse that matched her sandals and handed him her key. She wished she had a pair of elbow-length white gloves, but she didn't. Indeed, she'd never given a thought to wearing them. Her lifestyle had never included pretensions to elegance. She'd been content if she had a place to stay, transportation, tuition and enough to eat.

Jack parked in front of a restaurant, gave his car key to the doorman, took her elbow and walked with her to an elegant lounge where they seated themselves in beautifully upholstered chairs. She told herself not to let her jaw drop.

The maître d' appeared and bowed to Jack. "Your table is ready, Doctor Ferguson," he said and showed them through a room softly lit by chandeliers that glowed onto cream-colored linen cloths on which were set fine crystal, porcelain and silver. They reached the table, and as she sat down, she saw a large bowl of red and yellow roses nestled between tall, cream-colored candles.

"I hope madam enjoys the flowers that Doctor Ferguson ordered," the maître d' said. "Enjoy your dinner."

"Jack, this place is exquisite, and the flowers are beautiful," she said after the maître d' left them. "You're making me feel like royalty." He didn't have to know that he was the first man to give her flowers.

His wink unsettled her. "You deserve royal treatment," he said, "at least in my estimation. Melanie, I haven't previously known a woman like you. You have so many interesting facets, and I want to experience all of them. I know you wanted to be a nurse when you were little and that you wanted to learn to play the piano. What else did you want that didn't quite come off?"

"Friends," she said and stopped herself as she was about to clamp her hand over her mouth.

He looked up at the sommelier, accepted the beverage menu and asked her, "Would you like a drink now? I expect we'll have wine with dinner, and since I'm driving, I'll wait for the wine." Still mortified from the slip she'd made, she told him that she didn't want a drink. He handed the menus to the sommelier and focused on her.

"Are you telling me that you've never had friends?"

"Not real close ones. I couldn't bring people home with me, because I was always afraid my father would create a scene or be angry, so I shied away from close relationships. I didn't want anyone to know how mean he could be sometimes."

He shook his head from side to side as if bewildered. "That's awful. So you were always alone?"

"I was friendly with my classmates and people with whom I worked, but I've never had real buddies."

His brow wrinkled into a deep frown. "I've never thought about this before, but maybe Providence or God has a way of fixing things that are so outrageously bad we humans accept them as irreparable."

She sipped some water. "I guess being an only child made it worse than it would have been if I'd had siblings."

"Tell me about it. I used to wish I had a sister. I never wanted a brother, because I thought my dad might like him better than he liked me, and I guarded jealously the few crumbs of affection I got from him. Did you take up any sports?"

She shook her head. "I couldn't afford it. Besides, Daddy wanted me to work, take care of the house and cook for him. I went to school in spite of my father. He made it very difficult, but I didn't let him stop me."

The waiter brought a plate of tiny Maryland crab cakes, small pieces of barbecued spareribs, thumbnail-size quiches and a bottle of white burgundy. She looked at Jack inquiringly.

"I ordered the dinner in advance," he said. "This restaurant fills up, and I didn't want you to starve while waiting for the meal."

"If I tell you again how thoughtful I think you are, you'll probably think I don't know any other words."

"I try to be. I have enough shortcomings without adding thoughtlessness or insensitivity to them. You know, as I reflect, I also don't have a close buddy, a pal with whom I share practically everything. I hadn't considered myself a loner, either. I wonder why that is."

"Maybe you didn't need it."

"I don't think that's the answer." He raised his glass to her. "Here's to the loveliest, kindest, most gracious woman I know, and positively the sweetest. Congratulations. I hope this success will be followed by many more."

His lips were not in sync with his eyes, for they told her what she knew he was not prepared to say. She shifted in her seat, steadied her hand and raised her glass. "Thank

you for making this such a memorable day for me."
Clicking her glass against his, she said, "To the man—the
person—I admire most in this world."

She'd swear that he almost dropped his glass, but his
recovery was swift. "I hope you never want to take that
back, and I'll do what I can to be sure that you don't."

She didn't respond to that, for she knew she stood
at the edge of a precipice, and that one false move
could ruin her life. She sipped her wine, bit into one of
the miniature crab cakes and said, "This could not
possibly taste better." She smiled at him then, because
he made her happy.

"I'm sure you were a letterman in college, Jack, but
I don't imagine you played basketball or baseball.
Which sports?"

"I didn't. How'd you figure that out? I played football and tennis, and I was on the swimming team. I got
three letters."

"Your personality. I'd be surprised at your playing
football if I didn't think you were a quarterback."

He stopped eating. "Good heavens! Are you clairvoy-
ant or something like that?"

"No, but I understand your personality. In individual
sports, if you want to be the best, you must rely on
yourself alone. In football, the quarterback leads the
team, and it more often depends upon his wisdom and
skill. Both suit your temperament."

"And here I thought I was complicated, an enigma
that even I didn't understand."

She glanced at him, not sure whether he was displeased. "Don't worry. There's a lot about you that I don't understand."

"Really? I'm disappointed. I want you to understand me."

"Okay. I will, but you have to help. For instance, why haven't you kissed me all day?"

"Huh? Oh! When I was a kid, I used to put my ice-cream cone in the freezer, and contemplate it for hours until I was practically foaming at the mouth. Trust me, when I finally stopped torturing myself, I really enjoyed that ice-cream cone. Anything else you want to know?" Her face burned so badly that she put her palm against it to be certain that nothing untoward had happened to her smooth skin. He ate his coconut sorbet with relish. "I have a lot of patience, Melanie, and with you, I know I have to exercise it."

At the door of the famous restaurant, the maître d' handed Melanie a bouquet of red roses. "Congratulations on your graduation today, ma'am," he said. "It has been a pleasure to have you visit us this evening."

She smiled tremulously, barely able to restrain tears of happiness. "I enjoyed it very much. The food and service were outstanding. Thank you."

"I'm not done yet," Jack said, helping her into his car. "Gosh, it's a good thing I drove this one instead of the Porsche. How'd you get into this dress?"

"Easily. I poured myself into it," she said with a wink. "What's the matter, doesn't it fit?"

Happiness suffused him, for very little pleased him

more than bantering with her. "Fit? In some places, there's nothing to fit. I mean, they must have run out of cloth when they were making the top of this dress. Not that I'm complaining, but I sure as hell don't want you to wear it with any other man."

Pretending ignorance, she said, "What's wrong with it? I haven't gained or lost a centimeter anywhere since I bought it, and this is the first time I've worn it."

"The first time?"

She nodded. "Right."

"Thank God for that," he said. "Not that I'm complaining. But that dress is temptation personified."

"I'm sorry you don't like it. I wanted to look my best."

He parked in front of the Eubie Blake National Jazz Institute. "I probably should ignore that, because you've got to be kidding. Any red-blooded man who didn't like you in that dress would have to be asexual—race, religion, nationality and sexual orientation notwithstanding. Believe me! Let's go in here for a while."

He wanted to dance with her, and he couldn't think of another spot that offered the jazz he loved. The place wasn't meant primarily for dancing, but if the music moved you nobody complained if you danced. He got a table immediately.

"Would you like a drink or an espresso?"

"I'd love the coffee. Thanks," she said. He ordered two cups of espresso coffee, and settled back as Johnny Anderson raised his alto saxophone and began blowing the seductive strains of "In a Mist." He shifted his gaze from the musicians to her, and his heart seemed to flip over when he saw the naked passion in her eyes, as she gazed at him. Unguarded.

He stood and walked around to her chair. "Dance with me?" The words sounded to him like an order, but he hoped she listened with her heart and not with her ears. He held his breath until she stood, looked at him, smiled and reached for his hand. He walked with her to the little nook where another couple danced.

"Are we supposed to be dancing here?" she asked, opening her arms to him.

"Darned if I know. I've seen people dancing here, and I want to dance with you." She stepped closer, moved into him and swung to his rhythm. He'd swear that less than half an inch separated him from her warm, supple body. Her soft, firm breasts nestled against his chest, declaring her femininity. Without a warning, she tucked her head beneath his chin and moved with him as if she had done it daily all of her life. He could hardly breathe.

The music ended, and he stopped dancing, but if there was ever a mist, it surrounded and enveloped him then. He heard the first notes of "If," and she looked at him expectantly, but he pretended not to notice, for he couldn't risk the physical manifestation of his desire for her. Only a minute earlier, he'd been lucky to escape it.

"You dance beautifully," he said when they were sitting at their table again. "Anyone would have thought we'd danced together for years."

"Really? I consider myself a lousy dancer, but you made it so easy that I enjoyed it."

"We do a lot of things well together," he said. When she seemed uncomfortable with that comment, he changed the subject.

"My dad likes to go fishing, and I'd enjoy going with him if he didn't expect me to catch a lot of fish. I go fishing in order to sit in the boat with the rod and reel in my hand and go to sleep, or at least relax. If I don't catch anything, good for the fish. Would you go with me sometime, say, very early one Saturday morning? I will actually try to catch a fish, and we can cook it for breakfast right beside the river."

"I think I'd like it, but I don't swim. Daddy wouldn't let me learn. He said it was too dangerous."

He tweaked her nose. "I'm not suggesting that you dive for the fish, sweetheart. And as for drowning, you'll have a life jacket, and a man with you who was an Olympic swimmer."

"Uh…do you know how to clean a fish?"

"No, but I'll buy one and get Vernie to show me how." From the way her eyes widened, he knew that got her attention.

"Mind if I ask who Vernie is?"

No use trying to stop the grin that that he could feel taking control of his face. He felt good. "I don't mind at all," he said and let the laughter pour out of him.

She reached down and poked his thigh with her fist. "Very clever, but if you don't tell me, I'm not going fishing with you."

"That's blackmail. If you won't go, I'll have to take Vernie. At least she can clean the fish."

She pretended to pout. "If I'm that easily replaced…" She let the thought hang.

"You are not easily replaced," he told her, "not for fishing or for anything else."

"I was teasing."

"So was I, but I am not teasing now. Let's not tease about anything that could cause a misunderstanding between us, Melanie. What do you want from life, now that you've hurtled that huge obstacle? Do you…" It wasn't the right time, but he had a sudden compulsion to know. "Do you want a family?"

She didn't look at him, and somehow, he'd known that she wouldn't. "Of course I want a family," she said, her voice lower than usual. "But I'm already thirty-one and, with things as they are, well…you know."

"A lot of women have their first child late, nowadays. You take care of your health, so your chances should be as good as anyone's."

He'd never seen her so crestfallen, and he wished he hadn't brought it up, but at least he knew something about her that was so personal and so important to her that she couldn't talk about it.

"I'd like another dance," he said, "but keep a little space between us, please."

She livened up, winked at him and a smile bloomed on her face. "In that case, what's the point? Half the fun is snuggling up."

He intended the look he gave her to serve as a reprimand. "You're getting fresh with me."

"You don't like it?" she asked, looking at him from beneath slightly lowered eyelids.

"Of course I like it. There's someplace else I want to take you. Can we leave now?" He was not going to let her bamboozle him. Sitting across from her while she toyed with his libido—maybe not intentionally, but it was a fact—was getting to him. He stared at her cleavage and licked his lips. Damn! He walked around to her chair and held it for her as she stood. Now, how did she manage to get that close to him? He knew he hadn't moved.

"Thanks for a lovely time," she said, and strolled off like a queen who knew that her entourage would follow.

Oh, heck. It wasn't her; it was him, his head and his libido. If she could see how perfect she looked in that dress... He touched her elbow. "Let's stop by a little café that I like. Maybe you know it. Lovers' Snare. If you're tired, we won't stay long."

"I don't know the place, but I'd love to go there with you. I'm enjoying this evening too much to be tired." She reached for his hand, and he liked that. She didn't force a man to make all the overtures, but let him know that she enjoyed being with him.

Shortly thereafter, they entered what always looked to him like a dream: a small room with a dozen tables, clouds bedecked with a moon and stars replaced the ceiling, a single candle glowed on each table and grayish-blue furnishings and decor completed the dream.

He enjoyed her gasp as they walked in.

"I feel as if I've entered another world. This place is wonderful."

"Thanks. I hoped you'd like it. I'm going to have a dish of ice cream and some champagne. What would you like?"

"Since I don't have to work tomorrow, I'll have the same."

"A bottle of Veuve Cliquot, and two bowls of raspberry-vanilla," he told the waitress.

"You always remember what I like," she said. "That's amazing."

"Not really. I want to please you and make you comfortable." She lowered her gaze, and he wondered when, if ever, she would accept the fact that she was special to him and that he wanted her. He glanced toward a nearby table and back to her. The man at the other table was literally undressing her with his eyes, though she was obviously unaware of him. He looked straight at the guy and narrowed his right eye in what the man would understand as a warning. Pity the woman beside the guy if she was his wife.

"This ice cream is scrumptious," she said, "and by the time I get home you will have increased my weight by a good five pounds, and I won't be able to get out of this dress."

He sampled his ice cream. "I was wondering about that. If you poured yourself into it, you can't pour yourself out of it. I guess you'll have to wear it until you lose a few pounds."

"Very funny." The waiter poured the champagne, and he raised his glass to her. "You'd be surprised at the changes you've made in my life, Melanie. Congratulations on getting your degree and your cap. You are a very special woman." He clicked her glass and handed her the parcel that he'd carried in his trouser pocket.

"Oh, gee. Can I open it now?" She removed the silver ribbon and paper with unsteady fingers and gasped. "Fendi! Oh, Jack, I've never had a designer perfume in my whole life. I was wishing I had some to wear this evening, and I'd made up my mind that as soon as I got paid, that would be the first thing I bought. If we were someplace else, I'd hug you."

"You can hug me here."

Immediately, she got up, stepped around to his chair, leaned over and kissed his lips. "You've changed my life, too," she whispered, and before he could touch her, she swished back to her seat.

"Why can't you look at me, Melanie? You can kiss me, but you won't look at me."

"That's not true." She was miffed, and as usual, when he annoyed her, she had no trouble looking him in the eye and letting him know it.

"Oh, you'll even stare me down when I irritate you, but if we're like we are now, you look everywhere but my eyes. Why? Why are you afraid of revealing yourself to me?"

"When you reveal yourself to me, Jack, maybe I'll be able to reciprocate. Can we drop this?"

"Touché. Are you seeing a man on a regular basis?" He could see that his question surprised her. "Are you?"

"No. I haven't had time for a social life."

"Does it surprise you that I want to take up as much of your free time as I can, and that I don't want you to see other men?"

"Surprise would be an inadequate way to put it. I'm stunned."

He leaned forward. "Why? Do you think that because I wear that white coat with a stethoscope stuffed in the pocket I don't need love and tenderness, that I don't get lonely?"

"No, I don't think that, Jack, but I haven't let myself believe that you wanted it from me."

"It isn't a matter of want. I said need." She seemed flustered, but he didn't intend to let it drop until she admitted that she felt something for him. "If you've never imagined yourself with me, I don't want to know it."

"But, Jack, you're my boss."

"I know that, and if I thought I could get a nurse who suited me a quarter as well as you do, I'd fire you and pursue you like an outfielder after a fly ball. I'm serious, Melanie."

"I know, but how can we keep this separate from our work?"

"Easily. We're both adults, and we're both dedicated to what we do." She looked as if she carried the world on her shoulders, so he smiled. "It'll be all right. If you'd like nothing else, would you like to leave now? It's a beautiful night, and I'd like to walk along the river with you, that is, if you aren't too tired."

"I'm not tired, but this dress wasn't meant for walking. Still…I've never watched a river rush along beneath the moonlight." She reached for his hand. "Let's go. If I trip, you'll break my fall."

"In that and all things," he heard himself say.

An hour passed before he stood with her at the door of her apartment, looked at his watch and saw that it was a quarter after one in the morning. "It's late. I hope I haven't exhausted you."

"All you've done today is make me happy, Jack. I've never known a day such as this one, and it's etched in my memory. Thank you." He took her door key, and used it. But what was next? What did she expect of him?

She settled it when she said, "It's too late for me to ask you to come in, and I'd like this day to last forever, but I'm adult enough to know that isn't possible."

He didn't want to lose points with her, but he wanted more. Hell, he'd never backed away from anything he wanted, no matter how remote the chance that he'd get it. He wanted her, and he intended to have her.

"Nothing is impossible between two people if they both want it," he said, "and I want you." Her gasp gave him the opportunity, and he wrapped her in his arms and plunged his tongue into her waiting mouth. She gripped his shoulders, then slid her hands to the back of his head, adding pressure to his kiss while she sucked him deeper into her mouth. Stunned by the fierceness of her need, he gave himself to her, gripping her hips with one hand and her shoulder with the other, drowning in her sweetness. Her nipples became little hard pebbles pressing against his chest, and he wanted them in his mouth. When she began to twist against him, her groans mingling with his, he tightened his hold on her, and she took his hand and placed it against her left breast. He could feel the heat flowing to his groin, but he told himself to control it while he gave her what she wanted. He dipped his hand into the bodice of her strapless gown, released her left breast, lifted it and sucked her nipple into his mouth. He'd been dying for it all evening, and he didn't spare it, sucking as if his life depended on it. He wanted to devour her, to bury himself in her to the hilt. He wanted...

He eased her back to the wall, released her and braced his hands on either side of her head. "I know this isn't the time for what we want right now. My head is ruling my desires, otherwise I'd carry you to your bed, and I wouldn't leave you until we were both sated and weak from it." He kissed her lips as gently as he could without further inflaming his libido. "If we ever get this far again, we'll make love, sweetheart. Get used to the idea that you are going to be mine, and I am going to belong to you."

She shook her head as if in disbelief. "You can't imagine how difficult getting used to that's going to be. You're so special to me, Jack. If anything happened to destroy that, I don't know what I'd do." She reached up, pressed her lips to his, hugged him and opened the door. "Good night."

Nobody had to tell him that he wasn't the same man who attended her graduation ceremony that morning or that he would ever be the same. She was deep inside him, and he didn't doubt that she would always be there. What was he going to do about it?

Lacking the strength to collect herself and prepare for bed, Melanie sat on a chair in her living room musing about the evening. She and Jack cared for each other, but all that he showed her and the places he took her...his tastes...told her how far apart they really were. He was born with a sliver spoon in his mouth, she with plastic, so to speak, and she didn't believe that their worlds could mate. Still, she didn't know what she'd do if he took himself out of her life.

She opened the perfume, sniffed and dabbed some behind her ears. If she'd had her choice, she would have picked that one. How had he known that the delicate fragrance suited her? She went to her room, lit two candles on her dresser, undressed, took a shower and slipped into bed.

The phone rang, and she answered it, knowing that the voice would either make her happy, if it belonged to Jack, or miserable, if the caller were her father. "Hello."

"Gosh, I'm sorry if you were asleep. I thought you might be in bed, but I didn't think you'd gone to sleep."

"Hi."

"I couldn't sleep without telling you that this was the happiest day I've spent in years, maybe ever. I didn't want it to end, and I certainly didn't want to leave you. Will you go with me to a concert Sunday afternoon? It's at the Meyerhoff Symphony Hall at three in the afternoon."

She had never been to that concert hall or to any symphonic concert, but she loved music, although she'd learned it from the radio and CDs. "I'd love to go," she said, trying not to sound too eager. But she *was* eager; she wanted to see how his set lived, and she wanted to be with him.

Sunday afternoon, she dressed in a white suit—substituting a skirt for the pants—a ruffled lavender blouse and white accessories, considered herself as well-dressed for the occasion as she could be and sat down to wait for him. He rang her bell promptly at two o'clock and greeted her with a possessive kiss. He wore a pale-gray linen suit, a lighter gray shirt and a yellow-and-gray paisley tie.

"You always look perfect," she told him.

"Not any more than you do."

He held her hand throughout Mozart's "Symphony Number One," and, at intermission, he walked with her to the lounge. "Would you like a glass of wine?"

At least a dozen people greeted him while they stood there sipping wine, and when his expression changed to one of irritation, she followed his gaze and saw a tall, attractive and elegant woman staring at him with obvious disapproval.

Goose pimples formed on her arms. "Who is she, Jack?"

"We were friends. She decided that she owned me, but I had never given her reason to feel that way. We went around in the same set, my dad liked her, and she decided that counted for something. I told her and my father that I would not settle for a woman merely because we had the same friends, that I wanted to spend my life with a woman I loved and that I wouldn't need him to help me choose her."

"Oh."

"Don't worry. I have never been unkind to her, but I was honest."

She noticed that he nodded to the woman when they passed near her on their way back to their seats for the second half of the concert. She enjoyed the concert, and marveled at the difference between recorded and live classical music.

When she mentioned it to him, he said, "You're right. It's like the difference between seeing the Roman Coliseum in a movie and looking at it from a vantage point of fifty feet or less. We have some time before dinner. Would you like to stroll through the Baltimore Museum Sculpture Garden? It isn't too far from here."

She was with Jack, and nothing else seemed to matter. After they left the garden, they went to a restaurant not far from the Inner Harbor, because both wanted seafood. As they left later, a limousine stopped at what looked to her like a night club a few doors away.

"Say, that's my dad's car," Jack said and with his hand at her elbow rushed to stop his father and his companion before they entered the building. "Hi, Dad," he said and embraced his father. "You remember Ms. Sparks?"

Montague's lips didn't curl up, but she'd have sworn that they flattened out. "How do you do, Ms. Sparks," he said, turning to the woman with him and saying, "Helena, you've met my son, Doctor Jack Ferguson?"

"No," the woman said, "I don't believe I have, although I've certainly heard of him."

"Yes," Montague Ferguson said, "Jack is well-known. Jack, this is Helena Smith."

The woman nodded. "How do you do?"

If she's a jerk, I certainly won't be, Melanie said to herself. *Nobody snubs me.* Although she knew it was the place of the older woman to do so, she extended her hand. "How do you do, Ms. Smith? And you, Doctor Ferguson? How nice to see you again."

She wasn't sure, but she thought she heard Jack snicker. One thing was certain: the arm that slid around her waist and tightened belonged to Jack Ferguson. He was making a statement, and she hoped he wouldn't regret it. On the drive home, neither of them mentioned the incident, and she didn't know whether his dark mood reflected an attitude toward her or his father. At her apartment, he held out his hand for her key, took it, opened the door and walked in with her.

"I'm sorry that this evening wasn't as happy a time for us as it could have been, and I'm asking you, Melanie, don't let what you've observed come between us. Nobody makes up my mind for me but me." He tipped up her chin with his right index finger and stared into her eyes. "I'm asking you to give me a chance. Will you?"

"I… Jack, this is hard. He's your father, and you love him. I can—"

He sucked the unspoken words from her parted lips, as he gripped her to him and plunged his tongue into her. Sampling the sweetness of every crevice, every centimeter of her mouth, plunging in and out, letting her know what he planned to do to her, squeezing and caressing her breast, possessing, sending frissons of heat through her body until she could stand it no longer and slumped against him.

"I asked if you were seeing any other man, and you said no. I don't want you with another guy. You understand?"

She knew he was possessive. Everything about him said that he would guard jealously all that he owned and all that he cared about. But if he could lay claim, so could she. "And I don't want you with any other women," she said, looking directly into his eyes, "including the one I saw gazing at you during intermission in Symphony Hall today. Do *you* understand?" Six months earlier, she wouldn't have said that to any man, but she knew who she was now, and she'd learned that, with men, all things had better be equal.

His smile nearly unraveled her. "Fine with me. I haven't noticed another one since the first time I saw you. I'll call you tomorrow after my office hours. Thanks for being with me today."

"I enjoyed it. Oh, Jack… What did you think of my perfume? She couldn't help grinning. She wanted to know if he liked it on her.

"It's perfect for you. I wanted to say so, but I thought it would seem as if I was complimenting myself. It's wonderful on you, and I'm delighted that you like it."

She reached up, kissed him quickly on the lips and walked with him to the door. "Good night."

He stared at her. "First, you couldn't call me by my first name. Now you can do that, but you can't use an expression of endearment."

"If I do that, I may slip up and do that in the office, and it would be out of place."

"All right. Point taken. But this once?"

"You can be so much like a child sometimes. Good night, darling."

His faced bloomed into a smile. "Good night, love."

Alone, she looked toward the ceiling and asked aloud, "What am I going to do?" If she continued to work for him, seeing him almost every day, she knew she would go to bed with him as sure as her name was Melanie Sparks. And if she did that once, knowing the thorough man that he was, she'd be a goner. But she loved the job, and... She didn't let herself finish the thought. She didn't dare.

When Jack's phone rang that night, he lifted the receiver with a full-blown attitude. "Ferguson speaking."

"This is your father, and I presume you know that, because you should have been expecting me to call you. Do you mean to tell me you tossed aside a fine woman like Elaine Jackson to fool around with your nurse?"

He was in no mood to be reprimanded for minding his own business. "Be careful, Dad. You don't want to build a barrier between us. I disliked your date intensely, but I was gracious to her. She tried to put Melanie Sparks down, following your example, but Melanie gave both of you a lesson in good manners. I was proud of the way she handled that ugly situation.

"You know, Dad, one reason why I'm drawn to Melanie is her respect for people, all people. She doesn't look down her nose at people. Elaine Jackson and your date, Helena Smith, are cut from the same piece of cloth. You don't want my advice. I know it's been a long time, but before you plunge into anything, make yourself remember what it's like to have a warm, loving and tender woman in your life, and look for one."

"I thought this call was about you," Montague said, but Jack detected a strange, almost nostalgic tenor in his father's voice. "Are you serious about this woman?" his father then asked him.

"Dad, I can't tell you what I haven't told her. I want a woman like my mother, not some freeze-dried society clotheshorse who's incapable of feeling anything except money."

"I think you're being too harsh, but I know your mind's made up, and there's no use talking to you."

"Right," Jack said. "How's the foundation coming?"

"I'd planned to call you about that tomorrow morning. I've got the five we need, and I think you'll approve of them. Could you meet us at the club for lunch, say, one o'clock, and ask your attorney to come and bring the contracts?"

"If he doesn't have a previous appointment, we'll be there. That was fast work."

"They needed something to think about. Reading the paper and damning the Democrats can consume only so much of a day. They didn't need persuading."

"You have no idea how overjoyed I am, Dad."

"Next, you have to look for a good architect."

"That's the least of our problems. I'll use the Harringtons, three brothers that include an architect, engineer and builder. They're located near Frederick, but they've done a lot of work here and throughout the state. They're my frat brothers."

"We're leaving that up to you. You watch your personal life, though. These fellows lay great store by appearance."

"I know. And they lead a double life, too. You won't catch me doing that."

"You mark my word."

Chapter 7

Melanie arrived at work that Tuesday morning, hung her uniform and her cap in the closet, changed into a pair of sneakers and set about taking the monthly inventory. She had streamlined the process and didn't regard it as a chore. Although comfortable with the job's requirements, her relationship with her boss made her increasingly uncomfortable. Her feelings for him deepened daily, but his father had made it clear the previous Sunday evening that he disapproved of their socializing, and she didn't believe a man with Jack's background would risk his relationship with his father because of her. That clinic meant everything to Jack, and she didn't think Montague Ferguson would sponsor the clinic if he disapproved of Jack's social life and particularly of his choice of a woman.

* * *

Jack knew the risk, but he'd stand on his own, no matter what. His father had the contacts and had used them well, but he had some of his own, and he would not exchange his rights to a woman of his choice for a clinic or anything else. Besides, he doubted his father would expect that. He laughed at the thought that came to him. In recent months, he'd begun to think and act less and less like the son of Montague Ferguson, physician to the moneyed class and heir to the Ferguson millions, and more and more like his mother, whose values and outlook he'd found in Melanie.

He hated having had a confrontation with his father about Melanie, and it pained him that his father chose to dislike her because she wasn't a descendant of the so-called Talented Tenth. She was worth a thousand Helena Smiths and Elaine Jacksons, and he hoped his father would one day understand and appreciate that.

Shortly after four o'clock that afternoon, Melanie showered and dressed in her new uniform and, for the first time, she put on the cap for which she had struggled so hard and so long. She looked at the red cross at the center of the cap and blinked back the tears. For that evening, at least, she would wear white stockings and shoes to complete the transformation from LPN to RN. To her delight, several patients congratulated her.

"Just this way, Mr. Watson," she said to a patient, a man of about forty. "The doctor will see you now." She stood with Jack as he prepared to give the man an injection.

"Roll up your sleeve," Jack said, causing her to

wonder at his gruffness. She scrutinized the patient and saw that he was attempting to establish some contact with her. Watson smiled and winked.

"Ms. Sparks, you're so pretty. Coming to the doctor is a pleasure. Doc, you're one lucky man. You can look at her twice a week, at least, for hours. Ouch! Doc, that hurt."

"Sorry. Try to be still."

She put a Band-Aid on the man's arm and watched him leave the examining room rubbing the spot. "You did that deliberately," she said to Jack. "Shame on you."

"I told him to be still."

"Right. After you jabbed him. How could you do such a thing?"

"It was just a prick, and he shouldn't even have felt it. The guy was trying to get your sympathy. Hell, Melanie, you can smile and soothe the patients, but you've hardly spoken to me since I walked in here this afternoon. You could at least have given me a quick kiss."

"Jack, we have to have some rules for working together."

"I agree, but right now, I need to know that I'm important to you."

She gazed up at him. He wasn't joking. The need reflected in his eyes stunned her. "Oh, Jack. Darling, don't you know that I care for you?" Her arms went around him, and he seemed to soak up the love and sweetness that went out to him from her—a sponge absorbing life-giving fluid.

"I needed to hear it. I don't come down here an hour before this office opens because I can't find anything else to do. I do it because I can't wait to be with you, to see you."

"Don't worry," she said. "I can't wait until you get here. I'm going to call the next patient, otherwise we'll be here all night. Kiss me."

His lips settled on hers as he stroked her back, electrifying her. But it satisfied neither of them, and she knew that she, at least, wouldn't be soothed until she exploded all around him while he lay deep within her. She shook herself vigorously, discarding the thought.

"I can't believe how fortunate I am," he said. "Bring them on."

Melanie answered the telephone and buzzed Jack in the examining room. "This is Ferguson." He listened for a few seconds, sat down and took a deep breath. "I can't thank you enough, Doctor. This means a lot to me and especially to my patient. I'll see that she gets there Sunday afternoon. Thank you. I'll stay in touch." He finished examining his patient, a boy of eleven, gave him some medicine and bounded out to Melanie's desk.

"You won't believe this," he said, wearing what he knew was a broad grin. "St. Jude will take Midge. She's due there Sunday afternoon."

She stared at him. "What are you talking about?" He explained to her his association with one of the research hospital's doctors. "That was the call that just came in. Thank God they're taking her. They know how to care for patients with sickle-cell anemia. When she gets back here, she'll be able to lead a normal life." He shoved his fingers through the hair at the back of his head. "The problem is that we won't be getting those cranberry scones every morning."

"Why? You mean her mother's going?"

"Absolutely. It's all set. I'll get their tickets tomorrow."

"I'm beyond crying when something good happens, but if I'm not careful…" She blinked back the tears.

"I like you in your new cap," he said, hoping to change her mood. "The red cross, tiny black stripe, white shoes and stockings are making a statement. You're giving this joint class."

She sniffed and winked at him. "This office had class the minute you opened the door." She sniffed again and called to a patient, "Rodger Gaines, please come with me."

The next morning during a lull in his Bolton Hill office, Jack called his contact at St. Jude Children's Research Hospital. "As you know, about half of my patients are children, and I consult with you about some of them with increasing frequency, because our arrangement is working for me. But I think I could serve this community better if my nurse spent about a month at St. Jude talking with nurses, going with doctors on rounds. She'd have a better feel for some of the problems we've been facing here. She's a registered nurse, and a smart one at that. It would be solely at the expense of my office."

"Sure, we can certainly arrange that. Just let me know when you want her to come."

"I'll have to get her to agree, but I'm sure she'll be eager to have the experience. Thanks. I'll be in touch."

* * *

"I have an idea, and I hope you'll find it acceptable," Jack told Melanie after they had taken care of all the patients.

"Half of our patients are children. Would you be willing to spend a month as a nurse-intern at St. Jude Children's Research Hospital in Memphis? It would make all the difference to the children we take care of. I'd like you to observe patient care and the new treatments that are coming from the St. Jude research program. I can't leave here for that long a time, but you could, and we can both benefit from your experience there. What do you say?"

"I'd give anything if I could go there, but who will help you here?"

"I don't expect to find anyone better who's willing to work down here. If I can't get a nurse, I'll get a medical student who's on summer vacation. I should be able to get an LPN though. When can you leave?"

She looked at him as if he'd disappointed her. "What's wrong?" he asked her. "Look. You don't have to go if you don't want to."

"I want to, Jack, but... Are you sure this is what you want?"

The question didn't make sense to him. He studied her for a few minutes. He hunkered in front of the chair in which she sat staring at her hands. "Melanie, I will miss you every second that you're in Memphis, and I want you to know that no one can take your place, neither in this office nor here." He pointed to his heart.

The separation could prove to be what they both needed. At the end of it, they would either be starved for each other or greatly relieved.

"Don't get any ideas about my replacing you," he said. "Do you understand? It won't happen."

"I could be ready to go in a week," she said, letting her hand stroke his hair.

He got up. "Wonderful. Let's go someplace and get a slice of pizza. I'm starved."

"Me, too, and I want some raspberry sherbet."

"I want some peach sherbet," he said, locked the office and walked with her to his car.

"This has been a fantastic day, Melanie. I'm going to call Alice Hawkins tomorrow morning with the good news for Midge."

"Who'll keep her other two children while she's in Tennessee?" she asked him.

"Friends and neighbors promised to take care of the children. When you get there, Midge will be delighted to see a familiar face."

Once seated at a small bistro table in the back of the pizza parlor, Jack said, "Six months ago, I would have headed for the club and eaten supper there. These days, I almost never remember that the place exists. There's a saying that everything changes, and I suppose people also change. I know I have.

"My dad had a meeting at lunch today with the five men who've put up the money for the clinic, my lawyer and the two of us. It went so smoothly that I still can't believe it. They'll be silent partners—that is, they'll have no say in clinic practices, policies and procedures. They will hold an annual fund-raiser culminating in a gala designed to attract men with money and women who want to show off their designer gowns. In addition, their names will appear on the letterhead of our stationery, which we will design as soon as you get back from Memphis.

"I've begun working with an architect on the building, which will be erected across the street from my office. It's amazing how fast this thing got under way."

"Yes, it is. I was afraid that because of our encounter with him last Sunday night, you father would decide not to help build the clinic. I'm glad he's a bigger man than that."

"He's as anxious for its completion and operation as we are, and he thinks turning my office into a laboratory is a great idea. I'm considering converting the entire building. It's only two stories."

"Did your father mention our exchange?"

"You bet he did. But believe me I had my say. My dad and I can talk, and we can disagree without coming to loggerheads. It's a good thing, too, because these days, we almost always disagree."

After their supper of pizza and sherbet, he drove her home. Strangely, he had a need more urgent than ever to stay with her. The evening hadn't been one in which they had embroiled themselves in heated passion, yet his need to give himself to her felt stronger than it had previously. If only she'd give him a clue, any sign, that she was ready to share her body with him without reservation, he'd do the rest. But he couldn't push her, because he was her boss, and he didn't want her to feel that he took advantage of her. He didn't doubt that she wanted him and that she was physically ready to receive him, but she had reservations, and he didn't want her to regret making love to him.

Melanie didn't like the idea of leaving Baltimore for an entire month without telling her father where she'd gone. Yet, if she contacted him, her life would once more be as difficult as when she had lived in his home. For seven weeks, she had been free of his mean-spirited-ness, and she had learned that she could be happy without seeing him or hearing from him. Days had passed when she hadn't given him a thought. After musing over it, she decided not to contact him. She had much to do and only a few days in which to get it done, and dealing with her father would take more time than she had.

Jack thought he had his life where he wanted it, but that was because he was accustomed to having things always work out in ways that suited him. She wanted to tell him that, in the real world, you got bump after bump and kick after kick until your ship came in, and that happened only if you were lucky.

When he brought the Town Car to a stop in front of the building in which she lived, she wondered what he'd do and how she would respond when they got to her apartment door. She knew he wouldn't pressure her, at least not obviously. And why should he? By now, he had to know how easily he could turn her on.

"Would you like some coffee?" she asked him.

His gaze lingered on her, holding her in its clutches while he considered his answer. "Thanks, but I'd better not have any coffee this late. I have surgery tomorrow morning, and it's best that I sleep. I'm aware of the difference between 'Do you want to come in?' and 'Would you like some coffee?' and I appreciate your subtlety. I'd love to come in but I'd better be going."

His grin didn't communicate its usual warmth. "Let me hold you for a minute." She opened her arms, parted her lips and received him with her heart. He released her, stepped back and stared at her.

"Did you mean that? Do you feel that way about me?" He gripped her shoulders. "Tell me."

"I've never pretended with you, Jack. Never."

He had her back in his arms, kissing her hair, cheeks, neck, face and ears. "When you come back from Memphis, we'll sort this out for keeps. Don't forget this—you're precious to me. Good night."

How could they sort it out for keeps? She was at once exhilarated and scared to death. "It's time," she said to herself. "It's way past time."

On his way home, Jack saw a convenience store that hadn't closed, stopped and bought a copy of the *Maryland Journal* and drove on home. After showering and getting into bed, he opened the paper and was stunned to see his name in bold letters. "Dr. Jack Ferguson, noted cardiologist, will build a clinic in an impoverished section of South Baltimore. A consortium of five sponsors will be silent partners in the venture. They have established a foundation with sufficient funds to build and equip a state-of-the-art clinic. Ferguson is working with Harrington Brothers, Architects, Engineers and Builders to design the structure." Jack folded the paper and closed his eyes, thinking that the story would help ease their problems in making the clinic a reality.

The next morning after performing surgery, Jack removed his scrubs, dressed and fell in step with one of the operating-room nurses. "I've got a nasty hangnail here. Could you please clip it off for me?"

"Glad to," she said and walked with him into an examining room for a pair of scissors. "That was a good job you just pulled off. You must have nerves of steel."

He hated being buttered up. He'd have been pleased if she'd said he did a nice job, and it would have been enough. He shrugged. "Don't you believe it. I feel competent, but the only time I pray is when I'm about to operate. It's a wonder the Lord pays any attention to me."

Her raised eyebrows didn't surprise him. "You're joking," she said. "I would never have imagined it." She clipped off the hangnail on his right index finger and smiled. "There. It's as good as new."

Jack didn't imagine that she held his hand longer than necessary, but he pretended not to notice. "Thanks, Ms. N. I'll do the same for you." He ignored her wide-eyed look and headed for the cafeteria. He'd gotten to the hospital too late to get his coffee and doughnut before going to the operating room. He went through the line in the cafeteria, found a table and sat down to a breakfast of scrambled eggs, toast, grapefruit juice and coffee.

He'd had only two sips of coffee when his cell phone rang. He glanced at his watch and saw that it was five minutes to ten, thirty-five minutes before he was due at his Bolton Hill office.

"Ferguson speaking."

"Oh, Jack. I just read the most marvelous news about you. Your new clinic is the perfect project for my Altalux Society. We'd do fund-raising, and you wouldn't need any more volunteers. The members would take care of that."

So she still hadn't given up. "You mean to tell me, Elaine, that you're willing to take care of patients in their homes, babysit children, drive patients to and from the clinic? I can't believe you've changed that much." He could almost see and hear her confusion.

"But…but your clinic won't do that, will it? I mean, we could appear on radio and TV, do magazine ads, roll bandages and things like that."

Laughter would have been too unkind. "Roll bandages, Elaine? What for? Thanks for trying," he said, amused at her thinly veiled effort to resurrect what, in his view, had never existed, "but I don't see a role for socialites in the clinic's operations. I'm trying to help people, not to treat them as inferiors. If you'll excuse me, I want to finish my breakfast before these eggs get cold. Be seeing you."

He hoped not to hear from Elaine again, but he suspected that she was already looking for other ways to hold on to him. He wondered why a woman with her looks and background would be so willing to settle for a loveless relationship. How could social status and prestige mean more to a woman than a relationship with a man she loved and who loved her? It didn't make sense. He finished eating, bought another cup of coffee, got into his Porsche and headed for his Bolton Hill office.

He flirted with the temptation to cancel his regular Wednesday lunch with his father because he was certain that Elaine would have called him, and he did not want any more flak from his dad about Elaine Jackson. However, he also didn't feel like dealing with the aftermath if he canceled. His father liked to have his life run like a clock and, for him, a canceled luncheon date was tantamount to losing hours out of his life. Thank God he didn't allow himself to be that regimented.

Montague Ferguson rose as Jack approached his table. "How are you, Dad?" He embraced his father and enjoyed the warmth of that fleeting moment.

"Feeling great, son. What about you? How are the building plans for the clinic coming along?"

Jack leaned back in the chair, strummed the table lightly and gazed at his father. Why did they always talk about whatever concerned the old man? He shrugged and let it fall off him as he'd always done. "The Harringtons know what I want, and they say they can deliver it to my satisfaction. So my task now is to engage a top-flight medical engineer who'll help choose the machines and laboratory equipment. I have one in mind. He's a consultant to the hospital administrators."

"Good. The hospital has the latest and best of everything, so you won't have a problem. I leave it to you."

To his amazement, his father didn't mention Elaine Jackson, but exuded excitement over the clinic, what it could accomplish and the possibility of encouraging other groups to sponsor similar facilities in other neighborhoods, cities and towns that needed the service.

"Son, you don't know how proud I am that you're going to head up this project. It's not cardiology, but it's medicine, and you're still one of the best cardiologists practicing today."

He could hardly believe his ears. His farther had always been stingy with praise and had poured very little on him. "I wouldn't take it that far, Dad, but I sure am happy to know you're proud of what I've been able to accomplish."

"Nonsense! I've always been proud of you. Even as a little boy, you had some exceptional qualities. You know, son, a man's pride is in his work, his woman and his kids. When your mother was alive, I had everything a man could want—success as a doctor, a good marriage to a wonderful woman and a son I was proud of." He released a long and melancholy sigh. "I was happy then, and I knew it."

Jack had never thought of his father as a man who needed consoling, but he realized that his father had grieved so deeply for his wife that he hadn't been able to help his son accept the loss of his mother. *It's a lesson I won't forget,* Jack said to himself. *All these years, I blamed him, thinking him self-centered, but maybe I was unfair to him.*

"I still miss her," Jack said, keeping his voice soft in order to control the emotion he felt.

"Not more than I do," Montague said. "I miss her softness and her gentle sweetness. Soft as she was, she had an inner strength that I haven't found in anyone else. That's the only kind of woman who appeals to me."

That last comment relieved Jack's somber mood. He wanted to laugh. Didn't his father realize that the two of them liked the same type of woman, and that Elaine Jackson didn't fit the mold? It also put his mind at ease about Helena Smith, because in his estimation that woman was about as soft as steel. When he bade his father goodbye at the end of their lunch, he walked with light steps, whistling as he headed for his car.

Jack hated shopping, especially when he didn't know what he was looking for. What did you buy for a fifteen-year-old girl? After wasting more than half an hour at Macy's, he approached a saleswoman who suggested a pretty necklace, picked out an amber one, wrapped it and relieved him of further worry. Sitting in his car, he phoned his travel agent and ordered plane tickets for Midge and her mother to be hand-delivered to Alice Hawkins.

He'd done the easy part. The worst would be this visit to the Hawkins's home, for he dreaded telling Midge she had to go to a hospital, and he'd bet Alice hadn't mentioned it to her. He stopped at the corner from the Hawkins home, bought half a gallon of raspberry-vanilla ice cream and two quarts of orange juice and hoped the ice cream would make his task easier.

"Come right on in, Doctor," Alice said when she

opened the door. "I told Midge you'd be here today, and I sure am glad you're here. She's having a lot of pain, though it's easier than it was about an hour ago. And I tell you, Doctor, when that child walks half a block, she's tired, and she just can't seem to beat that cold."

He handed Alice the ice cream. "I thought the children might like this. It's rather hot today. And I'd like Midge to drink plenty of orange juice and take this folic acid. Don't be alarmed. It's only a vitamin."

"How are you feeling, Midge?" he asked the girl, who reclined in bed.

"Not so good, Dr. Ferguson. I was hurting something terrible a while ago." She coughed several times. "But it's a little better now. Can you give me something for this cough?"

He gave her penicillin and a painkiller. "You need rest and plenty of fluids. Your mother will give you some orange juice, and I want you to drink a lot of it."

"All right. I love orange juice."

He sat in a chair beside her bed. "Midge, I'm going to send you to a hospital in Memphis, and you'll feel better all the time when you come back. Your mother will go with you."

She sat up and fell back in bed. "What about Lennie and Jewel?"

"Your brother and sister will stay in a lovely home in Ellicott City while your mother is away. They'll be in good hands."

"Do I have to go?"

"Yes, and you'll be happy there. You and your mother

may stay at the Ronald McDonald House. I'm not sure. The hospital has special social programs and accommodations for teens. The people who work there are caring and loving."

"Like you and Miss Sparks?"

"Thank you. You won't miss school, because you'll have your regular studies with regular teachers there. It's a beautiful, colorful environment and, best of all, you'll get the very best care in the world. That hospital specializes in caring for patients with sickle-cell anemia, which you have."

"Where is the place, Dr. Ferguson?"

"St. Jude Children's Research Hospital in Memphis, Tennessee."

Midge's eyes grew large and round. "I've never been out of Baltimore. You mean I'm going all the way to Tennessee?"

"Right," he said, "and I brought you a going-away present." He handed her the necklace.

"Oh, I love it," she said, after hastily unwrapping the package. "It's cool. I mean it's da bomb. Gee. Thanks for my present. I'm going to try and get well real soon so I can come back and wear this to school."

"I have some more good news for you, Midge," he said and noticed that Alice had entered the room. "Ms. Sparks will be down there for a short while, so you may see an old friend."

"Gee. Did you hear that, Mom?"

"I sure did. Dr. Ferguson, you know I thank you. I just hope and pray that the Lord blesses you the way you're blessing us. I'd thought Lennie and Jewel would be upset when the social worker said they would stay with a family in Ellicott City, but they can't wait to get there. The family was here yesterday, and the kids took to them right away."

"You'll get your tickets this afternoon," he told Alice, "and the social worker will be here Friday morning to take you to the airport. She'll take the children to their temporary home tomorrow afternoon." He stood. "So you're all set." He knew that the social agency would give Alice money for incidentals, but nonetheless, he handed her an envelope containing one hundred dollars. "A Mrs. Russell will meet you at the airport."

After he turned to leave, a thought occurred to him, and he stopped. "Wasn't Midge tested for sickle-cell anemia in the hospital when she was born?"

"No, sir. She was born right here, and a midwife delivered her. I didn't know anything about this disease. She didn't get her shots till she went to school, and I don't think they gave her anything for this."

He patted her shoulder to ease her concern that she may have been remiss as a mother. "Were your other children born here, as well?"

"No, sir. They were born over at General."

"Good. If they had it, you would have been notified."

"Is it curable, Doctor Ferguson?"

"Only with a bone-marrow transplant, and that's not a simple matter, but St. Jude will teach her how to survive with it." He shook hands with her and left. If Midge had received good medical care as an infant, the disease would have less of a grip on her, but the poor can't provide the best for their children. With each passing day, he took his privileged status less and less for granted and considered it less and less his due.

Jack needed to be alone, to think about what had just transpired and figure out what he should learn from it. He couldn't discern from Alice Hawkins's demeanor her feeling about leaving her two children with neighbors. In her place, he would have been petrified with fear. How would he feel if he had to entrust himself and his child to "a Mrs. Russell" whom he wouldn't even recognize? And what if she didn't meet them at the designated place?

He stopped in a small café, ordered a cup of strong coffee, tasted it and realized that he didn't want coffee. He wanted and needed assurance that he'd done the right thing, that he wasn't orchestrating Midge and Alice Hawkins's lives because he could, but because they had no other option. He was their one hope, and he prayed that he hadn't raised their expectations too high. With his elbows on the table, he covered his face with both hands. His dad once told him that he couldn't change the world.

"But I can make a difference," he said, "and I will."

Jack had parked his car in front of his office, and as he walked the four blocks from the coffee shop to his office, it appalled him that in his thirty-four years he hadn't stepped over and around as much waste and refuse. He stopped when he saw several children climbing up and down a pile of rubbish, and it occurred to him that he was looking at the source of some of the ailments he treated. He walked on, crossed the street and had to stop and remove a piece of broken glass from the sole of his shoe. Boarded-up buildings caught his eye, and he jumped out of the way as two small boys raced to claim an old and deteriorating automobile tire that lay against the curb. Leaves, sticks, broken glass, paper and various other refuse littered the gutters on either side of the street.

Months earlier, he would have blamed the women, men and children who sat outside in chairs or on the stoops for the horrible condition of their neighborhood, but not now. He'd come to understand that the destitute do not worry about appearances, but about staying alive. He waved when he passed two older men he recognized as his patients, men he surmised had been out of work so long that they had become unemployable. By the time he reached his office, he was tempted to vow never to walk through that neighborhood again. When driving through it, one was removed from it, but that walk had put him square in the middle of it.

Once the clinic was built—and he intended to have its surroundings attractively landscaped—he hoped other businesses would move in, especially a pharmacy, and that the area's appearance would improve. He pulled air through his teeth. *How could people have hope in this environment?* A few doors from his office, a young boy rushed toward him. "Doctor Ferguson, do you remember me? I'm Tommy."

He couldn't help grinning. "Tommy, how could I

forget the person who gave me a bat with Derek Jeter's autograph on it? That bat is mounted and hanging in my office at home." He stroked the boy's shoulder. "You've grown a couple of inches since I saw you."

"Yes, sir. My dad was tall like you. Real tall. I'm gonna be like that, but I'm not gonna play basketball. I'm gonna be a doctor, and I'm gonna work in your clinic."

Now, that was news. "How did you learn about the clinic? We haven't moved the first shovel of dirt."

"I read the paper every day. When our neighbor finishes the paper, he gives it to me."

"How's your grandma?"

"Okay. She wasn't feeling so well, but we went to a dentist, and he found an abscess and took care of it. She's back singing in the choir again, going to prayer meeting every Wednesday night and visiting her friend in a nursing home. She sews, too. She's fine."

Were they talking about the same woman? "How old is your great-grandmother?"

"She'll be ninety in a couple of months I think."

"Let me know when she has a birthday."

"Yes, sir. I sure will."

"It's a while before office hours. Come in for a few minutes. I need a cup of coffee, and Ms. Sparks may have some juice and a doughnut or scone. What are you doing while school is out?"

"I work with a delivery man from six to nine every morning. Dr. Ferguson, out there in the Westmorland Ridge area, those people is stinking rich. You ought to see their houses. I made enough to buy my school clothes. I wanted to see you, 'cause I'm starting junior high next year, and I want to know what I should study."

The boy whose life he might have saved was determined, a child with a purpose in life. He needed no better proof that he had turned his life's ship in the right direction. "What kind of grades do you make, Tommy?"

"Mostly A's. I can learn anything."

Hmm. Confident, too. "Focus on biology, chemistry, Latin and math. You'll get the rest at the university." He walked into his office with Tommy at his heels. Within seconds, Melanie peeped into the room.

"Hello, Doctor. Hi, Tommy. How nice to see you again."

"How are you, Ms. Sparks?" Jack said.

"Hi, Ms. Sparks. Gee, you sure look good," Tommy said right behind him. He had to laugh. At age eleven or twelve, a boy could tell a woman he thought she looked great, but four years later, he either had to keep it to himself or learn how to communicate it some other way.

"She does indeed," Jack said, taking advantage of Tommy's license. "Have a seat, Tommy, and I'll get us something to drink." He made coffee, poured a glass of orange juice and warmed two scones. "Sorry I don't have any fancy plates," he told Tommy. "I also don't have any soft drinks, because they're not good for your teeth. A lot of sugar and little or no nutrition."

"I like orange juice, sir."

He observed the child who began work daily at six o'clock in the morning. "Will you work with the delivery company after school starts?" he asked him.

"I don't know, sir. Gee, these scones could stop a riot. Absolutely over-the-top. I'd like to, but I don't think my grandma is going to let me."

"She's right." They finished the scones and drinks, and Jack stood. "I have to get ready to work now, Tommy, but I want you to come see me again, and please give my love to your grandma." The boy shook hands with him, waved and left.

"He's quite a fine boy," Jack said to Melanie. "I hope my son will be as admirable."

"Any son you have will be like you, and that's all any parent could ask for in a child."

He stared at her until he convinced himself that she meant what she'd said. "You'd better be careful saying things like that to me," he told her. "One of these days, I may say I'd like you to help me make it real."

"Go ahead. See what kind of response you get."

He jumped up from his desk and grabbed her arm. "Are you challenging me?"

She knocked his hand off her arm and treated him to a careless shrug. "I'm not sure. There's only one way that I could help you make it real. You could say my imagination got a bit out of hand." She turned to walk off, but he stopped her.

"What did you imagine? I want to know."

"Do I ask you what you imagine about me? I do not."

"How do you know I imagine anything about you?"

The woman winked at him. "Oh, that's easy. I know because I am grown and have been for, let's see, thirteen years. You get my drift?"

Sometimes he wanted to shake her, like right now, but instead, he pulled her into his arms, lifted her and seared her lips with his own. "Yes, I get your drift, and yes, I imagine myself wrapped in your arms reveling in your body. I could go on and on, but you don't want to know. At least not right now." He released her, kissed her cheek and then hugged her.

"I only needed an excuse to do that," he whispered.

"And I did my best to give you one. Are you going to miss me while I'm at St. Jude?"

"More than you know. I don't want to think about it till I have to. No matter how much you like it there, Melanie, you come back to me."

"I'll always come back to you, Jack." He gazed steadily at her. Was she his soul mate? If only he could be sure.

Chapter 8

"You mean you're letting your nurse go off for an entire month?" Montague asked Jack. "How are you planning to handle that crowd you have there?"

"If I can't get a registered nurse, I'll try for an LPN. I'll even take a medical student. They're not in school during August, and every one of them can use the money. I'm doing the right thing, Dad, and I'll benefit from it almost as much as she will."

"Well, sure. That's a great institution down there in Memphis, and if she stays there a month, she'll be a better nurse. Try to get a medical student in her last year."

"I was hoping to do that." He hung up, finished dressing, got into the Town Car and drove to Melanie's address. She opened the door almost simultaneously with his ring.

"I thought you'd never get here, Jack."

He looked at his watch and relaxed. "I'm eleven minutes early. Are you eager to leave or eager to see me?"

"I'm a nervous wreck. I'm leaving all I know, and I'm headed for… I'm glad I'm going, but—"

He brought her into his arms and smothered her words with his lips. "I'll miss you, too. Call me every night, and use the office cell phone. Oh, hell, sweetheart. Let me know you'll miss me."

She wrapped her arms around him and parted her lips for his kiss, feasting on him, squeezing his shoulders as if she couldn't get close enough to him. Brought back to his senses by the warning signal that every adult male recognized, he eased her away from him.

"I'll take your two suitcases, and you take your carry-on bag. Let's go. If you need anything while you're away, even if it's a toothbrush, let me know."

"What am I getting a hundred dollars a day spending change for? My room and board are paid, and I won't be going to the movies, jazz joints or museums every day. Besides, I'm getting my salary."

He locked her door, took the suitcases and headed for his car. "All right. Don't tell me when you need a toothbrush. See if I care. But you will call me, won't you? And if you don't like it, you can come home."

At the airport, he wished he'd bought a present for her. He needed something to show her that he appreciated her. He shook his head, as if correcting his thoughts. Was he going overboard? After she checked in, he walked with her to a coffee bar, bought two containers of coffee and led her to a little round bistrolike table. "We'll probably lay the foundation for the clinic before you get back. I'm seeing Telford Harrington, the builder, in a couple of days to check final details. Think of a name for the clinic."

"Oh, that's simple. What was your mother's name?"

"Alicia Todd Ferguson. That's a great idea. You know, I'm sure she would have loved you." Both of her eyebrows shot up. He'd surprised her. Hadn't she ever thought of marrying him? He'd give anything if he could understand her. They heard the flight call, and he stood.

"That's for first-class passengers," she said, not bothering to get up.

He didn't look at her, because he didn't want her to read his feelings. "What kind of ticket do you think I bought for you? Let's go."

The perfunctory kiss he gave her did not reflect the deep hole that opened up in him. Her wobbly smile as she walked away didn't help. If she had cried, he would probably have taken her and run away from that plane.

What the devil's getting into me, and where am I headed with this woman? he asked himself as he watched her disappear into the plane. *She suits me in so many ways, but is she what and who I need for my life?* He had to deal with those questions, and he had to do it soon. He didn't string women along, and he didn't let them do that to him. He wasn't about to let her go, but was he ready to commit?

Melanie didn't feel like talking to her seatmate, an expensively dressed man whose elbow used more than his share of her armrest. "If you'll excuse me," she said after the plane was well into flight, "I'm going to sleep through most of the flight." To her delight, he didn't say another word to her during the flight to Memphis.

After the plane taxied to the gate, the man stood, took her carry-on bag down and handed it to her. "Some guy is lucky. I hope he knows it."

"There's a lesson here somewhere," she told herself as she headed for the luggage-claim area, "and I hope I figure out what it is."

Two representatives from St. Jude Children's Research Hospital waited for her at the luggage-claim area, and she was soon on her way to her hotel. That afternoon, entering the famous institution for the first time, she had a sense of great adventure; a partial tour of the facilities excited her, and she couldn't wait to tell Jack about it.

After dinner, which she ate in her hotel room, she went over her notes, organized them and prepared for bed. Forgetting that Memphis was on central rather than standard time, she phoned Jack and didn't get an answer. At nine-thirty local time, her phone rang.

"Hi. I thought you promised to call me."

"I did, but you didn't answer. I figured you'd be home by six-thirty."

"I was, but that would have been five-thirty your time."

They laughed. "I made the same mistake a minute ago," he said. "How did it go today?"

"This place is overwhelming. It's all about the children. The halls and public rooms are light, airy and eye-catching with interesting and beautiful drawings and paintings on the walls, very colorful and right at a child's eye level. Even the ceilings look like clouds. I imagine it's difficult to be depressed here, and I can't believe that anyone who's been here would decline to support this place. I just got here, and what I've learned of its policies and activities boggles my mind.

"Tomorrow morning, I'll be in the part of the hospital where they give patient care. I hope I get to see Midge. If not, I'll get permission to visit her."

"Make some friends. I'd hate it if you were lonely," he said.

"I met two really nice women today. One is from Australia, and the other is from Italy. This place is like a little United Nations. Did you know that a physician working here won a Nobel Prize in medicine?"

"Yeah, I knew it, although I haven't met him."

"Have you looked for a nurse?"

"Yes, and as you've no doubt guessed, I drew a blank. So I'm going to use a fourth-year medical student. She won't replace you, but I expect she'll do well."

"Are you looking for a female? What's wrong with hiring a guy?"

"One guy here is enough. I want somebody with some nurturing instincts, and men aren't known for that."

"Kiss me so I can go to bed. I have to get up at five-thirty."

"Kiss you so you can go to bed. Think about that statement, Melanie." He made the sound of a kiss. "Good night, sweetheart. Call me about seven your time tomorrow. You should be in bed by nine-thirty your time."

"Still bossy, I see." She made the sound of a kiss. "Good night, love." As she hung up, she heard, "Hey, wait a minute," and since she knew he intended to grill her about calling him *love,* she dropped the receiver into its cradle. She hadn't queried his having called her *sweetheart,* and he'd done it several times recently. Hmm. Maybe he wanted her to question it. Well, he shouldn't wait for it. When he wanted her to know something, he'd have to come right out and tell her, and he had to do it without any prompting from her. She lowered the air conditioner and got back into bed. Imagine not cooking or making a bed or shopping for food for an entire month!

The next morning, she went on rounds with three doctors and two nurses. "These are HIV patients." The doctor nodded toward a boy whose bed they approached. "This is Eugene," the doctor said, "but if you want to be on his good side, call him ET."

She walked to the side of the bed and extended her hand to the young boy. "How are you, ET? I'm Nurse Sparks. I have a young friend here. Her name is Midge, and she's about your age. If you see her, tell her I'm looking for her, and that I hope to see her soon. Will you?"

"Yes, ma'am. Yes, indeed, Ms. Sparks. I'll tell her to keep a cap on it, and you'll see her soon."

The doctors and nurses with her laughed, but she didn't because she didn't understand their amusement. When she asked, she learned that ET stayed to himself, was almost invariably melancholy and that his response to Melanie was, by comparison, jubilant.

"What caused the difference?" she asked.

"You made him important," one of the nurses said. "You, a stranger, asked him to do something personal for you. The boy is from a foster home, and he's filled with doubts and uncertainties about himself and the reaction of others toward him."

"I imagine he's scared, too," Melanie said. When one of the doctors confirmed that, she made a mental note to go back and visit the boy occasionally.

Shortly before noon, she found an opportunity to organize the notes she'd taken that morning and to get acquainted with some members of the staff who were engaged in research, policy and administration rather than patient care.

"I'll take you to see her," one nurse told Melanie at the end of the working day when she asked where she could find Midge.

"Ms. Sparks! Ms. Sparks!" Midge yelled when she saw Melanie. "They're going to give me a transfusion, and then I'll feel better. Did you see my mom?"

"No, I didn't." She hugged the girl. "But I'm sure she's nearby."

"She met a lady who wants her to do baking demonstrations on her TV cooking show while she's here. Isn't that da bomb?"

If she knew what *da bomb* was, she'd probably agree, but teenage slang was a different language, one that she hadn't learned. "I think it's fantastic," Melanie said. "I can't stay too long. Give your mother my regards."

"I will. Be sure and come back."

As she walked through the bright and cheerful hall, her nurse colleague pointed to a room and said, "That room is for the teens. It's their sanctuary, their haven. Your friend, Midge, will make friends there. They exchange information, talk, play games, listen to their music and dance if they want to. It's a place where they can be themselves, and they love it."

Melanie smiled at a child who lay in a duck-shaped wagon pulled by someone who seemed to be the child's father.

"That isn't a toy or a joy ride," the nurse told Melanie. "It's transportation made as pleasant as possible for a sick child. Here, it's all about the children."

"I like this building," Melanie told the woman. "It's so conducive to good spirits."

"By the way, it was designed by Paul Williams, the African-American architect who designed so many L.A. homes for Hollywood stars? Imagine! And he was orphaned when he was four years old."

"I didn't know he was African American," Melanie said, "but I do know that you can't stop genius. It finds a way."

When she finally got to her room a little after four o'clock, she flopped on the bed, kicked off her shoes and took a deep breath. Fatigue claimed every muscle she had, but she didn't mind. Indeed, she could hardly wait to review her notes, organize them and enter them into her computer. A glance at her watch told her that she had a three-hour wait before she could talk with *him*.

"I'm getting deeply in this man's debt," she said to herself. "His sending me here is as much for him as for me, but it is nonetheless an opportunity that I wouldn't have dreamed of, and I could not have afforded it within the next ten years. Imagine living in a four-star hotel. I don't even launder my uniforms." She made a cup of green tea in the coffeemaker that the hotel provided, walked over to the window and gazed at the Mississippi River in the distance.

She didn't care to go to the docks and dreaded the visit to the African-American Museum. She didn't want to see the stark evidence of the slave trade that had flourished in Memphis after Tennessee rescinded its ban on slavery in the 1840s.

Seven o'clock finally arrived, and she telephoned Jack. "How'd it go today?" he asked.

"Great, but except for the forty minutes that I ate lunch, I was on my feet from seven until almost four. I'll get used to it, though." She gave him an account of her day, omitting nothing of the things she saw and learned. "Midge was happy to see me. She said she's getting a bone marrow transplant that will make her feel better, and I noticed she wasn't coughing. When I meet her doctor, I'll ask about the diagnosis and what he prescribed. I made rounds with three doctors and two nurses. What an experience. It's all in my notes, and I've typed them out so we can discuss them when I get back."

"So you're excited. I'm happy that you're enjoying it so far. Did you see Mrs. Hawkins?"

"No. Midge said a TV cooking show host invited her mother to demonstrate her baking techniques. Not sure what she was asked to bake. It's a great opportunity for her. Tell me about you, Jack. Who's helping you?"

"I interviewed a fourth-year medical student, as I'd planned, and I think she'll work out."

"She, huh?"

"Well, yeah. I told you I needed somebody who'd soothe the patients. Why? You don't like the idea of my working with a woman? Three work in my Bolton Hill office."

If he was trying to upset her, he was inching toward it. "Humph! It's the idea of *her* working with *you*."

"Run that past me again. I don't see the difference."

"You wouldn't. You're a man."

"Hold on there. You bet your sweet bottom I'm a man. If I'd said something like that to you, you'd have labeled me a male chauvinist."

"No, I wouldn't have. I don't have quite enough evidence."

His voice rose. "You don't have quite enough evidence to call me a male chauvinist? Is that what you said? Listen here! You don't have *any* basis for calling me that. I'm crushed."

"You poor baby. If I was with you, I'd kiss you and make it better."

"Be careful. I can get to Memphis in two hours, and when I leave there, you'll be a different woman."

"Trust me. You'll be a different man, too."

His high-pitched whistle came through the phone sharply. "I detected a feistiness in you almost as soon as we met and, from time to time, you've given me little glimpses of it, but now that you're down there where I can't get my hands on you, you're really letting it all out. Let me tell you something, Melanie. I like this reckless side of you, this hell-for-leather attitude, and when I get you all to myself in a private place, I want you to bathe me in it. I want you to let me know who you are."

Stunned, she didn't speak for a while, and he didn't prod her to respond. "I, uh…I hope you don't mind if I don't say anything about that," she said at last.

"Don't tell me you fold up so quickly. A minute ago you had me dizzy with your come-hither sass. Right now, my mouth is watering."

For want of something clever to say, she asked him, "Have you had dinner?" Laughter rippled out of him until it seemed uncontrollable. "Jack, are you all right? You sound hysterical."

As quickly as the laughter began, it stopped. "Why would I be hysterical? Of course I'm all right. Have I had dinner? Babe, you sure are a graceful loser. You merely change the subject."

"Well, have you? Had dinner, I mean."

"No, but it's ready. I'm eating at home this evening, and I'd better get downstairs, or Vernie will be unhappy with me."

"Is she a good cook?"

"The best, but we're not off the subject of you and me. What did you call me last night when you told me good-night?"

She'd expected that. "I probably said, 'Good night, Jack.'"

"Liar. You said, 'Good night, love,' and I want to hear you say it again. That rang in my ears so softly and so sweetly that I couldn't get to sleep for hours."

"Surely you don't want to stay awake half of tonight, too."

"Woman, if you really put yourself to it, you'd drive me batty. Kiss me good-night."

She made the sound of a kiss. "Good night, love."

He returned her kiss, and after a few seconds, he said, "Good night, love."

Her hands shook as she placed the receiver in its cradle. They had talked to each other as intimates. He'd come close to telling her how he wanted her to make love to him, and she had let him know that she'd pull out the stops. He knew she'd told the truth.

She ordered her dinner and vowed that she'd find a dining companion the next day and be more sociable. If truth were known, though, she was so used to being with Jack or looking forward to being with him that socializing with others—men or women—never occurred to her.

While waiting for her dinner, she let her mind travel back over the past six months. Not only had her life changed for the better after she'd moved away from her father, but her personality seemed to have burst

into a new dimension. Or was it because Jack's appreciation for her work and his trust in her strengthened
her self-confidence?

Don't fool yourself, girl, her conscience niggled.
*When a man like Jack Ferguson shows a deep interest
in a woman, her self-confidence is bound to soar and
her personality can't help but bloom.*

Jack hung up, slipped his feet into his house slippers
and went downstairs to eat dinner. He took his dinner
in the breakfast room, a relatively small room whose
entire outer wall consisted of a huge picture window. He
liked to sit there on Sunday mornings and watch the
hummingbirds that came to the feeder. The small stream
flowing through the property had been one of his
reasons for purchasing this land on which to build his
house. And from the north edge of the window, he could
see the swimming pool. He could also see a part of his
deck. The thought occurred that Melanie might not like
living out there so far from the city.

"Where did that come from?" he asked aloud.

He had everything except someone with whom to
share his life. "I'm damned if I'll sink into that," he said,
then finished his desert and took his dishes to the kitchen.

"Vernie, that was a first-class meal."

"Thank you, Doc. It seems a pity, though, to cook
that kind of meal for one person. You need a dinner
companion."

"I know that, Vernie, so don't start lecturing to me about
it. My dad's on my case, and that's irritating enough."

"Well, I hope he makes some headway," Vernie said in her usual irreverent manner. He ignored it, went upstairs to his den and prepared for his meeting with Telford Harrington, whose company would build the clinic and restructure his office for a laboratory.

He thought of the changes he'd observed in Melanie since she began working for him and wondered how they came about. He knew that leaving her father had given her freedom, but he couldn't pinpoint the rest. She remained the sweet, feminine, soft woman who had a commendable work ethic, who knew her job and enjoyed doing it. And he figured she would always care deeply about people, especially those in need. But there was more, and he couldn't pinpoint it. Whatever it was, he wanted as much of it as he could get.

He didn't like doing business on Sunday, but Harrington was busy that Saturday, and he couldn't go to Eagle Park during the work week. He drove the Town Car into the circle at number ten, John Brown Drive in Eagle Park, not far from Frederick, got out and looked around. Wealth. No doubt about that. He rang the bell, the door opened and a man who seemed to be about seventy peered out at him.

"Hi."

He followed the sound, looked down and saw a charming little girl of around six. "Good morning, I'm Dr. Jack Ferguson. Is Telford Harrington here?"

"Hi, Dr. Ferguson," the little girl said.

"Come on in," the man said, "and have a seat right in there." He pointed to what Jack assumed was the living room.

The girl walked with him. "I'm Tara, and you came to see my dad. Do you want him to build you a house or something?"

Before he could say yes, she continued. "Please have a seat. Would you like some water while my dad's coming?"

If ever he saw a reason for a man to marry and have a family, he was looking at it. The child captivated him. Her warm smile and easy way with a stranger told him that she was loved and that she had a special niche in the lives of the adults with whom she lived.

"How old are you, Tara?"

"I'm six and a half, Dr. Ferguson, and I have a new little brother. Where do you live?"

"I live in Baltimore, Tara. I assume you go to school."

"Yes, sir. I love school, and I love to read and write and play the piano. Would you like to see Biscuit? He used to be my puppy, but he grew up."

"Hello. Sorry to keep you waiting. I'm Telford Harrington, and I see you've met my daughter."

Jack stood and shook the man's hand. "I'm glad to meet you. You're a lucky man to be the father of this charming child. An adult female couldn't have entertained me in a more delightful way."

"For a while, she was the only child among five adults—four men and her mother—and she learns quickly. She's also very much at ease with adults. My brothers will be here soon, so if you want any changes in the design, you'll be able to discuss them with Russ. I liked what he did, but you're the one we want to please," Telford said.

"I like it, too, very much, but I want to ask him some questions.

"How long do you estimate it will take to erect this structure? I figured about eight months."

"Maybe less," Telford assured him. "Russ looked at the plot, but I haven't seen it. I'll put my permanent crew on it, so we should bring it in about six months if there're no hitches in the installation of all this special medical equipment."

The doorbell rang, and he'd never seen anybody move as fast as Tara shot up from her chair and raced to the door.

"Uncle Russ! Uncle Drake!" he heard her exclaim.

"How's my best girl?"

"We've got company, Uncle Drake, and I think Dr. Ferguson—that's his name—wants to see Uncle Russ."

Jack stood when the two imposing men entered the room, each holding one of Tara's hands. He shook hands with them, and in only a few minutes he knew he'd done the right thing: the clinic was in good hands, and he understood the basis for the Harrington Brothers' reputation as builders.

"It will be completely wheelchair accessible," Russ said, and Jack relaxed, because he'd been concerned about that.

"I want to meet your medical engineer as soon as you can manage it," Drake, engineer for the company, told him, "because that engineer will have something to say about the placement of equipment."

The man who had opened the door for him walked

in and interrupted them. "Lunch is ready, and if you don't eat it now, it'll get cold." Tara jumped up, ran to the man, took his hand and walked off with him. Was the man the cook? He didn't wear a uniform, and he didn't mind interrupting, either.

"We may continue at lunch," Telford said. They entered what he guessed was the breakfast room, because a house that big would have a much larger and more elegantly appointed dining room. When they paused at the door, Tara looked up at him, smiled and said, "We're waiting for my mommy. She'll be here in a minute because she's never late for meals."

Jack resisted the urge to pick her up and hug her. He looked up just as a tall, willowy beauty approached. "My wife, Alexis Harrington," Telford said, with pride that even a child could discern.

Her smile welcomed him. "I'm happy to meet you, Dr. Ferguson. Please join us for lunch." Russ said grace and the man who had opened the door to him walked into the room with a huge covered tureen.

"Dr. Ferguson, this is Henry Wilkerson, our cook, surrogate father and judge penitent," Telford said. "Whatever you find that's wrong with us brothers, you can blame on Henry, because it's his fault."

"He's absolutely right," Henry said. "I should've taken a stick to 'em, but I felt sorry for 'em and didn't do it. Yep, it's me own fault."

Jack stayed with the Harringtons longer than he had intended. "It's insufferably hot," Russ said, "and I'm dying for a swim. One of Telford's bathing shorts should fit you," he said to Jack, "so why don't we cool off in the pool? Unless you have an appointment."

"Right," Telford said. "Man, it's Sunday. How about it?"

"Yeah," Drake said. "I'll call my wife, and tell her I'll see her around five."

"Velma's not expecting me back right away," Russ said. "Give us something to change into, Telford."

They were inside an air-conditioned house, so Jack didn't understand Russ's comment about the insufferable heat. Maybe the man just loved to swim.

By the time they'd swum for an hour, Alexis and Tara came out to the pool with a huge jug of lemonade, glasses, plates and a basket of cinnamon-raisin cookies. The four men sat on the edge of the pool with their feet dangling in the water, talking, drinking lemonade and eating some of the best cookies he'd ever tasted. It occurred to him that he missed a lot by not having buddies with whom to pass leisurely moments. Had he not been with these people right now he'd be at home on his deck reading a medical journal or, if he'd finished that, the *New York Times*.

"I'll be old before I begin to enjoy life," he said to himself, "and there are going to be some changes made." Until Melanie entered his world, his social life had consisted of appearances at various social affairs with different socialites and aspiring wives. That was behind him; he was through with all that superficiality. This was what life should be like: work that you loved and relaxation with your woman, your children, your friends and close relatives.

He'd done more than verify the plans for the clinic; he'd begun to sort out his life options, and he felt as if several hundred pounds had dropped from his shoulders.

"Come back to see us," they told him.

"Yes," Alexis said, "and bring your girl. You're welcome to spend the night. It's lovely here this time of year, and especially in the autumn when the leaves begin to turn."

"Right," Henry said. "I do the best barbecue anywhere near these parts. You come back. You hear?"

Tara ran to him and grasped his hand. "Bye, Dr. Ferguson. When you come back, I'll play the piano for you."

Totally captivated by the child's directness and charm, Jack knelt and hugged her. "You're a charming little girl, and I am really happy that I met you." He kissed her cheek. "Goodbye, Tara."

He told them he'd come back, and he intended to do that. He hadn't felt so relaxed and free of stress in he didn't know when. He'd love to have Melanie with him in this environment, away from the office and the hustle of the city. He could take her to his home, but their relationship was still at the stage where she'd be uncomfortable alone there with him. With others around, she would be much more at ease. Yes, it was the perfect setting for lovers. And if she didn't think they were lovers, he meant to show her.

He drove fast, because he had to be at home by eight o'clock when Melanie called. He wanted to share with her the splendor of his afternoon at Eagle Park. He arrived home minutes before the phone rang. She knew his cell-phone number, but he knew she wouldn't use it, because they had agreed that, in the evenings, she would call him on the house number. He didn't care one way or the other, but he had suggested it so she'd know he was at home and not out with a date.

"Hello, sweetheart," he said when he answered the phone.

"Suppose it hadn't been me," she said. "You'd have had some explaining to do."

"To whom? I'm free, unmarried and not engaged." If it had been Elaine, she'd have had something approximating a stroke, but that wouldn't have worried him. "Did you get any rest today?"

"No. I'd promised myself I'd try to make some friends, so I went to the African-American Museum against my best judgment. It is a fantastic, fascinating place and definitely worth several visits, but it pains me physically and depresses me to look at tangible reminders of slavery. It's something I'm happy to be ignorant about. I see enough of its consequences every day of my life."

"Can't say I disagree with you. You feel passionately about things, don't you? I like that."

"So do you, Jack. If you didn't, you wouldn't have that second office and you wouldn't be planning a clinic across the street from it. I saw Alice Hawkins today. She's a happy woman because Midge is getting care. She said Midge had the procedure this morning. She said she made cranberry scones on the TV show yesterday, and you should have seen her grinning."

He told her about his visit with the Harrington brothers. "That little girl sank into me like a hook. I've never seen a child with her manners, grace and intelligence. And charm. She has more than her share of that. As I was leaving, I hugged her. You will love her. I promised Telford's wife that I'd bring you to visit when I go back. So since I've committed you, you can't let me down." He'd shocked her, but he didn't care. He could almost see her jaw go slack.

"You told those people about me?"

"N-no, but I'm telling you."

"In that case, thanks for letting me in on it."

"Do you object?" he asked her. A cold dampness seeped into him while he waited for her answer.

"I…uh…I guess not."

"You *guess* not?" he roared.

"Actually, it makes me proud to think you'd introduce me as your girlfriend."

It was his turn to be speechless. "Thank you. That's one of the nicest things you've ever said to me."

They talked for nearly an hour. At last, he said, "Kiss me, Melanie. This is going to be one long month."

"I know. Very long." She made the sound of a kiss and he responded in kind. "Good night, love," they said simultaneously.

The month dragged by, and on the twenty-fourth of September, Melanie stepped into the terminal at BWI Airport. If her carry-on bag hadn't weighed thirty pounds, she would have run to the baggage-claim area where she knew Jack awaited her. She didn't see him but, swept up into arms that she recognized, she looped her arms around his neck and knew once more the feel of his lips firm and sweet upon her own.

He set her on her feet. "You lost weight," were his first words to her. "I sure hope you didn't lose it in any important places."

"Not to worry," she said. "I only lost it in my brain. Thanks for meeting me."

"What else would I do? I can't begin to tell you how much I missed you."

"I'm glad to hear it, because I missed you, too."

He stared down at her until her nerves began to rearrange themselves throughout her body. "We're going to do something about this. I don't like loose ends in my life."

She wasn't sure she liked the sound of that. Pressure from any source was not to her liking. "Am I a loose end?" she asked him, sounding frostier than she intended.

"You'd like to be, but I'm having no more of that."

Chapter 9

Melanie had been back to work as Jack's registered nurse for two weeks when the day of the clinic's groundbreaking finally arrived. She had splurged on an elegant burnt-orange suit of lightweight wool and brown leather accessories, the first time she'd ever bought a complete outfit for any occasion. It wouldn't hurt to wear her hair down, she reasoned. The bigwigs would be there—nothing like getting their picture in the paper at an event aimed to uplift the poor—and she meant to hold her own.

"You remember Ms. Sparks, don't you, Dad?" Jack said to his father as they approached the reserved seats facing the temporary podium holding each other's hands.

"Yes, of course. How do you do?" Montague said, his grudge as obvious as the nose on his face.

"Good morning, sir," she replied, giving him some of his own. Jack's arm eased around her waist and moved her closer to him. She looked up at him and smiled when she saw in his eyes the message that, for his affection for her, he apologized to no man.

"You look so beautiful," he told her as if his father were unable to hear his words. "I haven't seen you in this color. It suits you perfectly."

"Thank you," she said, and then, looking directly at Montague Ferguson, "Aren't there copies of the program somewhere?"

Forced to reply directly to her, Montague said, "Probably," and passed the task to Jack. "Have you seen any, Jack?"

Jack's shrug surprised her, and when his arm tightened around her, she realized that Montague Ferguson had wanted to get rid of Jack long enough to say something to her, and Jack had foiled his attempt. When Jack waved at someone, she looked around and saw Tommy, who joined them.

"See if you can find some copies of the program, Tommy."

"Yes, sir. How many do you want?"

'I think four will suffice." Tommy ran off to find the programs and Jack said to her, "Let's sit here."

"How often do you spar with your father, Jack?"

"With increasing frequency. But it doesn't bother me much—when it concerns my affairs, I usually win."

"But you maintain a good relationship with him, I hope."

"We're on very good terms. He won't stop trying to make me follow in his footsteps, and I won't stop resisting. We still hug each other."

She could feel her eyes widening. "Not today, you didn't. He froze the minute he saw me."

"He's thawed before, and he'll thaw again. I don't let it worry me. The fact that he's behind this clinic and here today for the ground-breaking is proof that he supports what we're trying to accomplish."

Tommy returned with the programs. "Here they are, Dr. Ferguson."

"Thanks, Tommy." He gave a program to his father, who sat two seats away, one to Melanie, one to Tommy and kept one for himself. "Sit over here beside me, son."

"Yes, sir," said the proud boy, smiling at Jack.

"Dad, this is Tommy Pickett. Tommy, this is my father, Dr. Montague Ferguson."

Tommy jumped up, walked around and shook hands with Montague. "How are you, sir? I heard a lot about you. My friend said you patched him up when Dr. Ferguson was away. He thinks the world of you. I sure am glad to meet you."

"Why, thank you, Tommy," Montague said. "I'm glad to meet you, too."

"Did Dr. Ferguson tell you he saved my life?"

"No, he didn't, but I'm certainly glad he did," Montague said.

"Tommy's very special, Dad."

I could love this man, Melanie acknowledged to herself. *I could really love him.*

The mayor opened the proceedings, took as much credit to himself as he could manage and then introduced Montague.

"I wouldn't be standing here if it weren't for my son, Dr. Jack Ferguson, the noted cardiologist," Montague said. "He had an epiphany one day and decided to open an office down here. It's right across the street." He pointed to the building. "I thought he'd lost his mind. But one night when he was out of town and there wasn't a reliable substitute, his nurse called me to look at a patient in Jack's office. I went, spent the next five hours there tending the patients—there must have been over twenty of them—and I decided that the area needs a first-class clinic. It's getting one.

"I and the other partners won't have anything to do with the clinic except to raise funds and keep the politicians in line. My son, Jack, will run the clinic, and he has decided to have the laboratory right where his office now stands. It's a good day for the people of this area. Jack, why don't you tell us your plans?"

"Thanks, Dad. I've engaged the Harrington Brothers, architects, engineers and builders, and I have a medical engineer on board to help in the selection and placement of equipment. We'll have a state-of-the-art facility, and we're getting physicians who are experts in specific fields to give us three free hours weekly. If patients have insurance, we'll gladly take that, but if they don't and cannot pay, we'll care for them anyway, as we do now, and we will not treat them as if they're receiving charity.

"I've learned a lot of things since I've had that office

across the street, the most important of which are to be thankful for what I have, that I'm blessed and that, but for the grace of God, I could be sick with no means of getting the care I need. I've learned that most people do not want charity, but that they sometimes need it to survive. If you contribute to the Alicia Todd Ferguson Memorial Clinic and Laboratory, you will be supporting a truly worthwhile establishment. Thank you."

Melanie could see that Jack's words touched his father, for the man's eyes clouded with tears. "I didn't know you planned to name it for your mother," Montague said to Jack after he sat down. "Alicia would have been proud, and she would have been right down here working with you. She would have found a way to help."

"I know," Jack said, "but it was Melanie's idea. I asked her to suggest a name. I'm glad you're pleased."

To Melanie's amazement, Montague Ferguson looked at her and nodded. "Thank you." Maybe he'd get around to thawing, but she wouldn't count on it.

Jack asked the mayor to remove a shovelful of dirt, he did and after a long and resounding applause, the mayor ended the ceremony, and the group dispersed.

"I should think you'd be happy," Montague said to Jack as they walked across the street to Jack's office. "Not many men get to see a dream take off like this so quickly. What's wrong?"

At the door of his office, Jack took the keys from his pocket, put his arm around Melanie and, without opening the door, said to his father, "I'm happy about the ground-breaking and the fact that the Harringtons are ready to begin digging for the foundation, but it saddened me that only one of the people for whom this is intended to help came to the service. Fortunately, Tommy is the one who came, for he is the reason why I have an office down here."

"Son, you have to realize that up and down cannot meet. It's impossible. The downs know it, and so do the ups."

Melanie tensed, and her sudden rigidity was at once obvious to both men. She pushed open the door. "If you'll excuse me, I have work to do. I'm one of the downs, remember?"

"Oh, no, you don't," Jack said, restraining her with a firm grip on her arm. "I'm having none of that. If my father prefers to live in the dark ages, there's no reason why you should join him there. You're not going to hold me in your arms and then act as if I'm not good enough for you."

"I never did that," she shot back, "and I've never held you in my arms."

"Liar! You haven't held me inside your body, but you've certainly held me and loved me until I was nearly out of my senses. If you deny it, I never want to see you again."

She hurt, and she didn't know what to do about it, but she didn't want to mislead Jack's father. "I misunderstood you, Jack. Yes, I've held you in my arms, and you've held me in yours, and it was the sweetest thing I've ever experienced."

She had to get away from them, but she knew Jack

wouldn't let her leave. She looked at him and saw his pain. "Oh, J-Jack," she stammered. "Oh, darling."

He pulled her to him with such force that her handbag fell to the floor. "This is between us, and nobody else, Melanie. I don't have to ask anybody's permission to be with you. I answer only to God. To him, there are no up people and down people. I'm pretty damn sure of that."

Still holding her as tightly as he could without hurting her, he looked at his father. "Tricks like that only bring us closer, Dad. This isn't something that you can call off the way you can call a bloodhound off a scent. What we have between us happened the minute we met. Do you want to come in for coffee? Melanie and I make great coffee."

"I know. I've tasted it. I hope you have some of those cranberry scones."

"We have some, sir," she said, "but they're not quite as good. These are from a bakery. The woman who made the others is in Memphis at St. Jude Children's Research Hospital with her daughter, who has sickle-cell anemia."

"If you were smart," Montague said to Jack, "you'd set that woman up in business and take a cut."

Jack lifted his shoulder in a quick shrug. "She needs some form of steady income, but it's all I can do right now to take care of my patients and plan for the clinic. Why don't you do it?"

"Who knows?" Montague said. "I'll think about it." He drank the coffee, ate two scones and stood. "With all the crime in this region, you really do leave your Porsche unlocked on the street in this neighborhood?" he asked Jack.

"When you go out, open the front door on the driver's side and see if I told you the truth. Your Cadillac will be out there, too."

"Why mine?" Montague asked.

"Because you're my father, and because you worked down here, helping these people. They do not forget a kindness."

"Hmm. Thanks for the coffee and scones. See you at lunch day after tomorrow."

Melanie was working in the supply room and heard their conversation, but she didn't feel like pretending, so she didn't go out to tell Montague Ferguson goodbye. He'd be able to figure out the reason, she surmised.

Jack didn't think for a moment that his father had accepted the idea of his son having a relationship with a nurse. Furthermore, he was about certain that his dad had hired an investigator to look into Melanie's background. He loved his father, but he knew that Montague Ferguson hadn't reached the level of prominence that he enjoyed without the toughness with which Jack was so familiar. His father had once advised him, "Never yell uncle, and never lose. If you can't come out on top, always make the other guy win. Don't give in." He assumed that his father would try another tactic, making his moves less obvious.

"Well, what do you think?" Jack asked Melanie after his father left. They sat in Jack's office with the aroma of freshly brewed coffee permeating the air. "I feel uplifted. Work on the clinic has actually begun, and you and I will see its progress day by day, like Venus rising from the Aegean Sea."

Her laughter caressed him like a warm blanket in winter. He couldn't help wondering how he had gotten so lucky. Every nerve in his body responded to her, and he had to resist the urge to hold her.

"What's funny?" he asked.

"Occasionally, you're poetic, and I like that. But I can't see any similarity between a building going up and a Greek goddess rising from the sea. That's pretty fancy thinking."

"Why not? I feel fancy right now, but this office is not the place to express it."

"Right. I have a feeling that your father will want to have a board of directors for the clinic, and he'll want the members to be his moneyed friends who can boast of their charity work, and who won't understand or care what we're trying to do in this community."

She knew precisely how to change the topic if she didn't want it to get personal. She also had a keen sense of decorum. He mused over her comment about a board of directors. "I hadn't given that any thought, but we should have one. We ought to be accountable to a board, not hour by hour and patient by patient, but I mean in respect to our policies and our patient-care standards."

"Yes, of course, though I can't imagine that any board member will have standards that are higher or more commendable than yours."

The woman had a way of making him feel like a giant, as if he could accomplish anything, but he knew she meant it. He sought to lighten the weight of her compliment, to control the urge to love her senseless. "Go ahead and butter me up. See if I care," he said, though it was far from the way he felt. "You make me feel as if I'm ten feet tall and bulletproof."

"That's the way you look to me," she said, and there was no smile on her face.

He pushed the plate of scones and doughnuts aside and grabbed her wrist. "If you keep talking to me like this, we'll be making love right on this floor, and you'll hate me and yourself, too."

A frown eclipsed her face. "Every office ought to have a sofa," she said and winked at him. "Libido, do not raise thy ugly head."

"Are you laughing at me?" he asked her.

She reached over and stroked his cheek. "I know better than to do that, Jack. I'm just trying to decharge the atmosphere in here. Now, back to the matter at hand. Since your father will demand that the clinic have a board, I suggest that you get ahead of him and select four people that you trust. They, along with your father, would constitute the board. As the director, you would automatically be a member. If I were you, I would present that to your father, before he approaches some of his cronies. He'd be very embarrassed if he had to rescind an invitation."

"You're way ahead of me," he said. "If I didn't know better, I'd think you'd known my father for years. I can think of three offhand—a doctor, a social worker and a university professor—but I want one more who's not a doctor. We ought to have somebody from the community."

"What about Alma's father? He served in Afghanistan, he's very intelligent, loves his family and people with money won't frighten him one bit."

"I thought of him. Do you think he can handle it so soon after his child's death?"

"He might do it as a memorial to her," Melanie said.

"Right. I'll name one of the examining rooms the Alma Powell examining room. Another one is going to be the Tommy Pickett examining room because he's the reason we're here and the clinic is being built. Tommy will love that."

She leaned back in the chair, glanced down at her fingers and said, "I'm glad I know you. I think we're really going to make a difference."

"Oh, we will, and that's all I want." He realized with a start that he thought of himself and Melanie as a couple. "I don't think I could do what we're attempting if you weren't with me. And I don't only mean your presence and your help. I mean your support and your caring."

She raised her gaze slowly and, he realized, reluctantly, and let him see in her eyes her feelings, bare and unprotected. But she didn't say one word, only looked at him and let him see what was in her heart.

"I need to get some work done," she said abruptly. "If I sit here with you, I won't accomplish one thing all day, and it will be your fault."

He didn't respond, but watched her open his office door and rush out as if she had to avert an impending disaster. He let her go without comment. They were in his office, and she was on duty. He respected her professionalism, but what he needed from her right then was a good session of pure woman. *Thank God one of them had sense.*

At home that night, Melanie mused over the many happenings of the day—the ground-breaking for the clinic, Montague Ferguson's snub, his rudeness to her, his thank-you for suggesting that the clinic have his wife's name and Jack's declaration to his father that theirs was more than a professional relationship. She knew she had endorsed it when she put her arms around Jack, but what else could she do when she could see the hurt in his eyes and almost feel the pain he suffered?

She had to decide whether what she saw as potential happiness was worth the battle. Montague didn't speak about Jack's demonstration of affection for her and hers for him, at least not where she could hear him, but she suspected that he would let Jack have a piece of his mind about it.

I'm too far gone, and it's too late to turn back, she said to herself. *I should have left when I could. He's as much a part of me now as my hands and my feet.*

After a supper of chicken and avocado salad, a roll and a dish of raspberry and vanilla ice cream, she sat down to write a letter to ET. She couldn't say why the boy had made such an impression on her. She wanted him to know that she hadn't forgotten him and that he had a friend in her, albeit a long-distance one. The next day on her way to work, she bought a book and a DVD on the training and care of birds and marked the chapter on falcons, included her letter, wrapped it and mailed it to ET at the St. Jude Children's Research Hospital. She suspected that he would respond to something different and exciting.

In the office, the telephone rang. She answered it, but no one responded, so she hung up. It could have been either her father or Jack's or someone with the wrong number. Certainly, one of their patients would have no reason to waste the cost of a telephone call. Maybe one of Jack's female friends who wasn't seeing enough of him. "Heck, if they try it again, I'll let them hear a thing or two," she said aloud, for the caller had blocked his or her own phone number.

When Jack came in at a quarter of five that afternoon, she told him about the crank call. "Who do you think is calling here just to annoy us?"

"Beats me. Next time, tell 'em that we've put a tracer on all incoming calls, and I'm going to have the culprit prosecuted. That ought to scare the bejeebers out of 'em."

"Good," she said. "I'll call the telephone company first thing tomorrow morning." When his eyes widened, she said, "What's the matter?"

"I was only planning to scare them, but go ahead. I'd like to know who it is."

"Do you have an idea?" she asked him.

"I know it wasn't my father. He's always sure he's right, and he'll stand up to anybody, male or female."

"Oh, well," Melanie said. "As long as they limit the harassment to an occasional phone call, I'll overlook it."

"Come here and give me a taste of honey," he said when she made no move to kiss him.

"Us kissing is bad office behavior," she said after soaking up the loving he gave her. "Suppose someone walked in here."

He looked at her and grinned, mesmerizing her. "If that happened, I'd move out of here like a bat out of hell. The front door is locked."

"Uh…right. Anyway, you behave." Even as she said it, she inched toward him, and within seconds he thrust into her parted lips. Suddenly giddy, she reeled out of his arms and rested her back against the wall. "Th-that's the reason why w-we have to k-keep this sort of thing out of th-the office."

"If you were sweeter to me, I'd behave," he said, obviously satisfied with himself.

She rolled her eyes toward the ceiling and, as she left his private office, threw over her shoulder, "Yeah, right. I believe that. I've also walked across the Atlantic Ocean from New York to London."

"You're saying you don't believe me?"

"Is that what I said? It's five o'clock, so get ready. I'm unlocking the door."

As soon as she opened the door, a tall, heart-stopping man walked in with his arm around a shorter, less-compelling figure of a man. "I thought you'd never open," the tall one said. "I'm Drake Harrington, engineer for your clinic. My worker cut his hand and, as you can see, it's bleeding badly."

"Glad to meet you, Mr. Harrington. Come right back

here," she said to the injured man and called Jack. "I have an emergency in room A. Have a seat in the waiting room, Mr. Harrington. I'll get you some coffee."

"I'd love some coffee," Drake said in one of the deepest and most musical voices she'd ever heard, "but my worker is the one in pain."

"I'm not sure the doctor would recommend that he drink anything hot at this point, but if he says it's okay, I'll give him some. What do you want in yours?"

"Milk, no sugar. Thanks." He looked around. "I wouldn't expect to find this kind of place in this neighborhood. It speaks well for Ferguson." He sipped the coffee. "This is good coffee." She brought him a blueberry scone. He tasted it and trained his large, sleepy, hazel-brown eyes on her. "I didn't realize I was hungry. This is great."

"We used to have some that were far better, but the woman who made them for us is in Memphis with her sick daughter. When she comes back, you'll see how good a scone can be."

"Well, I shall certainly look forward to her return."

Jack walked into the waiting room along with his patient. "It's good to see you, Drake. How are you?"

"Right now, I'm greatly relieved to see Lon smiling, and I'm glad to see you."

"Lon will mend properly," Jack said, "but I hate to tell you that he shouldn't use that hand for a week until that cut has completely healed. I wanted to put it in a sling, but he says he can manage not to let anything hit it. If you have any problems, let me know."

"My thanks. How much do we owe you, buddy?" Drake asked.

"Whatever your insurance pays. Drake Harrington, this is Melanie Sparks."

Drake looked from one to the other and smiled. "I'm delighted to meet you, Ms. Sparks. Bring her with you when you come to see us weekend after next, man." He directed his attention to her. "I hope you'll come. It's wonderful this time of year in Eagle Park."

She felt Jack's arm ease around her waist. "If she's reluctant, I'll persuade her. Give my good wishes to your brothers, Henry and that darling little girl."

"Tara," Drake said. "She twists every man, me included, around her little finger."

"She certainly got to me," Jack said. "See you weekend after next.

"You *will* go with me to spend that weekend with the Harringtons, won't you?" Jack asked her after Drake left with Lon. "They're a charming clan, three brothers, their wives, a crotchety old cook who's like a father to the brothers and one charming little girl who told me she has a new brother. Each of the men has his own home, but I gather that they congregate around Telford, the oldest, who lives in the family home. And trust me, that house is some mansion."

"So they're rich."

"Yes, they are, but they don't wear it on their sleeves, and they don't act like it. When Drake Harrington walked in here, did you size him up as a rich man? I enjoyed being with them. For the first time, I realized what I missed by not having brothers or a close male friend."

She wouldn't tell him that what Drake Harrington reminded her of was perfection in mankind, though she'd never be attracted to a man that handsome. "No, I realized he was one of the builders, but I didn't think about wealth. He accepted that mug of coffee as if he'd never had a porcelain cup in his hand. All right, I'll go with you, but you'll have to tell me what to expect so I'll know how to dress."

"I guess you take pants, sport shirts, a sweater, a casual jacket for day and a dress for evenings. Telford's wife looks as if she dresses for dinner."

"Thanks. I get the picture. Say, the waiting room's filling up. We'd better get busy."

"Right. Who's first?"

It made Jack uneasy that his father had said nothing more about his relationship with Melanie. He didn't know what to make of it. Montague Ferguson was like a diva waiting in the wings for an opportunity. He didn't get one, so he made one. Montague intended that his only son would marry a descendent of the "Talented Tenth," and Melanie Sparks was both too dark and too poor to fit that mold.

"Hello, Dad," Jack said, having seen his father's phone number on his caller ID. "How're things?"

"Just fine."

"Glad to know it. I have four names of people I want on the clinic's board of directors, five with you, and as the clinic's director, I'd serve on the board. That makes six. We should probably have seven, to ensure a majority vote on every issue."

To his surprise, his father said, "That's great. I hadn't gotten that far. I knew we needed a board, but I hadn't gotten so far as to choose the members. Who are they?"

Jack named his choices and his father said, "That's a good mix, but who's this Rodney Powell? Do I know him?"

He gave his father a brief description of Rodney Powell and added, "There must always be a member of the community of this board. We're not going to have a group with no vested interest in the area guiding the clinic's work."

"Mmm. Well, you'd better put that in the by-laws. Get your lawyer to take care of it. I hope the man is able to hold his own in the group."

Jack didn't comment. His father wasn't pleased but had chosen not to contest Jack's decision, which meant something else that Montague considered more important was in the offing.

"Uh…I'm giving a formal dinner for eighteen people at the Marriott Waterfront Hotel Saturday evening, and I want you to come."

So that was the reason for the call. "Since it's formal, I assume I may bring my date?"

"Well, I've got an uneven number of women and men, and I'd rather you didn't. I hate a dinner party with more women that men or the other way around. So come solo. I'll expect you at seven."

"I suppose you know this louses up my own plans for the weekend."

"I'm sorry, son, but I appreciate your helping me out."

He didn't like it, and he definitely did not look forward to spending the evening with one of his father's old friends, a society biddy who'd outlived her options.

He dressed appropriately in a tuxedo, added red accessories and black patent leather shoes. To his annoyance, his father met him at the door with a vapid-looking, long-necked woman of about thirty, bedecked in a pink chiffon evening gown and more jewelry, including diamonds, than a young woman could wear without appearing vulgar.

"Miranda Lucas, this is my son, Dr. Jack Ferguson, the cardiologist."

He glared at his father, not out of disrespect, but honesty. It was the only way that he could express himself short of turning on his heels and leaving. To express his resentment, he talked mostly to the woman on his right throughout dinner, since his date's only response seemed to be "Really?"

After dinner, a small combo played dance music, and when he could no longer avoid it, he danced with the woman and had to admit that she knew her way around the floor. He noticed that a photographer took pictures of practically every person present, but he declined to pose for one. He knew the pictures would be on the society page of the *Afro American* and in several magazines.

Near the evening's end, he spoke with the woman,

whose name he'd already forgotten, told he her was glad to have met her and wished her a good night. He hadn't brought her there, and he had no intention of taking her home. If that meant he was rude, so be it.

Montague caught up with him before he reached the elevator. "You're leaving? You're not taking Miss Lucas home? What's come over you?"

"Plenty," Jack said. "I didn't bring her here, so I am not responsible for seeing that she gets home. You could as easily have had a party for sixteen instead of eighteen, and I could have spent the evening with a woman who interests me."

"I can't begin to tell you how disappointed I am," Montague said. "She undoubtedly will expect more of a son who bears my name."

Jack took a deep breath and counted to fourteen. He didn't lose his temper with his father, and he was on the verge of it. "I had hoped you'd given up trying to or-chestrate my private life, Dad, but it's clear that you haven't. Do you really think I'd be interested in Miranda Lucas or any woman like her? Are these social man-eaters the type of mother you want for your grandchil-dren?" He shook his head from side to side, puzzled at his father's behavior. "Please let it lie."

"She's a good woman from one of the best families, and you'll know she isn't after your money."

"If she's got so much going for her, she shouldn't have a problem finding a man and shouldn't need anyone to arrange a blind date."

"You heard what I said. She won't be after your money."

What was the use? He threw up his hands in frustration and disgust. "You think that, at my age, I'm so stupid I don't know whether a woman cares for me or is merely posturing? Being able to discern that is precisely why I'm sick of the Elaines, Mirandas and other women in this social set. They check out a man's credentials and go after him. Their feelings have nothing to do with their choice of a man. *Is he a good catch, and if I get him will other women envy me?* That's their yardstick. Spare me. See you at lunch."

He headed outside, breathed in the night air, polluted though it was, and handed his ticket to the valet. Yes, he would ordinarily have taken the woman home, but he didn't like her and, moreover, he wanted to teach his father a lesson. He paced in front of the hotel, retracing his steps several times, as he waited for his car. By the time he got home, it was too late to call Melanie. He wondered what she thought about his having a Friday-night engagement that did not include her.

Melanie thought nothing of Jack's Friday-night engagement until Tuesday morning when she received in the mail a copy of the newspaper containing the pictures taken at Montague Ferguson's formal dinner party. She noted that the large manila envelope had no return address, and after a short debate with herself, she opened it.

"What's this?" she asked aloud, as she scanned the front page of the paper's society section. Her lower jaw dropped, and she found her way to the nearest chair and sat down. At least a dozen color pictures of Jack with the same woman. She figured the woman's dress had cost at least two thousand dollars.

"She sure gave him plenty to look at," Melanie said aloud, looking at the top of the dress that revealed the edge of the woman's nipples. "So that's what he was doing last Friday night." She pitched the paper across the room. "Damn him. I don't care what he does or who with."

She went to the kitchen for a cup of coffee, glanced out the window, saw two pigeons grooming each other and felt a lump in her throat. *Somebody sent me this, someone who knows my address, knows how I feel about Jack and wants it to stop.* She picked up the paper, folded it and replaced it in the envelope.

"I'll see what Jack has to say about this."

When he arrived at the office shortly after four o'clock that afternoon, he greeted her with a hug and kiss, and she reciprocated, but her heart wasn't in it. He gazed down at her with a question in his eyes, and what seemed to her an expression of hurt.

"What is it, Melanie?"

"Uh…I'll make you some coffee, and we'll talk."

"Forget the coffee. What's the matter?"

She handed him the envelope. "I know you didn't send this to me, but someone did, and that person wants me out of your life."

He turned back to the door, secured the lock and took her hand. "Come in here with me," he said, led her into his private office and closed the door. "Have a seat."

He took the newspaper out of the envelope and looked at the pictures. "You know I didn't send this to you. This was a dinner party that my father gave for eighteen people, including me, last Friday night. He asked me to come alone, because he wanted an even number of men and women. I left early, and he and I had some words.

"I thought then that he was matchmaking, but he didn't stop there. I'm ashamed of what he did. This is a very juvenile prank."

"You think he sent me these pictures?" she asked.

"Who else would have done it? I don't think that woman knows you exist."

"He doesn't like me, and he's going to do everything and anything he can to get me out of your life."

"I don't know, but I certainly am not pleased with this. He introduced me to that woman the minute I arrived and had already seated us together. I refused to take her home, and I left when the guests were still dancing and partying. He was very displeased."

"Did you know her before Friday night?"

"I'd never seen her, but I know a dozen women like her, and they are not for me."

Melanie wished she could understand why Montague Ferguson opposed her so strongly. "What was your mother like, Jack?"

"Oddly, you are very much like her in personality, outlook and values, and my dad was crazy about her. I can't see why he would want less for me than he wanted for himself."

"I have this feeling that I'm a wall between the two of you, and it shouldn't be that way. I don't like it."

"Don't worry about it, sweetheart. I don't have to choose between you. It will never come down to that."

"You hope it won't."

Chapter 10

"You real quiet tonight, doc," Vernie said to Jack when she topped his warm apple turnover with a scoop of vanilla ice cream.

"Is that why you're filling me with all these calories?"

"Well, I thought I could at least cheer you up with your favorite desert."

"Thanks. I appreciate that, but I'm fine. Just had a decision to make. Thanks for a great meal. It was up to your usual high standard." He patted her shoulder. At least one of them ought to be happy.

Bounding up the stairs, he was reminded of his childhood and his faith that his father stood for all that was good, right and just, a man whose integrity couldn't be shaken. He didn't understand the reason for his father's zealous crusade against his son's friendship with a woman similar to his own wife.

He can try as he might to torpedo our relationship, but I won't let him win. Jack walked into his den and stopped. Suppose his father made a move to oust Melanie from the clinic or even to demote her. No way would it happen. He would frustrate his dad by not mentioning those newspaper pictures to him, and he would protect Melanie's position. He sat down at his desk and drafted a new contract for her signature. When he got to his Bolton Hill office the next morning, he phoned his lawyer and read the contract to him.

"Will this stand in court?" he asked.

"If it has both your signature and hers on it, yes. The stipulation that she's head nurse is fine, but you should add a line that she answers only to the clinic's director. I'll run by and have a look at it."

It hadn't occurred to him that Melanie would balk at signing the contract. "Why do you want me to sign this? I have a two-year contract, and that's good enough for me."

"It's not good enough for me. That contract was signed when you were an LPN and before I knew your level of competence. It's only just that I take account of your status and abilities with a salary adjustment."

She locked her knuckles to her hips, slanted her head to the side and let her gaze travel over him. "There's more to this, Jack. Something's going on, starting with the pictures in that paper, and I want to know what it is."

He walked over to her, removed her hands from her hips and put them on his shoulders. "Either you trust me or you don't. I did this in full consultation with my lawyer. We've built something in this community. You and I. Yes, you are as much responsible for it as I am, and I insist that you have the status and the recognition that are your due. Please sign this contract, Melanie."

"What are you going to do when the clinic opens, Jack? It will be a different kind of operation."

"I'll be here two evenings a week, Tuesdays and Thursdays, and I'll have a direct line from my Bolton Hill office to the clinic."

"You may have to give up something. You're only human."

"Maybe, but I'll never give up the clinic, not until I can no longer practice, and even then, I'll direct it as long as my health permits. It's the one good thing I've done with my life. Tell me you're with me in this." He took a pen from his pocket and handed it to her.

"All right. As long as I work here, I'll know I'm doing some good, helping those who can't help themselves, and that's the reason why I wanted to be a nurse." She signed the contract and handed it to him.

He released a long sigh of relief. "With you at the helm," he said, "humanitarianism will always be the hallmark of our clinic." He took her into his arms and wrapped her close to him. "Has it ever occurred to you that we belong together? Has it?"

"I don't let myself engage in such fancy thinking, Jack. There're too many problems."

"When I encounter problems, I move them, Melanie. You and I care deeply for each other. I know you have a hard time accepting that fact, but it's the truth. I'm getting to the point where I need a resolution to this. I need you in my arms and in my bed."

She attempted to move away from him, and knowing her, that didn't surprise him, but he held her. "We're going to deal with it head-on, Melanie. You're important to me entirely apart from this uniform you wear." Her arms tightened around him, probably against her will, he figured. He told himself to keep it between the lines. In fifteen minutes, the first patient would ring the doorbell. "Kiss me, sweetheart."

Her parted lips welcomed the thrust of his tongue, and she pulled him into her, greedily, hungry for him and not bothering to hide that fact. He broke the kiss and hugged her close.

"When did you last kiss a man other than me like that?" he asked her, gazing into eyes that said he could have whatever he wanted. "When?"

"Never!"

He gazed at her until she seemed to swim before him, teasing and tantalizing his senses. "I'm… I'll m-make some coffee," he stammered, and left her, shocked as he was by the realization that she could do anything with him that she wanted to.

He couldn't say how he got through the next four hours. But with three emergencies and one nearly traumatized parent, Melanie went about her duties efficiently, calming the patients, even singing to one small boy until he lost his fear and wanted to follow her wherever she went. But Jack thought the evening would never end.

"What's ailing you?" she asked when they had a moment alone.

"I'm managing to take care of the patients, but that's about all."

Her soft hands stroked the side of his face. "Are you tired?"

"Physically? Not a bit. Don't worry. I'll deal with it, and soon." A quizzical expression flashed across her face. At first, he chided himself that he might have upset her.

He shrugged first his left shoulder and then his right one. *If I upset her, good. She's one hundred percent responsible for the way I'm feeling right now, breezing around here as if I didn't exist, as if she didn't knock the starch out of me and then stroll over to the door and open it to these patients. What ails me? She does. Dammit. But I'm putting a stop to this.*

Two days later, Melanie stepped out of Jack's Town Car and gazed up at the house that was, by any measure, a mansion. Until she'd agreed to spend the weekend with Jack at the Harrington home, she hadn't known that the hamlet of Eagle Park existed. Everywhere, she saw symbols of wealth. The perfectly manicured lawns and hedges, a custom-built Town Car and a Lexus in the circular driveway. The house itself was reminiscent of antebellum mansions of an earlier era.

Jack opened the trunk of his car, removed their bags, walked with her to the front door and lifted the knocker. When he looked down at her and smiled, she knew with certainty that, if she wasn't careful, her life would change before she left there. The door opened.

"Hi, Dr. Ferguson," a small voice said. "I was waiting for you."

"It's time you got here," an older man said in what was obviously an affectionate greeting. They stepped inside the house and, after shaking hands with Henry, Jack hunkered beside the little girl.

"Hi, Tara. I've been looking forward to seeing you again."

"Me, too, Dr. Ferguson." The little girl looked at Melanie. "You must be Dr. Ferguson's girl. My mommy said he was bringing you. She wants to meet you." Melanie looked down at the little girl and couldn't help smiling at her expectant expression. Completely disarmed, she bent, put her arms around the child and hugged her.

"I'm glad to meet you, Tara. I couldn't have had a more pleasant welcome. I'm Melanie Sparks."

"Hi, Ms. Sparks."

Still holding Tara, Melanie glanced up at Jack and caught him with his feelings raw, but he recovered quickly.

"Henry Wilkerson, this is Melanie Sparks. Melanie, Henry is surrogate father to the Harrington men."

She extended her hand to him. "I'm glad to meet you, Mr. Wilkerson."

"And I'm glad to meet you. It's been years since I heard meself addressed by the name Wilkerson. Call me Henry."

A tall man walked up to the door and said, "Well, so

you're Melanie. I'm delighted to meet you and to have you here. I'm Telford Harrington. My wife is getting the baby to sleep. She'll be down in a few minutes."

"I'm delighted to meet you, Mr. Harrington." She looked up at the man and couldn't help smiling inwardly. No wonder Jack liked the Harringtons; he and the two brothers she'd met were cut from the same cloth. "I've been looking forward to meeting you and your family. Jack fell in love with your daughter, and I can see why."

"Come on in, and be at home," Telford said, leading them out of the foyer. He looked at Jack and winked. "You hit the jackpot, man. Glad to have you both. Alexis will get you settled."

Tara looked up at Henry. "Mr. Henry, can I give them some of the lemonade you just made? It's real good."

Henry took Tara's hand. "Sure you can," he said and headed for what Melanie assumed to be the kitchen. As they walked away, Melanie's gaze lingered on the little girl, and her thoughts were of what her own life might have been if she had grown up in an environment of love as that child obviously had.

"Forgive me for not greeting you when you arrived." Melanie looked in the direction from which that silvery voice came and saw Alexis Harrington gliding toward her.

"I'm Alexis Harrington. I'm glad you'll be with us this weekend, Melanie. How nice to see you again, Jack." She took Melanie's hand. "Come with me."

Alexis walked with her a few paces and stopped. "Do you want a room with Jack or without him? We aim to please."

Melanie knew her eyes increased to twice their size. Then, recognizing a true sister, she grinned. "I should tell the truth and say I want a room with Jack, but I wouldn't like to give him a heart attack. We haven't gotten that far, but I wouldn't mind if he was within walking distance."

"Woman after my own heart," Alexis said, "but I may be able to do better than that." If she was surprised, she didn't show it. "I think what you need is privacy. He's a smart man, and he can find you. All right?"

At that point, Tara appeared carrying a pitcher of lemonade and two glasses on a tray and presented them to Jack. Melanie had a sense that Tara liked people but much preferred men, the taller the better.

"Mr. Henry makes good lemonade, and I helped him make the cookies," she said.

Jack took the tray and poured a glass of lemonade for Melanie and one for himself. "This really hits the spot, Tara. Thank you," he said. "If I had a little girl like you, I'd feel like a king."

Melanie couldn't believe it when Tara blushed with all the coyness of an adult female. "Thank you, Dr. Ferguson. Maybe if you ask my daddy, he can find one for you."

He walked right into that one, Melanie said to herself, but laughter poured out of Jack. "Thanks, but I know how it's done, sweetheart."

Alexis's face bloomed in a grin. "Tara thinks Telford hung the moon. I'm surprised she hasn't managed to get him nominated for president. Come with me, Melanie."

They walked down the hall to a large suite that consisted of a bedroom, sitting room and bathroom. "It's perfectly safe," she said after opening the curtains to disclose a garden surrounded by a fourteen-foot-high, metal, mini-wire fence topped with barbed wire. "If the barbed wire wouldn't work the electric sensors would certainly do it."

"This is a beautiful room," Melanie said as her gaze took in the elegant furnishings.

"I'm glad you like it. I'll put some candles on the mantelpiece in case you want to use them. I hope Tara didn't embarrass Jack," Alexis said.

"She may have pulled his chain a bit, but she certainly didn't embarrass him. He's enchanted with her." The thought of Jack asking a man how to make a baby brought a laugh from Melanie. "Imagine Jack asking a man how to do that! I enjoyed it immensely."

"Be careful, Melanie, unless you've decided you want him for keeps. Have you?"

Melanie sobered at once. This was girl-to-girl talk, and she wasn't used to it. Still, it was her nature to be honest and truthful. Besides, nobody had to tell her that Alexis Harrington knew what side was up when it came to male-female relations.

"I think he's wonderful, Alexis, but I don't fool myself. Jack Ferguson is out of my league. My background is nothing to brag about. Whatever I've accomplished, I've done it in spite of my background. Jack was born with a gold spoon in his mouth, and the whole world as his oyster."

Alexis stat down on the bed and crossed her knees. "Now, wait a minute here," she said. "If he had everything at birth and you had very little, who is the more to be admired for having achieved success? You're a credit to any man, and Jack Ferguson knows it. That's one reason why he's so proud to be with you, and let me tell you he is proud of you. That man stood beside you like a peacock in a yard full of peahens. He's crazy about you, and he doesn't care who knows it."

The muscles in Melanie's legs seemed to turn to rubber, and she stumbled to the chaise lounge and dropped herself onto it. "Alexis, I don't need that kind of encouragement. I'm in deep enough as it is."

"You love him." It wasn't a question. Melanie nodded. "Then you're blessed," Alexis said. "Go for it. To love a man who truly loves you and to share your intimate self with him is heaven on earth."

She hadn't expected to have such a personal conversation with another woman, and especially one she'd known for less than an hour, but she was a fledgling in the arena of love, and she needed all the insight she could get.

She leaned toward Alexis, propped her elbows on her thigh and supported her chin with the base of her hand. "Jack told me that when he was here before, he realized what he missed by not having a brother or a close male friend, and now I know what he meant. You're the first woman with whom I've ever had such a personal conversation. I've missed so much. Thank you for talking with me."

"I was lucky," Alexis said. "I have an older sister, and

she's married to Telford's brother Russ. You'll meet both of them. You've met Drake, my youngest brother-in-law. He figured out right away that you and Jack were in love."

"He did what?"

"Oh, don't be so surprised. Drake has an uncanny sense about people. He told us we'd like you."

"Well, I'll be darned. I never would have guessed that about him. Do you dress for dinner?"

"Let's say I try to look better than I've been looking all day," Alexis said and stood. "Your bag will be beside your door." A grin spread over her face. "Jack's upstairs, but I plan to give him a tour of the house."

Melanie got her bag and unpacked it, all the while musing over what Alexis had said. She had never met such a self-confident woman. Could she be right? Was Jack Ferguson really crazy about her? She made up her mind to give him an opportunity to clarify it one way or the other. Resolute, she unfolded her red string bikini and threw it on the bed. She'd never worn one of those things, but she hadn't previously gone away with a man for the weekend, either.

Telford knocked on Jack's door. "We'll congregate around the pool shortly for a swim prior to cocktails and hors d'oeuvres. So if you'd like to swim, I suppose you know to do that before cocktails. I remind everybody of that, including my brothers. When you're ready to come out, stop by and get Melanie."

"I'd be glad to, if I knew where she was." He heard

the testiness in his voice, but he didn't like not knowing where she was and suspecting that she was miles away from him.

"Not to worry, man," Telford said with what seemed to him like a muffled snicker, "Alexis is planning to give you a tour of the house. Tomorrow morning, we'll take you both around the Harrington estate. My brothers have built their homes on it not too far from here, but we're widely enough separated to ensure complete privacy and still be reasonably near each other."

"Sounds like a good plan. I'll look forward to it." Telford left, and Jack finished unpacking. Surely, a family as sophisticated as this one wouldn't deliberately separate him from Melanie to keep them out of bed together. He put on his bathing suit and the white terry-cloth robe that hung in the closet and strolled down the winding staircase.

"I was waiting for you," Alexis said. "I wanted to show you the house. I guess you've seen the four bedrooms and baths upstairs. The master bedroom also has a private sitting room that we use for the baby's room." She guided him through the living room that was decorated with matching blue silk fabric on the walls, at the windows and on all the chairs, except two leather, overstuffed ones. He liked the formal dining room that was already set for a formal dinner for ten, which he took to be the Harrington men and women, Melanie, himself, Henry and Tara. You've seen the breakfast room," Alexis said, "and this is the family room or den as we sometime call it." She smiled, a bit mischievously, he thought. Then she said, "You're getting nervous, but not to worry."

He followed her down a long hall. "There're several bathrooms on this floor, and that's one," she said, pointing to a closed door. She stopped, and knocked on another door.

"Yes?"

"It's Alexis with Jack. If you don't want company right now, we can come back later," Alexis said. "Jack's dying to know where you are, and we're all getting ready to go out to the pool for a swim. I have to go change. See you in half an hour?"

Alexis walked off and left him standing there in what he regarded as an invitation to do as he pleased. He knocked lightly. "Open up, Melanie, I want to see you for a minute."

The door opened at a snail's pace and she peeped up at him. "Hi."

He stared down at her, wrapped in a robe that matched his own, and laughed. "What on earth are you scared of? Can I come in or not? If you'd rather I didn't, I don't mind standing out here."

"Where's Alexis?"

"She went to put on her bathing suit."

"Oh. This is a really nice room. Want to see it?"

"Why did they put you so far from me?" Jack asked her. "We're grown, and we don't need anybody to oversee our morals."

She pulled the robe tighter and opened the door

wider. "I think you've got it wrong. Alexis gave me the choice of a room with you or one of my own. I told her not to put you too far from me, and I guess she decided to give me the privacy to do as I pleased. She can't be guarding your morals if she brought you here."

What was she telling him? At times, he didn't understand women one bit. "Okay. I was wrong, but, when I didn't know where you were and there was nobody to ask, I got hot under the collar."

He looked around the room, walked through it to the sitting room and then strode over to the window and looked out. Melanie raised both hands as if attempting to ward off an attack.

"Don't get upset. That fence has a sensor, and it's topped with barbed wire. Besides, only a pole vaulter could jump over it."

He pushed his fingers through his hair, punishing his scalp. "Oh, hell! Come here to me, baby."

For almost a minute, she stood there, as still as a statue, pulling the white terry robe tighter and tighter, as if warding off the cold in freezing temperatures. He spread his arms and reached out to her. She let the robe fly open as she sprang into his arms. She spread kisses on his jaw and cheek, and he thought he'd die of pure joy.

Holding her away from him, he gazed into her eyes; though he was attuned to her actions, he had to read her emotions. For once, she looked straight at him, deliberately opening to him the door to her feelings, exposing herself. Stunned, he pushed his hands inside her robe and immediately jerked them away when they caressed her naked flesh. Seeing that her gaze didn't waver, he gripped her to him and lowered his head. Her lips, soft and sweet, opened to him and, trembling from the awesome power of his passion, he plunged his tongue into her mouth.

He tried to hold off what he knew was coming, but his erection was swift and complete. When he attempted to move away from her, she held him with more strength than he would have thought she had.

"I'm sorry about that. It's the first time that ever sneaked up on me."

"You weren't the only one responsible," she said. "Ready to go? They probably won't swim long, because Alexis said they swim before they have cocktails."

"I know. Telford said the same." He knew that a frown covered his face. "Aren't you going to finish dressing?"

"I'm wearing the only bathing suit that I brought. In fact, it's the only one I have."

"But, you can't… I mean, there're men out there."

"Oh, Jack. Look at *you*. Do I want those women seeing you like that? I do not! Besides, nobody will pay the least attention to this bathing suit. This is what women wear when they're planning to swim or just relax near water."

He didn't want to appear grumpy, but he felt worse than grumpy, so he made an attempt at being funny. "I had my arms around you, and all I felt was flesh. That must be the skimpiest bathing suit ever made. Can I get a preview?"

"No, sir," she said, tightening the robe. "You'd censure me in a New York minute." Taking his hand, she smiled at him, heating the blood that rushed through his veins. "Let's go. They'll think we're making out."

"That's precisely what we should be doing," he said.

If I want to hang out with Jack, I'd better get used to this, Melanie said to herself after meeting Russ Harrington, his wife, Velma, and Pamela, Drake's wife. Russ appeared as self-possessed as a person could be, and she thought Velma and Pamela equally as self-confident and at ease as Alexis.

The entire Harrington clan had gathered for a swim and drinks and, from her observation of the dining room table earlier, she assumed that they would also eat dinner with them. She got a wonderful sense of belonging when Tara took her hand and said, "Miss Melanie, I have two uncles and two aunties. Are you and Dr. Ferguson going to get married so you can be my auntie and uncle?" Every adult present looked at her.

She grinned, hugged Tara and said, "I don't know the answer to that, Tara, but as soon as I do, I'll let you know."

"Maybe I'll ask Dr. Ferguson." Tara moved as if to go to Jack, but Melanie detained her.

"I wouldn't do that, Tara. He's shy." A roar of laughter filled the air, and because everyone around her was laughing, Tara laughed, too. Melanie blew out a long breath, glanced at Jack and read his unspoken threat: *I'll get you for that.*

Alexis dived into the pool, and Melanie knew she did it then in order to take the heat off her. Others followed Alexis, but Jack continued to lounge on a beach towel beside the pool, looking up at her, and she knew he wouldn't move until she removed the robe.

All right. She'd give him an eyeful. She didn't swim well, but she'd taken a few lessons at school and figured she could manage the breaststroke. Anyway, Jack and the Harrington men wouldn't let her drown. She stood, dropped the robe and, without glancing toward Jack, strolled to the pool and jumped in. His sharp whistle split the air, and the splash told her that he'd jumped in right behind her.

"I thought you couldn't swim," he said after nudging her to the edge of the pool.

"I took a class at school, but I never tried to swim on my own. I only learned the breaststroke."

He pinned her between himself and the cement wall. "You're practically naked. Suppose those little strings holding this thing up break?"

She braced her hands against his chest. "If that happens, you'll remove those skimpy swim trunks that don't hide a thing and give them to me."

"You're too fresh. Kiss me."

"Jack, there're a lot of people watching, and Tara's probably looking straight at us."

"I'm not moving till you kiss me."

She pressed her lips to his and quickly removed them. "You have to behave, Jack. If you don't, these people won't like me."

He appeared to think about that. "Okay. I'll swim along with you. If you get a cramp, scream."

"I don't know what's gotten into Jack," Melanie said later to Alexis as they stood together munching on tiny crab cakes and sipping white wine.

"I do," Alexis said. "Three other men here have their women with them, and he wants it clear that he has his woman with him."

"But I'm not his woman."

"Not yet, but give it a few more hours. That man means business, and from where I stand, you ought to mean business, too. He's a great guy."

Melanie looked at her hostess, a woman of whom she grew fonder with the passing hours. "Jack has finer qualities than you could guess. I've never known anyone like him and, in spite of my reservations about the differences between us, I've decided to stop being stupid. I…I need him." Her voice quivered as she realized how deeply she felt it.

Alexis's arms slid around her. "Let him know that, and you'll be a happy woman."

"Is anybody talking about me?"

Melanie turned around and found herself in Jack's arms. "You behave yourself."

He looked at Alexis and flashed his trademark grin. "Am I out of line, Alexis?"

"Not in my view, but when it comes to that, I don't think I count. You two come with me." She led them through the front door and around the side of the house to a flower garden in the center of which stood a white trellis that supported a swing.

"Telford and I used to sit there and make out," she said, pointing to the swing. "We'll have dinner in thirty-five minutes."

"You look so beautiful in that jumpsuit," Jack said. "What kind of material is that?"

She knew why he asked, but didn't allude to it. "It's silk jersey. I didn't want to be overdressed, so I figured this was somewhere in between."

"It's perfect, and you're stunning in red." He traced his fingers through her hair. "I like it down like this, but I know it's best to have it up when you're working." He put his arms around her. "Melanie, do you think you can stop pretending there's nothing between us and let's see if we have anything going for us? I mean the basis for a permanent relationship. You must have thought about it. I'm not seeing other women. Will you…I mean, can you agree not to see other men?"

She'd promised herself that she would give him a chance to tell her how he felt about her, so she snuggled closer to him. "All right. Does that mean I can tell you when I want a kiss?"

He held her away from him and gazed into her face. "Whenever you need a kiss or…if you need me, period, find a way to let me know it. That's all you have to do. Do you understand?"

She didn't answer, but moved back to him, stroked his cheek and nipped his chin with her teeth. Within a second, his tongue danced in her mouth, and his hands roamed over her body heating her almost to boiling point. She loved him so much that she wanted to scream it aloud, as he thrilled her with promises of a deeper and more satisfying loving.

The garden lights blinked, and Jack looked at his watch. "Alexis is precious, isn't she?" he said, referring to the reminder. "Five minutes before dinner." He flicked his index finger across her nose. "I hate the thought of four other men looking at you in this getup." He stood and extended his hand to her. "I'm actually hungry. Come."

"I'm properly dressed, Jack. Everything's hidden."

"It may be hidden, but it sure as hell is well-outlined." He took her hand and walked with her to the house, rang the doorbell and looked down at Tara when she opened the door. "My mommy said you were enjoying some privacy. What does that mean, Dr. Ferguson?"

A grin circled his lips and spread over his face. Anyone could see that he adored Tara as he lifted her into his arms. "It means we wanted to talk to each other. You promised to play the piano for me when I came back, so don't forget."

"I won't. I like to play."

He'll be a wonderful father, Melanie thought and heard herself telling him so.

He put Tara down, and his smile disappeared along with his light mood. "I'm longing for that day, Melanie."

What could she say? That she longed to give him a family? She squeezed his fingers and remained silent as they followed the little girl to the dining room. Russ said grace, Henry and Alexis served the food, sat down and she saw firsthand the wonder of having a large, loving family. It wouldn't do to cry, so she tried to focus on the good things that were happening to her.

"How is it that you said grace, and everyone expected you to do it?" she asked Russ. Her question drew a round of laughter.

"'Cause he doesn't want *me* to say it," Tara said. "Uncle Russ says my grace is too long."

"Right," Russ said. "If you don't like the way somebody does something, do it yourself."

And so it went, a full hour of camaraderie and love. "I missed a lot growing up without siblings and a real family," Melanie said to Jack later.

"So did I, Melanie, and being here with these folks brings it home to me forcibly. You think that we have vastly different backgrounds, because I grew up in wealth and you had a life of poverty, but in other important respects we had a lot in common. I wasn't physically abused, but I was ignored most of the time. We both lacked a warm and loving family life. My mother loved me, and after she died, I was alone. Did you bring a wrap of some kind? Let's join the Harringtons for coffee and cognac or something and then take a walk."

"I'll settle for coffee and port. Cognac's too strong for me."

"It seems like a nice evening," Jack told Telford as the two of them stood together sipping after-dinner drinks. "I presume it's safe for Melanie and me to walk outside?"

"Safe from humans. You could encounter a snake or

a deer, so stay on the road. The moon's high, and you can see far into the distance." He walked to the foyer, got a key and gave it to Jack. "Tomorrow's Saturday, so we eat breakfast around eight. If you need anything, Melanie, just let Alexis know. Have a pleasant walk. Good night."

He waited while Melanie went for a shawl. As he watched the movement of her hips, free and easy, he made up his mind that it was time they made love. And he didn't believe she'd worn that sexy jumpsuit to entice the Harringtons. When she returned, he took the stole from her, wrapped it around her shoulders and left the house. "I'm so glad you suggested we walk out here," she said. "It's idyllic, a fairyland. Imagine living here all the time!"

He wanted to tell her that he could give her that and more, but he didn't think it was time. "You wouldn't be lonely out here in the country?"

"If I were with the right person, I could live anywhere. Living out here wouldn't tax me one bit."

"It's a far cry from Southwest Baltimore." A raccoon and three small ones crossed in front of them, taking their time, as if they owned the road.

He stopped, pulled her close to him and realized that her breathing had quickened. His libido responded to it, and he locked her in his arms. "Open up to me, Melanie," he whispered, surprised at the urgency with which he uttered the words.

When her lips parted, he swallowed her breath and

went into her, crushing her to his body. Groans poured out of him and, stunned by his fierce longing for her, he attempted to break the kiss and lower the tension. But she held on to him.

"I need it," she moaned. "I need you. Don't you know I need you?" Frissons of heat plowed through him and his blood ran hot through his veins. He told himself to be careful, to move slowly and to take it easy. But he didn't want that, he wanted her. He had long since tired of fighting the sheets on his bed every night, of longing for her, needing her while she refused to admit that they belonged together.

"You're telling me you need me?" he asked, because he had to be sure she knew what that meant. She nodded.

"I... You know I'll always be there for you? Always."

She seemed impatient. "I know that, Jack. You've shown me in so many ways."

"I want you to need me in every way a woman can need a man. Do you understand?"

"Yes. I do," she whispered.

He wanted to pick her up and run with her. If only they were at his own house. With his arms around her, he headed back to the house. Drake and Russ had taken their wives and gone home, but the others would still be up. Well, he'd have to work around it. He saw the note when he opened the door. "Wine, champagne and glasses are in the bar in the family room; crackers, cheese and grapes in Melanie's suite, just in case you get hungry. Love, Alexis."

So Alexis had it all figured out, did she? Well, he was

definitely not going to disappoint her. He handed the note to Melanie. "I have to go up to my room. Either wait here, or I'll see you later. Would you rather have champagne or wine?"

She looked at him, and he could almost see her mind working. "Let's celebrate."

"What'll we celebrate?" he asked, testing her.

"Being together." She reached up and kissed his mouth. "I thought you were going to your room."

"Yes, ma'am." He couldn't get up the stairs fast enough. She'd all but told him that she had plans for them, and his whole body began to throb in anticipation.

"He knows where to find me," Melanie said to herself and headed for her room. She brushed her teeth and rinsed her mouth, freshened up and dabbed in strategic places a few drops of the perfume he'd given her for graduation. She used it sparingly, and she knew she'd have that bottle, though empty of the precious fragrance, for as long as she lived. She flipped on the radio to an easy-listening music station seconds before she heard his soft knock. She rushed to open the door.

"This place is so quiet you could hear a mouse," he said and placed the champagne in its iced bucket on the table beside the snacks. "Alexis thinks of everything," he said and frowned. "What's that song?"

"Something by Gershwin. Oh, I think it's 'Love Walked In.'"

A grin flashed across his face, and his eyes sparkled, making her weak in the knees. "Is that what I did?"

"I haven't had two glasses of champagne in my entire life," she said, ignoring his question. "This will probably make me giddy."

"It'll make you warm and cuddly, and that's the way I like you." He handed her a glass of champagne, poured one for himself and clicked her glass. "Here's to us."

"And here's to the wonderful man who changed my life." She sipped the bubbly wine.

He put his glass on the table and looked at her with eyes that seemed to grow darker with the passing seconds, eyes as turbulent as a storm. "Do you think I'm wonderful?"

The moment had come, and she had to let him understand that she knew it. She rested her glass beside his and looked him in the eye. "I know you are. At least to me."

He was in her room, and he'd be a gentleman to the end, so knowing she had to make the first move, she stepped closer with her arms open. He went into her arms, wrapped her so close that air couldn't get between them, and she parted her lips for his kiss. His body trembled when he plowed into her, lifting her from the floor. One of his hands gripped her buttocks and the other held the back of her head as his tongue darted here and there in her mouth, testing, sampling until she captured it and sucked on it until his groans filled the air.

Her hot blood rushed to her loins and, out of her mind with need of him, she put his right hand on her left breast and rubbed frantically. He needed no further encouragement, but freed her breast, lifted it and took it into his mouth.

"Oh, Jack," she moaned. "Jack, I can't stand this."

"Do you want me?"

"Yes. Yes. I've wanted you for months."

He locked the door, unzipped her jumpsuit and let it fall to the floor. "Oh, Melanie, you're beautiful." He ran his hands over her body, nude but for a tiny bra and a G-string, threw back the covers, picked her up and laid her on her bed.

"Are you going to regret this?" he asked, the words tumbling out of his mouth as if he didn't want to say them.

"Never!"

She watched him strip at breakneck speed and place one knee on the bed. "Do you trust me?" he asked her in a voice so soft that she strained to hear it, and it moved her that he could be so overcome with emotion.

She opened her arms. "More than anyone else I know or have ever known."

He stumbled onto the bed and nearly fell into her arms. "Sweetheart, love me. I need you to love me."

"I do. I always have."

He kissed her lips and began a scorching assault on her body, kissing her eyes, her ears, neck and shoulders before returning to her breast. He kissed her until she thought she'd go mad waiting to feel him inside her, and when her body urged him to join them, he ignored her and continued his onslaught until she nearly sprang from the bed in anticipation of his goal. He reached the ultimate prize and tormented her with the kisses of an expert until she grabbed the pillow and covered her mouth to muffle her screams.

He made his way up her body. "Take me in, love."

At last she had him inside her. He was hers for those few minutes, if never again. Suddenly, he unleashed his power, and she couldn't think. Stars raced above her, lightning cracked, wind seemed to howl and the sun burst into flames. He was in her, over her, under her and all around her until at last she exploded in ecstasy and flew with him to the sun.

"I love you. I love you so much," she said, flung her arms wide and gave herself to him.

"You're mine now. You hear me? Mine," he moaned and splintered in her arms. A few minutes later, he raised his head, looked down into her face, smiled and said, "I love you, Melanie. I think I fell in love with you when you walked into my Bolton Hill office, and every day since, I've loved you more. Promise me you won't put any more obstacles between us, and that you'll accept the fact that we belong to each other. Promise me."

"I promise," she said, but somehow, she doubted her own words.

Chapter 11

That Monday morning after an exhilarating weekend in Eagle Park, Jack awakened at six-thirty with the world on a string. He could still smell her woman's scent and feel her soft skin beneath the tips of his fingers. Whew! He headed for the shower. Life was good. He wanted to call Melanie just to say good morning, but it didn't make sense; she was probably still asleep.

He had to give a lecture in the operating theater that morning, a task that he always enjoyed, and that morning, he especially delighted in it. "You were really on this morning," a woman doctor said to him after his talk. "You think I could make your eyes sparkle the way they lit up when you talked about cholesterol-free arteries?"

He always became annoyed when his female colleagues made passes at him, but her remark sailed right over his head. He envisioned Melanie in the grip of passion, undulating beneath his body, and couldn't control the grin that spread over his face.

"Sorry," he said, "but if my eyes are sparkling, it's because of someone special." And how good it was to be able to say that!

In spite of the frustrating Monday-morning traffic, he got to his Bolton Hill office on time. "Good morning, sir," his nineteen-year-old, self-conscious receptionist said as she twirled the ends of her long hair extensions. "You have two calls—one from a Dr. Marsh in Memphis and one from your father."

"Thanks. Would you ring my father first, please?

"Hi, Dad. You called me?"

"Yes, I did. I had some raspberry scones at Brewster's the other day, and they were awful compared to the ones your patient's mother made, plus they cost me three dollars apiece. They claim to serve the best pastries in town, but those scones weren't worth fifty cents. I think I'm going to set that woman up in business. She'll be able to make a living, I'll get some decent scones and we can both make some money. I assume she can bake something other than scones."

Knowing his father's passion for money, Jack asked, "What kind of deal are you going to offer her?"

"If we find a nice spot, I can furnish a bakery/coffee shop for about twenty thousand. If it doesn't serve coffee, around fifteen thousand. I put in the money, she donates the labor and we split the profits sixty for her and forty for me."

"Seventy-thirty would be more equable."

"Well, I could make it sixty-five for her. You think she'd take it?"

"Considering her situation, she'd be crazy not to."

"Where can I reach her?" Montague asked. "Is she back from Memphis?"

"Not unless she came back this weekend. Let me check and get back to you. If this works out, she'll be one happy woman. By the way, where would you put the bakery?"

"Why, next door to the clinic, of course. That way, we'd have a built-in clientele."

Jack laughed aloud. It made sense, and he didn't have to start thinking of his dad as a humanitarian. That would be too much of a stretch. "Remember that's a poor area. If people have two dollars, they'll spend it on chicken and rice."

"Don't worry. I'll market it all over the city."

"Great idea."

He phoned Dr. Marsh and said, "This is Jack Ferguson. Glad to hear from you."

"I want you to know that your patient, Midge Hawkins, is being discharged tomorrow. I've given her mother a set of instructions, but I am e-mailing them to you along with her prescriptions, which you may copy. If you have any questions or problems, please call me. I'm sending her to you with a two-month supply of medicine which I've put in a package addressed to you. I think she'll do well if she follows the regimen I've prescribed."

"Thank you, Doctor. I'll keep you up to date on her progress. If you don't mind, I'll have their plane tickets sent to you electronically."

"Not at all. We'll see them safely to the airport. Call me whenever you need me."

Jack hung up, greatly relieved that Midge had a chance to grow into adulthood. He had a patient due at that minute, but that would have to wait. He needed to call Melanie and tell her about Midge.

"That's the best news you could give me," Melanie said after learning of Midge's progress. "I'll phone her neighbors and tell her when Alice Hawkins will be home so she can get the children ready to go back to their mother."

"I hadn't thought of that. I'll send someone to meet them at the airport and bring them home." He told her about his father's plan for a business venture with Alice. "I think her ship's about to come in. Dad doesn't throw money around, so I suspect he's already done some research and had his scouts busy."

"Jack, you're a blessing to a lot of people."

"Really? What about you? You haven't kissed me, and you haven't told me you love me, and we've been talking at least ten minutes." Her laughter soothed him like a cool breeze on a hot summer evening.

She made the sound of a kiss. "As for the rest, you shouldn't have any doubts."

"I don't, but I need to hear it. Melanie, I'm in love with you. I'm in deep, baby."

"I love you, Jack. This past weekend…will stay with me forever."

"Me, too, sweetheart. We'll talk later."

Melanie hung up and tried to settle down to work on the mundane things that keep a doctor's office in good working order, but she couldn't concentrate. All that made life worthwhile, she'd found in Jack Ferguson's arms the previous weekend in Eagle Park, Maryland. All the times she'd dreamed of him and imagined what it would be like to lie in his arms with him buried deep within her had come nowhere near approximating the pleasure he gave her and the pure joy of giving herself to him.

"I'll love him as long as I live, and then some," she said aloud and tried to focus on her work.

She phoned Alice Hawkins's neighbor and made arrangements for Alice's two younger children to return home the day after she arrived with Midge from Memphis. Then, knowing that the Hawkins kitchen would be bare, she ordered milk, bread, potatoes, rice, olive oil, vegetables and a chicken and stored them in the office refrigerator.

For the third time that day, the telephone rang and when she answered, the caller hung up. She locked the door, but the possibility that the caller could be her father preyed on her mind. She decided not to mention it to Jack.

"Now what?" She answered the door and accepted the mail and a package from the mailman. Seeing that the package came from a supplier, she put it aside, thumbed through the mail, found a letter addressed to her from ET and sat down to read it.

Dear Ms. Sparks,
I wanted you to know that I have a new friend.
She's just like you. Real nice, and I like her a lot.
Her name is Michaela Landry, and I'm going to
live with her. I don't know for how long, but for
a few weeks will be a lot better than that foster
home. This is my address in case you want to
write me again. I missed you a lot after you left.
ET

Melanie read the note several times, folded it and put
it into her pocket. She would answer him and send him
a book. She'd learned a lot in the one month she spent
at St. Jude Children's Research Hospital, but she cher-
ished most having been exposed to people who regarded
helping others as a privilege and a blessing. She placed
the week's orders for supplies, updated her log, wrote
a note of thanks to Alexis Harrington and had decided
to heat a can of soup for lunch when she heard Jack's
key turn the lock in the office door. She raced to the
door. He kicked it shut, lifted her into his arms and
settled his mouth on hers.

"I couldn't wait to get here for that," he said. "Don't
ask me how I plan to discipline myself and treat this
place as an office, because I have no idea. I'm going to
try, though, so you won't be lecturing to me all the time.
I don't respond well to lectures, and especially not if
they reach the nagging stage, so I'm going to try to
keep it between the lines."

"All that, and I haven't said a word. I wanted that

kiss as much as you did, and I would have been disappointed if I hadn't gotten it," she said, reached up and kissed his bottom lip. "Still, we do have to be circumspect, don't we?"

He rubbed her nose. "You're precious. I was in no mood to eat pizza, so I brought us some lunch." He cleared the top of his desk, made a tablecloth out of paper towels and spread out their lunch of lobster salad, whole-wheat rolls, cheesecake and grapes. "I'll make us some coffee."

"This is wonderful, Jack. It's like dining in a gourmet restaurant."

"Do you think I'd bring my sweetheart anything less than the very best? You wound me."

She observed him carefully, because she wanted to know whether he was joking. He wasn't. So she said, "You've always given me the best, Jack. I don't ask for or demand the best, only what I need, but you always go that extra step for me. Don't think I haven't noticed or that I don't appreciate it. I have, and I do."

He looked at her with as sober an expression as she'd ever seen on him. "I will always do the best for you that is within my means, and I want you to remember that."

She stopped eating and looked directly at him. "The likelihood of my forgetting anything about you is practically nil, and I want *you* to remember *that*." Suddenly, she threw her arms wide. "Do I look the same to you? I'm not the same. I don't feel the same, and I'll never be the same."

He stared at her, his eyes ablaze with passion and his

nostrils flaring. She could almost taste his breath. "No, you're not the same. Beginning last Friday night, you're my woman and you love me. I'm your man, and I love you. Most important of all, we know each other, we suit each other and we know we belong together. I know I'm not the same, and I wouldn't take a million dollars for what changed me. I don't want to be the same."

Her heart seemed to swell with the happiness she felt, but she had to get them off that topic before they found themselves on the floor making love. "I put some groceries for Alice Hawkins in our refrigerator. When she gets here tomorrow, I'll take them over to her."

"They'll be home a little after two," he said, "and I'm anxious to see how Midge looks. I'm sure she'll have a lot to tell us."

"Maybe it would be a good idea for you to examine her before she goes home."

"We'll see. I'm considering going to a meeting in New Orleans. We'll be discussing the health needs of inner-city adolescents. Would you come with me?"

She thought for a few minutes. How easy it would be to settle into an affair with him, and the likelihood of that would increase if they went to New Orleans or anywhere else together. When he'd had her beneath him, he'd rocked her out of her mind, and all she could think of was that she wanted more and more and more.

"One of us should stay here and look after the office," she said. "You'll tell me about it when you get back."

He remained silent for a few minutes, and she wouldn't say that his eyes seemed sad, but his demeanor suggested disappointment. "You really don't want to go? New Orleans is still beautiful."

"I know, but I-I'd rather not this time." She rested a hand on his left wrist. "It doesn't mean I care less, only that I think it best I don't go. Can you understand that?"

He nodded. "I suppose I do, and you may be right. In my euphoria, I want to be with you every second, and although I want to go to that conference, I hate the thought of being away from you for an entire week."

Hoping to lighten his mood, she said, "Just think how glad to see you I'll be when you get back."

"That's damned little compensation." He discarded the remains of their lunch, kissed her cheek and went to the bathroom.

My cue to put on my uniform and get ready for work, she said to herself as she left Jack's private office. *He can't have everything he wants the way he wants it, and neither can I, but he just showed me that he hurts easily, so I'd better be careful.*

Half an hour later, the door buzzer rang, and Terry Jordan, the young boy she'd met sitting on an adjacent stoop when she arrived to work that first day, walked into the office.

"Hi, Ms. Sparks. I just wanted you to know that I'm entering the University of Maryland next week on a full scholarship. I'm gonna be a doctor."

"Congratulations, Terry. I'm so happy for you. You'll be a fine doctor." She knocked on Jack's door, told him that Terry wanted to see him and went into the waiting room that was already filling up with patients. She hadn't worked so hard since her first night there.

Around seven o'clock, with the office still crowded with patients, she started into the waiting room and stopped short when she saw Ralph Sparks walk in. "Hi, Daddy. Are you all right? Do you need to see the doctor?"

"I need to see him, all right, miss, and you, too." The smell of beer reeked from six feet away, and she knew her father meant to make a scene. But if he thought she'd cower before him as she'd done all those years, he was in for a surprise.

"If you're not sick, Daddy, I suggest you call the doctor if you want to talk with him. He has seventeen patients who are sick, and he doesn't have time for a social visit right now."

"I see you're full of sass. If you give me any mouth, you'll swallow your teeth. You're throwing yourself at this so-called doctor like some street woman just because he's rich." The room suddenly buzzed with the sound of voices. "You're a disgrace."

She couldn't believe what she was hearing. He'd come here deliberately to embarrass her, and to ruin her relationship with Jack. Anger boiled up in her. "I'd like you to leave this second. If you don't, I'll call the police."

He took a step toward her, but she didn't move. "You'd call the police on your father, would you? When your belly is full, don't come running back to me." She saw a woman who sat near the water cooler leave the room and figured she'd gone to the women's room, but seconds later, Jack appeared followed by the woman.

"What's going on here?" Jack asked.

"Oh, so you're the doctor with so much money he can buy this daughter of mine. You enticed her out of my house so you could use her, and—"

"Shut up! How dare you impugn this woman's character. She's a respectable woman, in spite of you."

"Don't get uppity with me. She's living with you like a shameless tramp. I'll—"

"You're a liar. She has never set foot in my house. And you'll do nothing, because you are a coward. A man who would treat his own daughter as you have and as you're doing now isn't worth the salt that goes into his food."

When Ralph Sparks headed toward Jack, three of the male patients jumped up as if on cue and placed themselves between Ralph and Jack. "Do you want us to get rid of him, Doc?" one of them asked.

"I want him to tell me who sent him here and why," Jack said. "Otherwise he's going to jail for harassment and disturbing the peace."

An eerie sensation weakened Melanie, and she stared at her father, anticipating his answer because he had the look of a man who held all the cards. She had covered her tracks. She had an unlisted phone number at home, her cell phone belonged to Jack's office, she had never mentioned Jack's name or his office address to her father, and he didn't know where she lived.

"I don't know what you want with this trifling woman," Ralph said, slightly subdued.

"Listen here. If you want to curse at somebody, try me. I'm your size, and I'd love to give you what you

deserve. Neither you nor any other man is going to stand
in my presence and berate Melanie Sparks. If you do it
again, I'll be merciless with you. Who sent you here?"

"I ain't going to no jail. Your old man don't want you
with this…this woman, and he told me to see that she
leaves you alone," he said, backing out toward the door.

"I don't believe a word you say," Jack said and
looked at the three men. "Please show him the door, but
don't hurt him." He looked at the patients who had witnessed the ugly encounter. "Not a word he said is true.
I apologize for the disturbance."

"We know his type," a woman said. "He ought to be
proud of his daughter. But she got out of his clutches,
and he'll never forgive her for it. If she was my child,
I'd be on my knees thanking God."

Melanie struggled to hold her head high, smile as usual
and do her work. When the last patients walked out of the
office, she collapsed in her desk chair. Oh, they had seemed
sympathetic, but the situation had embarrassed her.

"Please don't be sad, Ms. Sparks," one older man
said to her. "He doesn't deserve to have a daughter like
you. We know he wasn't telling the truth."

She'd thanked the man and added, "But it hurts that
he would try to ruin my reputation. I've been a good
daughter to him."

"Don't worry," a woman said, "we don't believe him.
We see how you are here with us, and that's what we
care about. Dr. Ferguson should've let Miles knock the
stuffing out of him."

She appreciated their efforts, but she wasn't placated, and she sat slumped in the chair, all but oblivious to the silent emptiness around her, making up her mind. The touch of Jack's hand on her shoulder brought her upright.

"I'd give anything if this hadn't happened, Melanie. Even overworked, in life-threatening situations, tragedies and near-tragedies, I've never see you dispirited as you are now. Sweetheart, please don't let it get you down. I can't bear to see you like this."

She patted the hand that rested on her shoulder almost absentmindedly. "I'm leaving, Jack. My father has made it impossible for me to work here after his awful accusations. These people won't respect me."

"What do you mean, you're leaving? Leaving where?"

She stiffened her back for she could see his objections coming and knew that she would need all of the willpower that she could summon if she were to stand her ground. "I can't work here any longer, Jack. I'm sorry, but I...I can't. I've never been so mortified. He's found me, and this is just the beginning."

He walked around to face her, his mouth agape as he stared into her eyes. "You...you're mortified because someone will think you live with me, that you sleep in my bed?" His words had a strangely staccato cadence, and his voice had sunk to a lower register, almost menacing. "Is that it?"

"Oh, Jack. How could you think that? If my father doesn't respect me, why would anyone else? And why shouldn't some of those patients believe him? I can't stay here."

"Our relationship means nothing to you?" he asked her.

"Are you saying that what we mean to each other is valid only as long as I work here? If that's true, it won't kill me. I'll send you my resignation tomorrow. I'm sorry."

His face contorted, whether in furor or sadness, she couldn't figure out which, but no matter; she was not going to let his feelings derail her. "Don't tell me you're sorry. I don't want to hear it. You signed a five-year contract, and if you quit before it expires, I'll sue you for breach of contract, and I will be merciless. Woman, you changed my life. You opened up a whole new world to me. You made me need you. Damn you!" She heard the tremors in his voice, but steeled herself against his obvious pain. "You can lock up or not. I don't care," he said, striding out and leaving her sitting there.

She'd walked home many nights, and she wasn't afraid to do it on that night. She changed into her street clothes, locked the door and headed home. She didn't feel like walking thirteen long blocks, but she'd do it.

She had almost forgotten how the youth hung out on the corners and how the automobiles rarely bothered to stop for red lights and stop signs.

"Hey, miss. You dropped something." She didn't pause for fear that the boy was up to some devilment. He caught up with her and handed her a folding umbrella. "I think you dropped that." Recognition bloomed on his face. "Ms. Sparks!"

She took the umbrella and scrutinized him. "You don't remember me," he said, "but I'm one of the guys who makes sure nobody parks in Dr. Ferguson's spot. You got any idea when Midge is coming back home?"

"She's supposed to come back tomorrow. I heard that she's doing nicely."

"Gee, that's great. She was real sick. Want me to walk you to the avenue? It's kinda late."

She'd be the last one to discourage gentlemanly behavior in a sixteen-year-old boy. "Thanks. This is so kind of you."

"Call me Takk. You know, the whole neighborhood changed after Dr. Ferguson opened his office. It's like we're a different community. Everybody treats everybody nicer. He's a real cool guy. I'm thinking of studying to be a doctor. My dad says I'm crazy, but my mom says I'm not."

"Go with your mom," she said as they reached the avenue. "And thank you for walking with me."

"Anytime. You look after us—we look after you," he said and headed back to his friends.

His words and sentiment stayed with her, and as she prepared for bed, she couldn't shake the feeling that he would be disappointed in her if he knew she'd quit the job.

As soon as he could get away from his Bolton Hill office, Jack headed for his office in South Baltimore. The past fifteen hours had been the roughest since his mother had died. Once he'd stopped resisting, he'd opened himself completely and wholeheartedly to Melanie, and he loved her to the recesses of his soul. The mere contemplation of a life without her caused him heart palpitations. He had committed himself to the needy in the Morrell and Cherry Hill communities and others like them, but with her sweet, caring and loving ways, she had lightened the burden of his long hours. Some would say they hadn't stood a chance, but he had more in common with her than with any woman he'd known. Two girls ran out to remove the orange cones in front of his office building, and he eased the car to the curb.

"You spoil me," he told them, "but I appreciate it. Thanks for helping me out."

"Everybody loves you, Dr .Ferguson," the younger one, who he guessed to be about eight, said. He put a smile on his face, patted the girl's shoulder and went inside.

"What on earth? I thought you quit," he said when he saw Melanie sitting at her desk.

"And I did. But I remembered that Midge and her mother are coming home today and that I had stored some food for them in the refrigerator. When can I expect that court summons?"

He ignored her question. "I sent someone to meet them, and they're coming here directly, so I can examine Midge and make certain she's all right after that plane trip. It's good you're here. I don't know what shape she'll be in." He hated talking to her as if she were a stranger, when what he wanted, what he needed was to put his arms around her and love away her hurt and pain. And he needed to know that she was his and that she wouldn't allow her father's stupidity to come between them.

He went to the closet, exchanged his jacket for his white coat, walked back to her desk to ask her to fold back his sleeves an inch, as she usually did, and stopped when his gaze caught hers. The naked passion in her eyes nearly clobbered him. He started to her, and the door buzzer sounded.

"Damn," he said aloud. In another second, she would have been in his arms. He opened the door.

"Midge! My goodness. You look wonderful. Come on in. How do you feel?" Melanie rushed to the door and, standing there beside her, he knew he couldn't let her leave him.

Melanie leaned down and hugged the girl, then wrapped her arms around Alice Hawkins, Midge's mother. "It's so good to see Midge looking so healthy," she said, took the girl's hand and walked with her to the examining room.

"My father is going to call you," Jack said to Alice. "He's got some kind of deal in mind."

"Really? I hope it's a job. I made a little money in Memphis appearing on that TV show, but it was just enough to pay next month's rent and get the children ready for school."

"It's a job, and don't let him stiff you. He's got the money, and he does his best to keep it."

"Who can blame him? If I ever get any, that's what I'll do. If he's half as nice as you, I'll be glad to hear from him."

Jack read the St. Jude doctor's report and examined Midge. "You're to rest for the remainder of the day and follow the instructions the doctor gave you. I'll continue

your treatment precisely as he ordered. You look wonderful, and we want to keep you in good shape."

"Yes, sir. Thank you, Dr. Ferguson. Mama said I
wouldn't have had this chance if it hadn't been for you."

"Don't thank me, Midge. Do something good for
someone else. That's all the thanks I need."

Melanie brought the two shopping bags of food. "I'll
walk home with you," she said to Alice. "Your other
children will be home tomorrow morning."

"I can't thank the two of you enough," Alice said.
"When I think what you all have done for me, and my own
family pretends I don't exist… Well, it makes me humble
and grateful. See you in two weeks, Dr. Ferguson."

He hung the white coat in the closet, put on his jacket
and left. As he was about to get into his car, he looked
across at the building that seemed to be rising out of the
earth like a well-fertilized, growing plant. Soon, they
would begin the roofing. He walked over to speak with
Drake Harrington.

"He just left, Dr. Ferguson," a man told Jack, "but
he'll be back around four. Can I give him a message?"

"No, thanks. I can't believe how fast this building
is going up."

"We'll top if off next week."

If only Melanie had been there to rejoice with him.
She'd left, and only nodded in his direction. Not a word
of goodbye, because she didn't want anyone to think her
father had told the truth about her, and he knew that
before twilight, Alice would know about that encounter.

He stopped at a convenience store, bought a bag of

peanuts and drove to Druid Hill Park. He needed to think, and he'd always done that best when completely alone with no voice or music to disturb him. He threw nuts to a couple of squirrels, and soon several of them frolicked around his feet. He tossed the empty bag into a refuse bin and went home, unsure what to do with himself.

"What would you do?" he asked Vernie at supper, "if you loved someone who walked out of the relationship for reasons that had nothing to do with you personally?"

Her eyebrows shot up, and she stopped chewing her food. "I'd go to her and shake the living bejeebers out of her. If you didn't do anything bad, don't stand for it. Besides, she's waiting for you to straighten out the mess she's made. Believe me." That didn't sound much like Melanie, but what could he lose? He showered, dressed and headed for Melanie's apartment. If she wasn't at home, so be it. He rang her doorbell and tried to breathe when he heard her slip the chain.

"Jack! What're you…"

"May I come in?" He was half into the apartment as the words left his lips. When he heard the door close and lock, he swung around to face her. There was no point in preambles.

"Do you love me? Did you ever love me?"

She didn't look at him. "You know the answer to that. I hardly remember my mother, so you're the only human being that I have ever loved. How could you doubt my feelings for you?" She turned away from him, and by the time he reached her, tears cascaded down her face. "Oh, Jack. I hurt. I hurt."

"I don't want you to hurt, or be unhappy, sweetheart. We love each other, and we belong together." He put his arms around her, and it seemed as if she dived into him. "Kiss me. Love me," he said, shocked at the urgency in his voice.

She parted her lips and he went into her, unashamed of his trembling body. She sucked his tongue into her mouth and loved him as if she'd never get another chance. He picked her up, carried her to her bed, peeled every scrap of clothing from her body, stripped himself and joined her.

"I don't need finesse, Jack. I need you," she said, swaying beneath him as an ocean wave undulates beneath a rising moon. He took her with a powerful thrust and thought he'd lose his mind as she rocked him senseless. In the end, he gave himself to her as he'd never done with her or with any woman, and collapsed in her arms.

When he could summon sufficient energy, he smiled down at her. "Don't think I'm going to give you up. It won't happen. Did you ever tell your father my name and where my office is located?"

"No, I haven't, and after he left your office last night, I went over it carefully in my mind. The night I'd planned to tell him was the night he bumped into me and I fell down. So, I never told him. He doesn't know where I live, and my phone number is unlisted. I didn't even give that information to the school, so I don't know how he found us."

"I do." He separated them and sat up on the side of the bed. "Will you be hurt if I leave now? My father has some explaining to do."

"He said your father put him up to it, Jack, but I'm not completely sold on that idea."

"I am. My father probably hired a private eye to delve into your background. The rest is easy to figure out."

After washing up in her bathroom and dressing, he sat beside her on her bed. "If you break your contract with me, I won't sue you, because I would never do anything to hurt you. But I want you to know I've only once been as miserable as I was last night, and that is the day my mother died. I'm happy when I'm with you. When we're together, working or just being with each other, life is more than I ever dreamed possible. Melanie, please don't throw this away."

Her fingers stroked the side of his face, drawing him to her as a magnet draws iron. He kissed her lips. "I'm leaving you because I intend to see my father before I sleep."

"Jack, please don't argue with him. I don't want to cause a rift between the two of you."

"He knows me, so he's expecting me. Will you come to work tomorrow?"

"All right. I'll be there."

He hugged and kissed her until he was tempted to stay. "I'd better get out of here. Be sure and lock the door."

"I knew it was you when the bell rang," Montague said to Jack. "Everybody else knows that nine forty-five is too late to visit."

Jack cut to the chase. "Why did you send Ralph Sparks to my office to embarrass me in the presence of my patients?"

"Embarrass *you?*"

"Yes, *me.* He made a scene. Do you dislike Melanie so much that you'd hurt your only son's reputation?" He could see from his father's demeanor that the man hadn't thought of the effect on Jack. "Three of the male patients wanted to do a number on him, but I wouldn't let them hurt him. Why did you sink to that?"

"A man in your position should have a woman who's his equal in status and achievement. It's the woman who determines the family's social status, and who—"

"Dad, I don't give a damn about social status. I'm sick of women who do nothing but marry a rich man. Love doesn't occur to these women. It's sex in exchange for diamonds, a big house, expensive car and other trappings.

"I want a companion, a help-mate, a woman who shares my dreams, goals and values, a mother for my children who'll teach them what's important in life, and I won't settle for anything less. I love Melanie. Deeply. And I am proud that she loves me. Unless she figured it out from seeing my Porsche, she doesn't even know that I'm rich, and she doesn't care.

"Dad, please stop parading those empty-headed clotheshorses past me. They have about as much sex appeal as a paper bag. Do you really want your grandchildren to have one of those women for a mother? Can you imagine one of them as a mother?"

"Do you intend to marry your nurse?"

"Would I be the first doctor who did it? So far, she's given me no indication that she'll have me, and you are not helping one bit."

"I suppose you're displeased with me, and I guess I deserve it, but I meant well. It's funny how history repeats itself. Until you told me just now how you feel about Melanie—and if I'm honest, I already sensed it—I had let myself forget how I battled my own father forty years ago about my choice of a wife and the medical specialty I chose. Right now, I see myself in my father.

"I've done my best for you Jack, and you've exceeded my greatest hopes. You're a fine man, and I'm proud of you. I'm here to help you in any way that I can."

"I know that, Dad. Open your heart to Melanie. She's a warm, caring and loving woman. By the way, Alice Hawkins and her daughter, Midge, returned from St. Jude Children's Research Hospital today. Midge looks like a different girl, and I told her mother to expect a call from you." He gave his father the phone number.

"You didn't mention a seventy-thirty deal, did you?"

"No, I didn't, but you know the standard for silent partners."

"All right now. I'll see you at lunch tomorrow. Give my regards to Melanie."

He looked at his father, the first time he'd ever seen him give in gracefully, hugged him and said, "Thank you. I will. If I'm lucky, you'll find out what it's like to have a wonderful daughter."

Chapter 12

As Jack embraced his father, he fought to contain his emotions. Knowing that his dad no longer held a grudge against Melanie made him feel as if a weight had been lifted. Melanie loved him, and his father at last respected his choice. Life was good. That night, he slept peacefully, and arose early the next morning feeling young and alive.

Later, in his Bolton Hill office, he thumbed through the mail, made a note to send two hundred dollars to each charity and was about to push the remainder aside when he saw a return address that caught his attention. He opened and read a letter from the chairman of the International Conference on Cardiovascular Disease in Children inviting him to lecture on a topic dear to him. He could hardly believe his good fortune, for an invitation to lecture to that august group of specialists from around the world confirmed that he had reached the pinnacle of his profession. He had worked hard, but he hadn't dreamed that he'd attained that level of respect. He phoned his father.

"I can't believe it, Dad. These guys are a generation ahead of me. I would expect to get an invitation like this when I turn seventy."

'You've earned it, son. I wish I could be there to hear you. I'm so proud of you, and I know your mother is smiling right now."

"You're going to accept it, aren't you?" Melanie said when he told her about it that afternoon in his South Baltimore office.

"You bet I am. The conference is in Paris, and it's been at least five years since I was there," he said, smiling down at her, the one woman whose mere touch could make his heart flutter and his arms feel like wings capable of flight.

"I've never been to Europe," she said. "Do you speak French?"

"I did the last time I was in France. Come with me, Melanie. We'd have a wonderful time together. Paris is nice at the end of September, and it's a good time for a vacation. The kids have had their health examinations for school, and I can close for a week and give all of my employees a rest. What do you say?"

She'd give anything to see Paris, and especially with Jack. But she remembered her father's accusations.

Even if Jack didn't expect her to share a room with him, she'd be in the same hotel, and...

"I'm happy for you, Jack. It's recognition of your achievements, and you deserve this invitation. But as much as I'd like to see and hear you give that lecture, I...I think it best that I don't go. It's too easy to fall into a convenient affair, Jack, and I...I just don't want that with you."

She didn't look at him, but she could feel the fire of his stare searing her. "You want to run that past me again? You're afraid of this becoming a convenient affair? Is that what you said?" He sat on his desk and propped his right foot on the chair beside it.

"Let me tell you something. I can find a dozen women willing to be with me just like that." He snapped his finger. "And they won't give a damn whether I care two hoots about them. If that was what I wanted, I'd have it already. In spite of what we've been to each other, what we've experienced together, you can suggest that you'd be a convenience for me? I thought we were on the same page, but it seems we're not." He whirled around, took a seat at his desk and opened his computer.

Melanie gazed at Jack for a few seconds, realized that he didn't plan to take his attention from the computer, shrugged her shoulders and walked out of Jack's office. He had practically dismissed her. Her father had preached that if she gave a man everything, after a while he wouldn't want anything from her. Why couldn't the man understand that her only bargaining chip was herself, her pride and her dignity?

She braced herself against pains that were more excruciating than the point of a knife. *It won't kill me, not after what I've been through in this life. He'd have to drop me off a cliff to make me feel worse than I did when my father walked in here and said those awful things to me. He stands on his principles, and I intend to stand on mine. If that means we separate, I can't help it. If he wants assurances that I'm his, let him commit to me.*

She opened the door for their first patient, and gazed at Midge. "Ms. Sparks, my mama sent these. She said she won't be home to deliver them tomorrow morning, because she has an appointment with Dr. Ferguson's father. They're going into business together."

"Thanks, Midge. That's wonderful. How do you feel?"

"Real good. I'm going to be on the girls' basketball team this year. Hug Dr. Ferguson for me." The girl leaned over and kissed Melanie's cheek. "Bye." Melanie went back to Jack's office and knocked on the door.

"Come in."

She handed him the package and explained why Alice had sent them. "Midge sent you a hug, but I have a feeling you don't want it, since I'm the person who has to deliver it." Without awaiting his response, she closed his door and went back to work.

A minute later, he was standing at her desk. "How is Midge?"

Deciding to give him some of his own medicine, Melanie didn't look up. "Fine. She's playing on the girls' basketball team this year."

"That's good news." When a full minute elapsed and he hadn't moved, she stopped typing at the computer and looked up at him. No one had to tell her that her impertinence annoyed him and that, as her employer, he was affronted.

Too bad, she thought, looked him in the face and shrugged her shoulders. If he didn't like receiving it, he shouldn't dish it out. Love didn't cover everything.

He punctuated his perusal with a frown, left her and a second later called her through the intercom, nearly frightening her when she heard the static, for he had never used it before. He had always walked out to her desk if he wanted anything.

"Would you please get me a syringe?" he asked. "I'm in room A."

She didn't like the sound of that. If he was in room A, he needed only to open the top drawer, stick his hand in it and get a syringe. And why did he want a syringe, anyway? The only patients in the office were the three who were at that minute sitting in the waiting room. She took her time walking down the short corridor.

As a child, she'd learned that she stood a better chance of winning when she attacked than when she defended herself. "What's this all about, Jack? Making sure that I earn my salary?" She opened the top cabinet drawer. "You want to stick your hand in there and get it, or will that syringe perform better if I hand it to you?"

"I dislike sarcasm, Melanie."

"You probably like it as much as I like having people act out at my expense. I've been dismissed a few times by people who considered me a nobody, so when you did it a few minutes ago, it was a clear reminder of who

I am. I suppose I ought to thank you." She left the room
without handing him a syringe.

He caught her before she reached the waiting room.
"We're both angry, and we're both hurt. Please give it
a rest, Melanie, before we hurt each other more. I didn't
need a syringe. I just wanted you to come in there to…
Oh, forget it. Let's just try to be civil to each other until
we can get past this. I'm sorry if I upset you."

The pain that she saw in his eyes moved her as deeply
as any kiss he'd ever given her, but she couldn't reach
out to him, not when she needed all of her strength to
avoid breaking down and crying. She had believed she
could have a life with him and now she wouldn't bet
fifty cents on it.

That does it, Jack said to himself as he headed back
to his private office. *Why can't she trust me?* He made
it through one of the busiest evenings he'd had at his
South Baltimore office, and Melanie's conspicuously
perfect professionalism didn't ease his task. When she
had to work beside him, she put as much distance
between them as she could. And when she had to look
directly at him, her facial expression was such that he
could have been a statue undeserving of her admiration.

"May I drive you home or do you want me to phone
the taxi company?" he asked her as they were closing
the office. He didn't want any more cold water dashed
in his face.

"Whichever will inconvenience you the least."

It wouldn't help if he shook her, but his fingers itched

to grab her shoulders and give them a real workout. "Neither will inconvenience me, so which will it be?"

"You listen to me," she said, whirling around and grabbing his arm. "I'm not happy. I hurt, and you're making it worse."

He pried her fingers from his arms, stunned at her viselike grip until he remembered that emotional pain could generate energy. Unshed tears glistened in her eyes, and as she faced him, defiant and regal, he knew she wouldn't shed them. He also knew why he loved her. He took a step closer and, when she didn't move, he risked getting so close that their uniforms touched.

"You couldn't have hurt me if I didn't love you," he said. "You hurt me because you don't trust me. Maybe you don't realize it, but you're asking me to pay for things that I didn't do and won't do, for…your father's selfishness and meanness, and for some guy who didn't know how to cherish you."

She inhaled deeply and closed her eyes so that her long, dark lashes shadowed her high cheekbones. "What about you, Jack? I'm always going to be honest with you, letting you know exactly how I feel about any issue facing us. I know you're not used to that, and maybe it isn't feminine for a woman to be candid, but what I feel for you is important to me, and I am not going to play games with it. I won't tell you I'm sorry for what I said, because I am not. It's what I feel. I only wish you could have accepted it for what it was, because I'd rather hurt myself than cause you pain."

His arms opened as if of their own volition, and

when she moved into them, he folded her in an embrace. Not the hot and fast passionate connection that had characterized their loving; he didn't want that. Their coming together was like a healing potion, taken with hope and faith. Her hands skimmed the stubble on his cheeks and chin, caressing his face in what he knew was her song to him without words, her confession that she adored him.

He gripped her tightly, lowered his head and sipped the sweet nectar from her parted lips. "I'll drive you home," he said.

It wasn't perfect, she hadn't promised to accompany him to Paris, and the invitation had lost some of its meaning for him, but she was still his, and for that, he was thankful. That night, he sat on the deck off his den until long after midnight. Funny how the night silence brought a man close to nature, reminding him that, in spite of his greatness, he wasn't God. He could repair arteries, replace a heart valve and even change one heart for a healthier one, but he couldn't make one tree leaf, one tiny flea or anything that lived and breathed. By morning, he had decided that he didn't need to go to Paris, that it wasn't necessary for him to be any more important than he was.

Melanie's conscience didn't trouble her that night. After Jack kissed her at her door, she heated a can of soup, ate and sat down to watch television. If she insisted on being candid, she would have to find a way to be so without hurting Jack. She had to remember that, in spite of his prominence and power, Jack hurt easily, and not because he'd been spoiled, but because he had an almost tormenting need to be loved for himself rather than for his accomplishments, status and material worth. She wondered if being a father would change that.

She washed the pot, spoon and bowl, wiped the kitchen counter clean, turned out the light and went to her bedroom with the intention of getting at least nine hours' sleep. The phone rang, sending her heart into a skid as she anticipated hearing Jack's beloved voice.

"Hello," she sang.

"This is your father." She held the receiver away from her, staring at it as if by doing so she could communicate to it her feelings. "You still there?"

"Hello, Daddy." She didn't know what to say to him, for she didn't know why he'd called. So she waited.

"I know you weren't expecting to hear from me again after…uh…what happened the other night, but—"

"You mean after you embarrassed me in front of my patients and tried to make Jack Ferguson think I'm a tramp? Frankly, I was sure I wouldn't hear from you again."

"I was wrong to do that, and I shouldn't have done it. I didn't expect to see you looking like a real nurse in a place like that one. Ferguson said I should get you out of the hole you'd dug for yourself, and I assumed you were living with your boss. I—"

"If you went to Montague Ferguson and told him to get his son out of the hole he'd dug for himself, do you believe he'd have gone to his son's office and embarrassed him? And particularly on the basis of anything you said? Do you? Montague Ferguson respects his son, and that's more than I can say of your feelings and attitude toward me."

"I said I was sorry. Seeing you in that uniform was a real shocker. You looked just like my mother, God bless her soul. Well, Baltimore's getting kinda small, so I'm going to Texas when the company moves the business down there. We're gonna start building prefab houses. I'll mail you my address."

She was leaning forward now, trying to deal with his surprises. "Do you know my address, Daddy?"

"Yeah. I located you the day after you moved in. You could at least have told me where you went."

"You and I could have done a lot of things differently, Daddy. I hope you're happy down there in Texas. Good luck."

"If you marry that doctor, don't let him make a fool of you. Stand up for yourself. Goodbye."

"Goodbye, Daddy." She consoled herself with the thought that her father probably cared, but had never learned what caring meant. She wished him well, but she wouldn't miss him.

"What do you mean you aren't going to Paris?" Montague stormed when Jack visited him several evenings later. "Have you lost your mind?"

"It isn't a matter of life and death, nor the end all and be all, Dad. I decided not to go. That's all," Jack said, kicking at the carpet in his father's dining room.

"Is anything happening with the clinic? I mean is

the construction going the way you wanted?" Montague asked him.

"It'll be ready to open by Thanksgiving, if Harrington can get all the equipment installed. The building's almost ready. They had sixteen men working on it, and that's a comparatively small building. Drake said he'd normally have a maximum of twelve on a building that size, but he increased the work force because I was in a big hurry."

"Good. Then you're not hanging around here because of the clinic. If you're having trouble getting someone to take care of your patients down in South Baltimore, I'll do it. So what's your excuse?"

He didn't like being shoved into a corner, and his father knew that. The problem was that he'd never told himself the truth about his reasons for not accepting the invitation to lecture at the conference. He'd had a couple of days to muse over his decision, and the rationalizations he gave himself didn't bear close scrutiny. Still, at his age, he refused to be grilled by anyone, including his father.

"Let it rest, Dad. I have to chart my own course, and you know I won't allow you or anyone else to do that for me. I'd better be getting home. See you at lunch Wednesday." He hugged his father and ambled down the stairs. He'd lost some points with his dad, and he wasn't happy about it.

Jack had not fooled Montague Ferguson. "I know my son, and he has an ego and ambition to match it. What he's doing is tantamount to refusing to be president of the United States without having to win a political campaign. Well, we'll see about that."

He phoned the private investigator he'd hired several weeks earlier. "Dodson, I need Melanie Sparks's address and phone number."

"It's on the report I gave you."

"I have no idea where that report is." In fact, he'd burned it, because he didn't want anyone else to read it. The man had recorded more personal information about Melanie and her father than he'd needed. It had pleased him to read that she had moved into her own apartment.

Jack had said she'd be a wonderful daughter to him, but he had to be certain that she wasn't the reason Jack decided not to go to Paris and capture the prize of a lifetime. He also had to mend some fences with her.

He telephoned her at nine that Saturday morning. "Ms. Sparks, this is Montague Ferguson. If you have time, would you do me the honor of having lunch with me today?"

"Well, Dr. Ferguson, this is a stunning surprise."

"I know it is, but it's extremely important. Will you please join me for lunch? There'll be just the two of us. I don't think you will regret it." He wasn't used to begging, but if he had to, he'd get on his knees to her. "Please."

"What time and where, sir?"

He released a long breath in relief. "At one o'clock. If that suits you, a car will be at your place at twelve-thirty to take you to the Harvard Club. I'll meet you in the lobby. I can't thank you enough for agreeing to join me."

* * *

Melanie hung up and sat for a full minute staring into space. Why did he want to talk with her? Well, no matter. She said she'd have lunch with him, and she would take advantage of the opportunity to tell him what she thought of him for sending her father to Jack's office to embarrass her and his son. She dressed in her softly styled burnt-orange wool suit and added brown boots, gloves and pocketbook, but decided to let her hair hang down. Gold hoops adorned her ears.

The doorman buzzed her at 12:25. "Dr. Ferguson's driver is here for you, ma'am."

"Thanks. I'll be there in a few minutes." She applied a bit of the perfume Jack had given her, said a prayer and headed downstairs. As she strolled toward the elevator, she wondered why she hadn't phoned Jack and told him that his father had invited her to lunch. She shrugged. What would be would be.

She entered the Harvard Club thinking that months earlier she would have felt out of place, but she didn't now, for she had learned that luck, money and opportunity counted for most of the differences she saw in people. As she stepped into the lobby, Montague Ferguson hurried toward her, tall, elegant and still handsome, the man Jack would be years into the future.

He extended his hand, and a charismatic smile covered his face. "Thank you so much for coming, Melanie. I have to ask your forgiveness for more than one thing, but right now, let's go claim our table."

He'd just taken the bite out of her animosity toward him, but she still meant to tell him a thing or two. They followed the maître d' to a table, and Montague told her that he always sat there.

"So you're a Harvard graduate?"

"Yes, I am, but my only son decided to go to my school's greatest rival," he complained, almost like a spoiled child.

"Yale's good," she said and laughed at his stern expression of disapproval. Then he laughed, too, breaking the tension.

"First, I want to tell you how deeply I regret interfering in your relationship with Jack. And involving your father in it was a terrible thing to do. Jack let me know what he thought of my doing that, and it wasn't one bit complimentary."

"I assure you it was the most embarrassing experience of my life, but our patients stood by me, and if Jack had let them, several would have thrown my father out of there. Why did you want to have lunch with me?"

"I'm going to have my usual," he told the waiter. "What would you like, Melanie?"

"Crab cakes with asparagus, thank you."

"Would you like wine? I don't drink wine at lunch, but you're welcome."

She couldn't help grinning at his facial expression. Take away a few years, and she could be sitting across the table from Jack. "I almost never drink it," she said. "Never got into the habit. It didn't belong with corn bread, collards and pork chops."

An expression of nostalgia flashed across his face. "I haven't had any good corn bread since Jack's mother died seventeen years ago. She was a wonderful cook."

"My corn bread's to die for. Next time I make it, I'll send you some."

His frown was off-putting until he said, "Uh…could you just make some for me? I'll come get it."

Like son, like father. Charm personified. "I'll make you some."

Their food arrived, and as he began eating, she realized his mood had changed. "Melanie, I need your help. Jack is deeply in love with you, so you're probably the only person who can change his mind. I want you to talk some sense into him."

She stiffened, put her fork on the side of her plate and looked at the man in front of her. "What is this about?"

She didn't like his painful facial expression and braced herself for the worst. "I suppose you know about Jack's invitation to lecture at that conference in Paris." She nodded, holding her breath. "He told me last night that he's not going."

She grabbed her water glass half a second before she knocked it over. "What? What did you say?"

He repeated it. "Melanie, I would just about die for that kind of recognition, to be invited to lecture on the hottest topic in my field and before the world's leading experts in it. How can he possibly decline? As far as you know, is he ill?" She shook her head.

"I would have expected him to ask you to go with him. When a man shines like that, he wants his woman to share it with him. I don't understand this. You've got to make him accept it."

She blew out a long breath. "I thought he had accepted. He asked me to go with him, and I told him I wouldn't and why. Are you saying he told you that he won't be attending the conference?"

"Yes. Last night. Mind telling me why you won't go with him?"

It wasn't his business, but she knew he wanted the best for his son. "I told Jack that I don't want to risk becoming a convenience for him, and that upset him. We made up, but our relationship is still a little strained. He tells me that he loves me, but he is not committed to me. As much as I love him, I am not going to let him have his cake and eat it, too."

Montague stared hard at her. "I see. You remind me so much of my wife, Jack's mother. Soft and sweet, but strong as iron. She loved me, but she did not let me take advantage of her. I wish you would reconsider though. Jack loves you deeply, and he needs you. I guess he feels he'll get no joy out of being there alone."

"He could take you with him," she said and nearly laughed at the thought.

Montague raised one eyebrow. "Tell me you're joking."

They finished lunch with a bowl of mixed fresh fruit. As he drove her home, he talked. "I hope you can bring yourself to reconsider, and please continue to support Jack as you've been doing. He's a different man since meeting you, and he knows it." He walked with her to her door. "Love him, Melanie. That's all he needs."

She looked up at him. He hadn't been an affectionate father, perhaps, but he loved his son. She opened her arms, hugged him and kissed his cheek. "I'll let you know when to come for the corn bread," she told the startled man, put her key in the lock, opened the door and left him.

She went to her closet and checked the clothing that she thought suited travel in the fall of the year. Deciding that she wouldn't have to shop, she put away the burnt-orange suit and the accessories she wore with it and phoned Jack, hoping that he wasn't on the golf course.

"Melanie! How are you?"

"I'm fine. Are you...uh...busy for dinner?"

"No. I was planning to sit here on my deck and read a couple of reports. Why?"

"Want to eat dinner at my place? It won't be very fancy, because I don't have much time to prepare it, but it will be good."

"What time? Tell me what you need, and I'll be right over there with it. I can read these reports while you cook."

"You can bring whatever kind of wine you like to drink, but not till seven. Okay?"

"Absolutely okay."

Hmm. He was in a good mood. What had happened to the morose Jack who'd left her at her door the previous Thursday night? She wondered if he'd talked with his father within the last half hour.

She told him goodbye and dashed out to the supermarket. She purchased a duck, a box of wild rice and a bunch of asparagus, two leeks, a bag of oranges, sour cream and four cans of chicken stock. At the corner florist, she bought a bouquet of orange chrysanthemums and yellow marigolds and hurried back to her apartment. She had everything else she needed at home.

She told herself that a dinner of leek soup, roast duck l'orange, wild rice, asparagus, green salad and sour-cream lemon pie should do it for a short-notice invitation. Half an hour before Jack's expected arrival, she remembered his father's love of corn bread, mixed some, poured it in her old iron skillet and put it into the oven. If father liked it, chances were great that son liked it, too. She finished dressing in a long black skirt and a dusty-rose sleeveless, silk-jersey top that had a deep cowl neckline. Not too sexy, but not prim, either. She let her hair down, dabbed some perfume behind her ears and looked at her watch. Seven o'clock. The doorbell rang, and she raced to answer it.

She opened the door, saw the lights glistening in his eyes and the grin playing around his mouth and raised her arms to him. His kiss didn't fool her. In spite of its brevity, it communicated warmth and love, and after nestling close to him for a second, she took his hand and led him to the kitchen.

"I have to stir this sauce for a while," she explained, "then I'll treat you like a proper guest."

"I don't want to be treated like a guest, proper or not. Where's a vase?"

She glanced down at the long-stemmed red roses in his hand. "Oh. I didn't see those." She handed him a vase and a pair of kitchen shears. "Oh, they're beautiful. Thank you. Would you clip the ends at an angle before you put them in water?"

He did that, and put the vase and a bag containing wine on the table. "Melanie, let's straighten something out right now." She turned toward him. "Oh, don't stop stirring that stuff. I wouldn't want to cause you to ruin it. Are things all right with us? Would you cook dinner for me if you were mad at me?"

She returned her attention to the saucepan and proceeded to stir. "No, I wouldn't, and I wouldn't enjoy your kiss so much, either. Are you still hurt?"

"Not as much as I was. I'm… Being here with you eases it a lot."

She pushed the sauce to the back of the stove, covered it and poured two glasses of wine. "I can't drink anything stronger than this. If I did, you probably wouldn't get a decent dinner. Next time I fix dinner for you, I promise to plan it properly."

"I don't really care, Melanie, as long as we're together."

She looked at him for a long time and realized that he meant what he said. "Okay, go sit at the table, and I'll serve the meal." She ladled soup into two bowls and carried them to the dining room.

"Would you say grace, please?" He held her hand while he said it, and from his solemn expression, she had a feeling that he also said an unspoken prayer for them.

"I've always liked leek soup, and especially on a chilly day like today. This is delicious."

She removed the bowls and served the remainder of the meal. "You *are* a good cook," he said, savoring the food. "Say, what's that? Corn bread? How'd you know I love corn bread?" He bit into a piece. "Melanie, this is just like my mother's corn bread. I haven't had any this good since she got too sick to cook. I could make a meal of this. Why'd you decide to give me corn bread?"

"Well, I figured that if your father loves it, you'd love it, too."

He rested his fork on the side of his plate, stopped chewing and looked hard at her. "How did you know my dad loves corn bread? It's his favorite thing to eat."

"I had lunch with him today at the Harvard club."

"Come again. You did what?"

She repeated it, and added, "When he brought me home, I hugged him and kissed his cheek. I also promised him some of my corn bread."

"Wait a minute. How the hell did that happen?"

"Never mind. I've decided that I want to go to Paris with you when you give that lecture. Nobody should have that kind of recognition without someone dear to share it with. When do we leave? I'm applying for a passport Monday morning before I go to work."

"Slow down, Melanie. I had decided not to accept."

She let an expression of horror cover her face. "You told them you wouldn't accept, that you wouldn't go?"

"Well, no, but I was planning to."

"You can't do that. It's an opportunity that you deserve or they wouldn't offer it to you. Why would you do that?"

"Triumph is no fun alone, Melanie. I didn't feel like going to all that trouble if I didn't even have anybody to…to so much as take a photograph."

"I didn't think of that, Jack. And I won't play games with you, either. The truth is that your father invited me to lunch today and told me you weren't going to accept. He looked as if he had the weight of the world on his shoulders. He didn't know why you decided not to go, but when he told me that, my heart sank. He asked me to talk to you, but the minute he told me, I decided that you were going if I had to ride a horse through Baltimore dressed like Lady Godiva."

A smile creased the side of his mouth. "Lady Godiva was nude."

"That's what I meant. Will you go and take me with you?"

He got up, went around the table, kissed her lips and returned to his dinner. "What are you going to do with the remainder of this corn bread?"

"You're going to take it to your dad. Are we going to Paris?"

"I love my dad, but I sure as heck am not giving him this corn bread, and if you think I am, you're nuts."

"Okay, so you won't give him the corn bread. I'll make some in the morning, call him and he can come and get it. When are we leaving for Paris?"

"What are we having for desert?"

She cleared the table and brought the pie and pie plates to the dining room. "I had no idea you were so stubborn. When are we going to Paris?"

"I don't make important decisions when I'm eating. Digesting food takes the blood away from the brain, makes one lazy and lethargic, mentally as well as physically."

She served the pie. "You're full of it, buddy, and you're not getting off so easily. I'll ride that horse right through Southwest Baltimore, and my contract does not give that as grounds for firing me."

As if he hadn't heard her, he tasted the pie, savored it and looked toward the ceiling. "I knew I was clever when I hired you. If I'm guaranteed corn bread and this pie whenever I ask, we'll go to Paris, and I'll give the lecture."

Joy suffused Melanie, and she wrapped her arms around his shoulders and hugged him. "That's blackmail, Jack, but I'll agree to most anything if you're reconsidering. Please call your dad, and tell him you changed your mind."

"He's not worried. When he asked you to talk to me, he knew you would and that I'd do whatever you asked me to do. And he knew it, because he knows I love you. Why'd you hug him?"

"Because I… I don't know. I was feeling happy, and I realized I liked him a lot and that he loves you."

"Sure he loves me. He just doesn't know how to show it. You can teach him."

"Would you please get me a weather forecast for the time we'll be in Paris? What are the dates?"

Three weeks later, she sat spellbound in the grand ballroom of the Paris Marriott Champs-Elysées Hotel as three hundred and fifty doctors of every race and culture stood applauding Jack's lecture. Realizing that she was probably the only person present who remained seated, she pushed herself upright, wiped the tears from her cheeks and clapped her hands. At least fifty percent of what he'd said was beyond her comprehension, but she understood that he said it with authority.

"Let's take the boat ride down the Seine," he said later, walking with her back to her room in the five-star hotel. "I'll meet you downstairs in half an hour."

"You were wonderful," she told him. "You were like an Adonis bestriding the earth. I'm so sorry your dad wasn't in that audience."

"So am I."

She smiled, proud of her foresight. "Not to worry. I grabbed a DVD for him."

"I didn't know they filmed it. Thanks. He'll keep it forever."

After the boat ride down the Seine, he took her to the Eiffel Tower. As they strolled along, she enjoyed watching women of all ages salivate, coveting him, and then looking at her as if she wasn't good enough for him. Her heart raced when he looked down at her, smiled and eased his arm around her waist.

"Tomorrow, if you like, we'll go to the Louvre, Notre Dame Cathedral and maybe do some people-watching at the Café de la Paix across from the Paris Opera."

"I don't care what we do, as long as we're to-gether," she said, deciding that it was time for him to show his colors.

"Why don't we have a drink around five?" he asked her. "That'll give you an hour to rest."

"I have a little balcony. We could sit out there, look at the Arc de Triomphe and have the drinks."

"Right. I'll send up some stuff." He held her hand, staring down at her until she thought she'd catch fire.

Shortly before five o'clock, she adjusted her short red dinner dress, slipped on her only pair of three-inch-heel slippers and refreshed her perfume. The waiter brought drinks and hors d'oeuvres. "Thank you, ma'am, but Dr. Ferguson took care of the tip."

"I remember that dress," Jack said when she opened the door. "You look like an angel and a siren in this thing. How'm I going to keep my wits if I have to handle both you and the alcohol?"

She closed her left eye in a long, slow wink. "Forget the alcohol. Just deal with me."

He glanced at the bed. "The balcony is a good idea."

"You've been here five minutes, and you haven't kissed me," she said with a pouting expression on her face.

"Ever hear of prudence? I'm wrestling with it right now."

"Hang prudence," she said. "I want you to kiss me."

He put the glasses back on the tray, lifted her into his arms and rimmed the seam of her lips with the tip of his tongue. She sucked it into her mouth, and within seconds he bulged against her. She had him the way she wanted him, and in no time, he lay above her gazing down into her face.

"If you want me, take me. I'm yours," he said, his voice hoarse and unsteady.

She took him into her body and gave herself into his care as he drove them to ecstasy. "I love you so much," she whispered after he'd taken them to their own secret place, possessing her totally time and again, draining her of her last bit of energy.

At least half an hour passed, and then she said, "I'm still spellbound, Jack. After hearing your talk and seeing all those doctors—old enough to be your father—hanging on to your every word. You were far from the Jack I know, a powerhouse of a mind. I am so proud of you."

"Then why were you crying?"

"Maybe because I thought of what you almost missed, or because I was so happy that you had your moment in the sun. Or because you seemed...untouchable. I don't know. It was wonderful."

"My dad said you had refused to come here with me originally because I wouldn't commit to you. That hadn't crossed my mind, because in my heart and my head, I committed to you the night you came to the hospital to be with me while I waited to hear what happened to Alma. She was the first patient I ever lost. From that night on, I belonged to you. Will you marry me, Melanie? I love you, and I will take good care of you and our children." He got on his knees. "Will you be my wife?"

"Oh, yes, Jack. I've loved you since that day you came to the office and found me taking inventory."

"That was three days after we met." He put his mother's diamond engagement ring on her finger.

"I know. It was ordained."

Epilogue

On Christmas Eve of that same year, Jack Ferguson stirred the coals in the fireplace of his living room and looked at the massive Douglas fir tree that stood near the window with its myriad lights and trinkets dazzling all who saw it. His bride of three weeks put an iron skillet filled with corn bread on the hot coals at the edge of the fireplace and banked the coals around it. Montague Ferguson walked into the living room with a tray of drinks and sat down.

"I'd say we should have let someone cater Christmas dinner, if it wasn't for the fact that Melanie is such a great cook." He put an arm around his daughter-in-law. "But you won't have to clean up after dinner. Vernie will take care of that. I hope you're planning to give me some grandchildren."

"Try not to meddle, Dad. Pressure leads to stress, which leads to—"

"I know. I know. But I can hope, can't I?" Montague said. "Melanie, did you call your father?" She nodded. "Good. This is Christmas, and a time for love."

That night, after Jack made long, sweet and satisfying love to her, Melanie lay in her husband's arms. "My period is late, so I took the test and it was positive."

"Good Lord! When?"

"I took it this morning. What's the matter?"

He pulled her into his arms, and his tears soaked her face and her hair.

"I love you so much," he murmured.

"I know, darling, and I love you with all my heart."

Tyson Braddock was not a man to be denied....

Second Chance, Baby

Book #3 in The Braddocks: Secret Son

A.C. Arthur

Except for one passion-filled night, Ty and Felicia Braddock's
marriage has been cold for years. Now Felicia is pregnant.
Unwilling to raise her baby with an absentee workaholic
father, Felicia wants a divorce. Ty convinces her to give him
another chance. But as they rediscover the passion they'd lost,
will it be enough to make them a family?

THE BRADDOCKS

SECRET SON

power, passion and politics are all in the family

Available the first week of October wherever books are sold.

NOVELS OF LOVE & HOPE

SUPPORTING ST. JUDE CHILDREN'S RESEARCH HOSPITAL

As a longtime supporter of St. Jude Children's Research Hospital, I believe in its mission of finding cures and saving children. Please join me in supporting St. Jude by becoming a Partner in Hope, and help keep the promise that no family will ever be turned away due to an inability to pay.

Together we can fight childhood cancer, sickle cell disease and pediatric HIV/AIDS and make a difference in the lives of the precious children of St. Jude.

Please visit
www.novelsofhope.org
for more information.

ARABESQUE®

Thanks,

Gwynne Forster

For All We Know

NATIONAL BESTSELLING AUTHOR
SANDRA KITT

Michaela Landry's quiet summer of house-sitting takes a dramatic turn when she finds a runaway teen and brings him to the nearest hospital. There she meets Cooper Smith Townsend, a local pastor whose calm demeanor and dedication are as attractive as his rugged good looks. Now their biggest challenge will be to trust that a passion neither planned for is strong enough to overcome any obstacle.

Coming the first week of September 2008, wherever books are sold.

ARABESQUE®

www.kimanipress.com

KPSKI040908

Will being Cinderella for a month
lead to happily ever after?

A Gentleman's Offer

DARA GIRARD

Wealthy Nate Blackwell offers dog groomer Yvette Coulier
an opportunity to live among the upper crust if she'll let him
pose as her valet. But it's not long before their mutual passion
forces them to take off their masks...and expose their hearts.

Four women. One club.
And a secret that will make all their fantasies come true.

Available the first week of October wherever books are sold.

www.kimanipress.com

KPDG0851008

Was her luck running out?

GAMBLE ON Love

The second title in The Ladies of Distinction…

MICHELLE MONKOU

"Black American Princess" Denise Dixon has met
her match in sexy, cynical Jaden Bond. But as their
relationship heats up, she knows their days are numbered
before her shameful family secrets are revealed.

THE LADIES *of* DISTINCTION:

They've shared secrets, dreams and heartaches.
And when it comes to finding love, these sisters
always have each other's backs.

Available the first week of October wherever books are sold.

KIMANI
ROMANCE™

www.kimanipress.com   KPMM0861008

She was beautiful, bitter and bent on revenge!

Tender SECRETS

ANN CHRISTOPHER

Vivica Jackson has vowed vengeance on the wealthy
Warners for causing her family's ruin—but that's before
she experiences Andrew Warner's devastating charm.
After the would-be enemies share a night of fiery passion,
each is left wanting more. But will her undercover
deception and his dark family secret lead to a not-so-
happy ending to their love story?

"An exceptional story!"
—*Romantic Times BOOKreviews*
on *Just About Sex*

Available the first week of October wherever books are sold.

KIMANI™
ROMANCE